Adult Supervision Required

SARAH PEIS

To all the moms out there. You got this. Just don't forget where you hid the chocolate.

Chapter One

Note: Sötnos = Sweetheart

"I want cockporn," Lena wailed.

"Don't we all," I muttered under my breath, then looked around the crowded supermarket, hoping nobody had heard her. "Not today, Sötnos. We still have some at home."

"But I want—"

I clamped my hand over her mouth and speed-walked my way to the checkout, hoping Luca wouldn't join her out of sympathy. He was two years older, but hadn't outgrown the tantrums yet.

She didn't like having her shriek interrupted and her little face went red with anger. But I'd rather deal with my daughter's wrath than once again be the talk of the town. We made it outside in record time, Lena wailing the whole way, Luca holding his hands over his ears.

I was running late, my shift starting in less than twenty minutes, and I still had to drop my kids home and drive to work. After wrestling them into their seats and dumping my bags in the trunk I hightailed it back to the house.

Lena made sure we knew her displeasure at not getting any popcorn for the duration of the drive. My friend Stella was sitting on the front steps waiting when we pulled up.

"Sorry we're late," I greeted her, unbuckling the little hellions. She watched my kids for me on the nights I had to work.

I couldn't really afford a babysitter, so when she offered, I had to put my pride aside and let her help. She was my friend—one of the few I had—and I just couldn't do it on my own anymore. I worked two jobs, barely keeping my head above water, and needed any break I could get.

My day job was a virtual assistant, something I could do from home while watching the kids. Luca had recently started preschool, so I only had Lena most of the time. My second job was waitressing at Pepper's, a strip club. It paid well, but the hours sucked. I never thought I'd end up where I was.

"Don't worry, I only just got here. Mason dropped me off," Stella said, cuddling Lena to her and holding Luca's hand. "But aren't you going to be late for work?"

I checked the time on my phone and sprinted up the steps. Definitely going to be late if I wasn't ready in the next three minutes.

I dropped the bags in the kitchen and raced to my room. My clothes were at work, so I would change there, and I'd ask the girls at work to help me with my hair and makeup since they could accomplish more in two minutes than I could in an hour.

Stella was getting the kids dinner when I came back out.

"Thank you so much. I'm sorry to run out like this. It's been one of those days."

She pulled the pasta out of the microwave and snickered at me. "As long as you don't make me cook, we're good. And it's good to see you've been making sure the kids eat balanced meals."

"Shut up. They're on a pasta bender by choice. I didn't make them."

"Go, or you'll be late," Stella said, waving a spoon at me.

I kissed Luca and Lena goodbye and drove to work. Thankfully the roads were empty at this time of night since everything closed around five.

Even though I had less than ten minutes, I stayed in my car once I'd parked. My hands were clammy, my throat dry, and I had to take a few breaths to calm myself down. It was the same overwhelming emotions I had every time I got here.

I hated my job. I hated what I was forced to do. But most of all, I hated that I hadn't been stronger and cut ties with my ex sooner. Because without him, I wouldn't be in this situation.

I grabbed my bag and dragged my ass out of the car. It was just another job. No big deal. Anyone could do this. After all, I'd been doing it for over a year.

I made it to the back door and stopped again. Maybe today I only had to count to three hundred rather than the usual five hundred before I could force myself to go inside. But no such luck; not even being late could push my brain to count faster. When I reached five hundred, I forced a deep breath into my lungs and went inside.

Hastening my steps, I rushed through the hallway, clutching my bag to my chest.

"You're late," Smitty yelled at me as I rushed past his office.

"I know, I'm sorry. It won't happen again," I called back, stopping in the doorway.

He didn't look up from the papers on his desk. "It better not. I have a business to run."

I kept walking and burst into the dressing room a few seconds later. Most of the girls were in there getting ready, looking up when I stumbled inside.

"What happened to you?" Elle asked, watching me in the mirror.

Tia's eyes widened at my disheveled appearance. "You didn't use the conditioner I told you about."

Star eyed me with raised brows. "What did you do to your eyelashes?"

They sat me down and fixed me up in ten minutes.

I was so grateful I nearly burst into tears.

"Thank you so much," I said and hugged them when they declared me ready.

They all towered over me, mostly because of the sky-high heels they wore, but also because I was short, having inherited my Japanese mom's build instead of my Swedish Viking dad's height. I shot them a shaky smile and rushed out to the bar.

It was still early, but the club was already filled with patrons. Business was definitely booming, and it helped that this was the only strip club around for miles.

I pulled out my order pad and greeted the two bartenders, Martello and Stephen. They were here most nights and good guys if you didn't try to give them a shitty tip.

My eyes didn't linger on them long; instead, they were drawn to the man standing next to the stage. I could find Sebastian no matter how crowded the room was. Call it my secret superpower. The most useless one at that, but I always seemed to know where he was.

His blond curly hair was sticking up like he'd been running his hands through it. The muscles in his arms bulged when he crossed them over his chest, making me swallow. He was perfection in a six-foot-three package, and I'd felt an inexplicable attraction to him from the moment I first saw him a year ago.

Our interactions were limited to the occasional nod and looks—creepy stalker stares from me and assessing gazes from him.

Not that I'd tried to get his attention. I had no time to date. And the head of security, who was also a member of the local motorcycle club that owned the strip club, was definitely not a suitable match for a single mom.

Word was they'd gone legit, but nobody seemed to believe it. And I didn't really make it my business to find out more about the motorcycle club. All I knew was Sebastian moved to town about a year ago when he also started working at the strip club.

I'd never seen him with a girl, but he might have one stashed away somewhere and didn't bring her to the club.

Once I finished staring at him for the five seconds I allowed myself, I got to work.

The rest of the night kept my creep level to a minimum since I didn't have time to do more than take a few sips of water every now and again. They really needed to hire more staff.

After fending off another slap to the butt, I leaned against the bar, eyeing the clock. One hour to go.

"Take a break. You look beat," Stephen told me and nodded to the door.

I wasn't about to argue since my feet felt like I was walking on nails. My new shoes would find a new home tonight in the trash can. Definitely not as comfortable as they looked.

"I'll only be five minutes," I called out, quickly

making my way to the back.

Once in the dressing room, I pulled out my phone to check my messages.

Stella: Your kids are savages. They didn't eat any of the cheese sauce, only the pasta. And who doesn't love ice cream?

Stella: I mean, not that I gave them any. At least not much. Sorry, but they asked so nicely.

Stella: And they're now sleeping like the little angels they are.

Stella: Hope you're not creeping on hot security guy again.

I rolled my eyes and replied.

Me: They're allowed ice cream, just not too much or the sugar will keep them up. It's really more for your benefit than mine.

Me: And I'm not creepy. It's only natural that my eyes would pass over him every once in a while. He's here all the time.

Stella: Of course…

Me: Shut it, you're making it sound like a bigger deal than it is. I should never have told you about him.

Stella: You are very talkative when you're drunk. I especially enjoyed the part about his butt. Never knew there were so many words for lickable.

I wanted to die of mortification. This was why I never drank; I talked nonstop and had no filter.

Me: You better not have told anyone about this.

Stella: …

Stella: Only Malena.

Stella: And Willa.

Stella: Oh, and Maisie.

Me: You are the worst friend.

Stella: xx

I put my phone back and took a deep breath. I'd almost survived another night with only minor incidents. I could do this. I was a kick-ass bitch who took charge of her life. Even if that meant working at a strip club.

I made my way back out to the floor and finished my shift, making sure to catch another glimpse of Sebastian before driving home.

Chapter Two

"My knees are cold," Luca complained.

"I told you to wear long pants."

He was looking out the window, never once taking his eyes off the front yard. "But I want to wear shorts."

The small stool he was standing on provided him with just enough height to look outside so he wouldn't miss my friend Malena pull up.

I put the last of the clean dishes away and walked over to him. "I know. That's why your knees are cold."

"Malena," he exclaimed, cold knees forgotten. He raced to the door and opened it, disappearing outside. I followed at a slower pace, watching him come to a sliding stop in front of my best friend.

"Hey, buddy, how's it hanging?" she asked and fist-bumped him before ruffling his hair.

He giggled and ran off with her son, Felix, the two

disappearing inside the house. We probably wouldn't see them again for the rest of the day.

Lena skipped up to Malena, who picked her up and carried her to where I was waiting.

"Thanks so much for watching him," Malena said and hugged me, squashing Lena between us.

"No problem at all. We were just going to hang out at the house today anyway."

It was one of those rare days that I didn't have to work at either of my jobs. And it really didn't make a difference to me if I watched another kid. Especially one as gentle as Felix. And he loved playing with Luca, so it was a win-win.

"I'll pick him up around five," she said and handed Lena back to me before leaning her head inside the house. "See you tonight, mijo."

I waved her off. "No rush."

She left to go to work, even though it was Sunday. She was a lawyer, and her job was the second most important thing to her, right after her son. Usually her parents watched Felix, but they were on a weekend trip to celebrate their fortieth wedding anniversary.

And I was all too happy to help. Usually I needed people to do me favors, so whenever I had the chance to pay them back, I jumped at it.

We spent the day playing in the backyard, then walked to the playground just across the street. I watched them go down the slide 2,876 times and get on and off the swing 5,409 times before I convinced them that going home was a great idea.

It was getting dark, and I didn't want to be outside too late, no matter how safe the neighborhood.

The boys disappeared inside the kids' room as soon as we got back. Lena was happy playing with her dolls, and I used the rare moment of reprieve to start dinner. It was another pasta night—no judgment required, I did enough of that myself.

"Kidlets, dinner is ready," I called out after dumping the sauce in a pan. The pasta was done, and the sauce would only take a minute to heat up.

I put the plates and cutlery on the table and called out again. When there was still no movement, I walked to the room. When I opened the door, I was greeted by a toy Armageddon. The floor was covered in them, and the kids had ripped the bedding off the bed.

I took a step inside and landed right on one of Luca's transformers.

"Merlin's rabbit," I called out, jumping back out of the room. That hurt just as much as the last twenty times it happened.

"Mommy ouchie," Lena said, toddling over to where I was still hopping.

"Big mother puffin ouchie," I said and picked her up when I was sure my foot was going to recover. "You hungry?"

She nodded, her mind successfully redirected from my injury to eating food.

"Luca, Felix, it's time for dinner," I told the boys and sat Lena in her highchair.

The boys finally joined us after I threatened to take away their dessert if they didn't eat a real meal first.

Dinner was messy, but the kids ate most of it, and that's really all I cared about. The new stains mingled with the old ones, and it would probably be another week before I cleaned them off the floor.

When Malena came back, the kids were sitting in front of the TV in their pajamas, watching *Paw Patrol*.

"Fed, cleaned, and ready for bed," I said, beaming at her. This was one of those unicorn moments that only came around once every hundred days.

"How did you convince them to take a bath? Felix keeps telling me that the dirt on his feet is clean dirt and he doesn't need to wash himself."

"Ha, yeah, he tried that one on me as well. I told him you would go to Fun World with us if he got in the bath."

"I hate that place," she groaned. "Besides, I'm working weekends for the foreseeable future. I want to make partner."

"Every weekend? That's crazy."

"You have two jobs. Aren't you throwing rocks out of a glass house here?"

She had a point. We were both hopeless. The only difference was that she loved her job. I didn't.

"I know, I know," I said, helping her collect Felix's

things that were strewn around the house.

After we found everything, she hugged me close. "Call me if you need anything. And thanks again for today."

She wrestled Felix out the door, and I dropped onto the couch, ready to go to bed. And my kids looked like they were almost tired enough to nod off as well, giving me hope that they'd go to sleep for once.

There was a knock on the door, and I reluctantly got up again.

"Did you forget something?" I asked and opened the door, expecting Malena.

But instead of my best friend, it was my ex standing in front of me. He looked like he hadn't eaten in a while, his face looking gaunt, his hair greasy and longer than I'd ever seen it.

"Jim."

"Sugar," he greeted me with the nickname he knew I despised. "Can I come in?"

"Can you come in?" I sputtered. "Are you insane?"

He looked behind him and then squeezed past me before I could stop him.

"Get out," I said, finally finding my voice.

"I came to see my kids," he said, already walking into the living room.

I slammed the door and sprinted after him. But my

legs were too short, and when I made it to the living room, he was already talking to the kids.

They both stared at him, trying to figure out who he was. They were too young to remember a dad who barely ever showed up.

"Good to see you, kids," Jim said and saluted them.

He'd never been great with them, and they never asked for him. I always thought kids that young would love their parents no matter what. But Jim proved that if you were a big enough barnacle, you could scare off even the most devoted of children.

"It's bedtime," I sang, pushing down my discomfort and concentrating on getting the kids away from him. "Who wants to read a book?"

They grumbled when I turned their show off, but they both loved reading, so after a few more complaints, they followed me to their bedroom.

We sat on Luca's bed and read two books before I declared bedtime.

When they were both settled, I took a deep breath and got ready for battle.

Jim was sitting on a bar stool, drinking one of my beers. Good to know he still had no boundaries.

"What do you want?" I asked, standing on the other side of the counter.

He took a long drink of his beer, making my blood boil. "I just wanted to see my kids."

I crossed my arms to stop myself from slapping

him over his big head. "So you just decided to show up here? Why the sudden change of heart?"

He grinned at me, showing the dimples I used to find adorable. "Don't be mad. You used to like being spontaneous."

"I also used to like *you*. Guess I finally grew up," I said, clenching my teeth.

He took another sip of his beer, and I noticed his hands were shaking. His hair was greasy, and he'd lost weight. "I need a place to stay for the night."

Luca came into the kitchen before I had a chance to reply. "Mommy, there's a fly in the room."

I took his hand and walked him back to his and Lena's room. "Come on, Sötnos, let's get you back to bed and find that fly."

Lena was already fast asleep, sprawled out on her mattress like a starfish. I pretended to catch a fly that wasn't there, and after making a big production out of throwing it out the window, Luca was back in bed. His eyes were already half closed when I pulled the blanket over him and kissed his cheek.

I straightened back up, took a deep breath, and wished for things that could never be. Like a meteorite falling on Jim. Just a teensy tiny one that wouldn't do any damage to anything or anyone but him. I rounded the corner back into the kitchen, watching Jim drink his second beer. The empty bottle of his first sat forgotten on the counter.

"It's only for one night," he said, as soon as he noticed I was back.

"Are you out of your mind? No."

"You won't even know I'm here," he pleaded, peeling the label off his beer bottle. "I'm in a bit of a jam."

When is he ever not in a jam? The only thing that had changed was I was no longer willing to bail him out.

I pointed to the front door. "Get out."

"There are people looking for me. I just need one night to sort myself out."

Did he just bring his problems to my doorstep? I went from trying to have a calm conversation to a nuclear explosion.

I stalked up to him and then stopped before I did something I'd regret later. *Oh, who am I kidding? I'd never regret punching him in his smug face.*

"Are you out of your mind? Do you ever think of anyone but yourself?" I whisper-hissed, praying he didn't endanger us by coming here.

"Of course I do. I was thinking of you. That's why I'm here," the woodhead replied.

I shrieked and threw a sponge at him. He was too slow to duck, and it hit him on the cheek with a satisfying thud.

"You would willingly put us all in danger just so you can hide somewhere for the night?" I asked, glaring at him.

He leaned back, his eyes not meeting mine. "If you put it like that—"

"That's exactly how I'm putting it."

I was fuming, looking for something else to throw at him that I wouldn't miss if it broke, when Luca came back into the kitchen.

"Mommy, I'm done with sleeps. I'm awake now."

I turned to my son standing in the entry to the kitchen, hoping my smile didn't look as fake as it felt. "It's still night, honey. Let's go back to bed and try closing your eyes again, okay?"

He put his arms around my neck when I picked him up, and I hugged him to me. I instantly felt better.

When I had him back under the covers, I'd come to a decision. Jim would never just leave, and it was easier to let him do what he wanted.

I hated myself in that moment for giving in to him once again. When would I ever learn?

As much as I loathed him now, I used to love him. Used to think he was everything that mattered in the world. So with a sigh, all the rage drained from my body and I felt defeated. When I came back, I said, "Fine. You can stay on the couch. But I want you gone before the kids get up."

He grinned and held his beer up in a toast. "Thanks, sugar. You won't even know I was here."

Without another word, I stomped to my bedroom.

He was gone the next day, leaving empty beer bottles and dirty dishes behind. But at least he wouldn't confuse the kids more than he already had.

They looked for him for a hot second before their mind was on breakfast. I was distracted, my thoughts on last night. Something the little hellions took full advantage of. I ended up agreeing to make them pancakes, and we were running late by the time they finished eating.

Luca was going to preschool, and Lena would stay at home with me while I worked. After dropping my son off, the day was as chaotic as always. I'd have to play catch-up tonight since I wasn't working at the club.

Lena was taking a nap and I was typing out an email when I heard the loud roar of motorcycles. It was a common occurrence in the small town, and I hardly noticed anymore. They had their clubhouse on the outside of town and often rode down my street to get there.

Only this time the noise didn't fade but rather sounded as if they'd stopped right outside. I looked out the window and choked on my spit when I saw three bikes parked in my driveway.

There was a knock at my door and I shot up, unsure of what to do. *Should I call the police? Open the door? Call Malena?*

Another knock, this time more insistent. As I didn't want Lena to wake up, the decision was made for me. I had to open the door.

The three guys who were on the other side didn't look like anyone you'd want to invite inside. They were big and brawny and wore varying degrees of displeasure on their face. Lots of frowning and narrowed eyes.

"Hi. Hello. Hi," I mumbled, my hands shaky. "How can I help you?"

"You need to come with us," one of them said with a scowl on his face.

I took a step back, my eyes going wide. "What are you talking about?"

"This can all be over in a few hours as long as you cooperate," the same guy said.

I gasped, taking a step back. "Cooperate?"

Is this guy on drugs? Of course I wouldn't willingly go with them. That just screamed bad slasher movie. They looked like they could kill me with their bare hands.

I tried to close the door so I could call the police like I should have done as soon as they knocked. Instead of the click of the latch, there was a grunt, and the guy who'd talked to me stepped inside, pushing the door open. It hit me in the head, and I fell back.

"Shit," I howled, clutching my forehead. When I pulled my hand away, there was blood.

"Clean up and let's go," the big guy barked at me.

I stumbled to the sink, grabbing paper towels and

pressing them to my head. "I can't just leave."

Big Guy crossed his arms over his chest, the other two men flanking him. "This isn't a negotiation. We're taking you to the clubhouse with or without your cooperation."

Okay. Think, Nora. Oh God, what if they start cutting off my fingers? Or lock me in a room and only feed me once a week? What would happen to my kids?

I stopped thinking mighty fast when I saw Lena standing in the doorway, clutching her stuffed octopus to her chest. The guys followed my line of sight and shifted when they spotted my daughter.

"Mommy, me hungry," Lena said and came up to me, holding her hands up.

I picked her up with one arm and sat her on my hip, my other hand still holding the paper towels to my face.

My eyes met the cold glare of the guy who'd been speaking. "I can't leave her here."

"Fuck," he yelled.

"Language," I scolded immediately, and my eyes went round when I realized what I'd done.

He didn't seem to mind, or maybe he didn't hear me, because he talked to the other two guys in hushed whispers, and they disappeared shortly after.

"We're taking your car."

I didn't think I liked that option any better than the last. "Let me just call someone to watch her. She doesn't have to be involved in this. She's only a toddler. She wouldn't even be able to describe you."

Or pick them out in a police lineup. Me, on the other hand...

"No phone calls. Now get her ready. You have two minutes."

I stood unmoving, staring at him. *How did this happen? Why did this happen? I must have done something really bad in a past life. And two minutes? To get ready to go with a two-year-old? Is he delusional?*

"One minute thirty seconds."

"No way, that wasn't thirty seconds," I said, narrowing my eyes at him. "You didn't even look at your watch."

When he stepped forward, I sprang into action, dumping the paper towels in the sink and rushing to find Lena's bag. She had snacks and diapers in there that should hold her for the next however many hours we'd be gone.

I grabbed it off the kitchen table where it was buried under a pile of clean laundry and turned. "Ready."

He didn't respond, just herded us out of the house and to my car. The other two guys were sitting on their bikes, ready to pull out. They'd moved his bike to the end of the driveway, so it was sitting in front of the garage that I only used as storage.

My car was so old, putting it under any sort of cover would just extend its suffering. I hoped it would die a swift death soon so I could claim insurance and buy another rust bucket.

I strapped Lena into her seat and got in on the passenger side. Big Guy needed a few attempts before he figured out the best way to fold himself into my tiny car. I would have laughed if this situation weren't so scary.

"Phone," he barked, and I jumped in my seat.

At this stage, I thought it was better to cooperate. I'd done nothing wrong, after all. Maybe if I didn't piss them off too much, they'd just let me go.

I handed my phone over, and he put it in his pocket. There was no way I was going to try and get it back from there. He turned the key and was greeted with a cacophony of warning lights. I noticed my fuel light had joined the choir, beeping alongside the engine and battery lights.

The biker raised a brow at my brightly lit dashboard and backed out of my driveway. The drive was short but still gave me enough time to work myself into hysterics. If they hurt my little girl, I would go nuclear on their gang. It was one thing to threaten me, but if they thought to do anything to my kids, they'd learn what a pissed-off mom could accomplish with wet wipes and large toys.

We pulled up to large gates, and the biker talked to the guy manning them. He waved us through, and we pulled up to a warehouse-looking building that had seen better days.

"Get out and follow me," he barked, heaving

himself out of my small car.

I did as I was told, getting Lena out of the back and holding her to me. She didn't like being held so close and started to wiggle, but I couldn't put her down because then we'd never make it inside. And I thought it wasn't a good idea to piss them off this early in the game.

The interior was bright, windows covering the top part of the walls. The space was open, only one hallway leading off to the left. There was a second-story landing winding in a circle along the outside wall and looking out over the warehouse floor. Doors were evenly spaced apart, making it look almost like a hotel.

I had taken about three steps inside when a loud crash sounded and an angry voice called out, "What the fuck happened to her face?"

I turned toward the familiar sound and locked eyes with Sebastian. And what eyes they were. A little green, a little midnight blue, and a lot pissed off.

"I—" I started to say even though he wasn't talking to me, his attention on the man who drove me here.

"Prez asked us to bring her in, so I brought her in," Big Guy said.

Lena decided she'd had enough and started pushing against me in her efforts to get down. She turned into a little eel and slipped out of my hold. As soon as her feet hit the ground, she let out a triumphant squeal and tried to bail.

I managed to grab her by the back of her sweater and her escape attempt came to a screeching halt. And

I meant that in the most literal sense, because she let out a screech so loud it could shatter eardrums.

"What the hell is going on here?" another voice joined in.

The guy who came with the voice was just as built as the rest of them, making me think they all took steroids. Didn't they know that stuff would shrink other parts of their bodies?

"Sorry, she just woke up," I said, looking back at my daughter, who was now shadowboxing.

"Ace, take care of the kid. You"—he pointed in my direction—"come with me."

"What? No. I'm not leaving my daughter with a stranger," I protested, my eyes jumping from the new guy to Sebastian.

Now I wasn't just worried but terrified.

Before I had a chance to argue further, Sebastian stepped forward and scooped Lena up off the floor. She was so stunned from being picked up by a stranger that she immediately stopped screaming and stared at him.

I could get behind that. If I could, I'd stare at him as well. Even though he was part of the same group of people that had basically just kidnapped me. But tell that to my eyes. They were only interested in his broad shoulders and the sharp angles of his face.

"She'll be here when you come back. I won't let anything happen to her," Sebastian said, leaning down so nobody else could hear him but me. "Go with our prez."

I wanted to scoff at him, but I didn't get a chance to do more than widen my eyes as someone grabbed my arm and dragged me away.

Sebastian growled and pierced the guy pulling me behind him with a glare. I had to admit I was feeling better knowing he was the one watching Lena. Irrational, but still reassuring.

They led me into a messy but clean office and pushed me down into a chair. My breath hitched and my whole body trembled.

"Your man owes us a lot of money," said the guy Sebastian called the prez.

He took a seat behind his desk, making me feel like I was in the principal's office.

"He's not my man," I responded, my voice quivering.

"Then why did he stay at your house last night?"

Jim, you buttgoblin. I'd always known that waste of space only thought of himself, but this really took the cake. If he'd even cared about his family at all, he would never have come to me. And now they probably thought I was helping him with whatever shady business he'd cooked up.

"He came by last night because he needed a place to stay," I said, forcing the words out of my dry throat.

And I let him. One of the worst decisions I'd made in a while. Right after adding red highlights to my raven hair last year.

"Where is he?" Prez asked.

I jumped at his loud voice. "I don't know."

"He borrowed money from us that he never paid back."

I gritted my teeth and took a deep breath before saying, "That mother puffin banana sucker."

Why would he borrow money from a motorcycle club? Had he completely lost his mind? Wait, that was a stupid question, because evidence suggested he was one cup short of a set.

"Since you have no money either, we'll have to get it back another way," he said, and my eyes went wide.

"Oh God. Oh no, please don't cut off my fingers," I called out, jumping out of my chair and burying my hands in my armpits. "I have kids. I need to work. If you maim me, I'll be out of a job."

"Why would we cut off your fingers?" he asked, frowning.

"Or my toes," I added, looking at my sandals. I'd painted my toenails a deep red last night, and they looked too pretty to be cut off. They weren't even chipped yet.

"Calm down," Prez grunted and got up. "You won't lose any body parts. But we'll put someone on you until Jim shows up."

I looked up at him with wide eyes. "What does that mean?"

"Someone will be with you at all times. If Jim is

stupid enough to show his face again, it'll be a win for both of us. You get rid of us, and we get Jim."

"But I have to go to work. I can't just show up with a stranger," I said, glad my shaking hands were still safely stuck in my armpits.

Prez leaned closer. "You won't be showing up with a stranger. Ace works at the same place as you. And since he's the one who will be glued to your side, it won't be a problem. You'll just have to line up shifts. Which is also no issue since we own Pepper's."

I gasped, blinking at him, not comprehending how things could get worse.

And who is Ace? Why does everyone here seem to have a ridiculous nickname?

"We've been watching you for a while. But you had no contact with Jim until yesterday. Knew we'd get lucky eventually," he said and I jolted back, dropping my hands to my sides.

"You've been watching me?"

"It's the only reason I believe you when you say you don't have much to do with him anymore," he said, watching me with a glint in his eyes. I didn't think much would get past him.

Guess his stalkerish ways worked out in my favor. Even if it was creepy. How had I never once noticed anyone watching me?

"Does that mean I can go home now?" I asked, a small flicker of hope coming to life in my chest.

He nodded at the guy behind me. "Gears will take you back to your kid."

I scrambled to follow Gears out the door, falling over my own feet in my haste.

"Thanks for not cutting off a finger," I called over my shoulder, my manners getting the best of me.

Instead of replying, he shook his head at me, one side of his mouth pulled up into a teensy grin.

"Ace," Gears called when we got back to the main room.

Sebastian looked up, and my stomach dropped. Was he the one who was supposed to watch me?

"You finished with the prez?" he asked my escort, not once looking in my direction.

He was holding Lena, looking like a wet dream come to life. Because hot guys holding toddlers were irresistible in my books. Especially if said toddler was currently playing with the hot guy's hair and he didn't care how hard she tugged on it.

When I got closer, I noticed a hair tie in her hand, and my mouth dropped. *Is he letting her do his hair?* It was a little longer on top, just long enough to put one side together.

I stopped in front of him and he finally acknowledged me, even if it was with an empty look. How could I have been so wrong about him? All the girls at work loved him. He was the first one they turned to if there was a problem with a customer. I hoped that wasn't all a front and he really was a good guy who was just battling indigestion at the moment, which would explain his pinched expression.

Lena spotted me and cheered, throwing herself forward. Sebastian caught her and then handed her over.

"You're with me," he grunted. "Stay where you are. I have to grab my stuff."

I was too stunned to utter a word in reply. His voice was the right amount of deep and growly, and my body wanted to go right back into swoon mode. But my brain was finally shaping up and kicking in, forcing my body into submission.

He didn't wait for a reply since me waiting for him was a given due to the twenty or so big guys sitting around, and only one and a half of me to go up against them. Not that the half part, Lena, would be much help.

I stood awkwardly among the rough bikers, wondering how I had gotten to this point. I guess I still had all my fingers and toes, so things could have been worse.

Sebastian came back a few minutes later, a black duffel slung over his shoulder.

"Let's go," he said, walking past me.

"Okay, alrighty, well, nice to meet you all," I called out to the room and then sprinted after Sebastian.

His long legs carried him across the vast space much quicker than my short legs could, and by the time we made it to the door, I was huffing and puffing.

Sebastian wordlessly reached for Lena, who again just stared at him. I was too stunned to stop him when he took her.

We walked to my car—well, he walked while I continued my slow jog—and he placed Lena in her car seat.

He stepped back and put his duffel in the trunk while I strapped my girl in. She seemed in surprisingly high spirits after just having spent time in a den of sin.

I got in the car, and as soon as my seat belt clicked into place, Sebastian took off.

He looked just as ridiculous as the guy driving me before, and I had to work hard not to laugh. His teeth were clenched, and I wondered how I would survive him in my space for the unforeseeable future.

Chapter Three

"I have to go into work tonight," I said to Sebastian as we walked into my house.

He grunted something akin to an agreement and put his duffel bag down next to the front door.

"And it's almost time to pick Luca up."

Another grunt.

Great. I hoped my kids wouldn't start communicating like that.

I saw Lena pick up her book in the living room and open it. I was about to turn to the kitchen to get dinner started when I saw her pull something from between the pages and stick it in her mouth.

"Was that a ham slice?" Sebastian's raspy voice sounded next to me.

I suppressed the shiver that was desperate to make its way down my spine at his nearness and nodded. "Looks like it."

She must have hidden it in there this morning. I'd put ham sandwiches together for Luca's lunch, and Lena wanted a slice. Guess she wasn't intending on eating it right away. I just hoped she wouldn't get sick from it.

"If you're ever hungry, just lift up one of the couch cushions. Plenty of snacks under there," I said and watched his eyes widen. I suppressed the snicker trying to escape and left Lena to her dolls and Sebastian to his mortification.

While I had some time, I set about making a lasagna for dinner. It was all about quick meals in my house. The simpler, the better.

"Button, it's time to get Luca," I called into the living room once I'd put the lasagna in the oven, ready to turn it on when we got back.

When there was no response, I went to look for her. Picking up her brother was usually her favorite thing to do. Especially since we walked, and she loved looking at every crack in the sidewalk, bug, and plant along the way. Which was why we had to leave now or risk being late.

What I didn't expect when I walked into the living room was to find Sebastian sitting cross-legged in front of my daughter, helping her put a dress on her favorite doll, Clara.

I stared, mouth wide open. *What is happening right now?*

Sebastian looked up and dropped the doll like it was lava. He then jumped up and left the room without a word.

I was too stunned to say anything; instead I watched him walk out and disappear into the bathroom. The back view was just as delicious as the front. The best thing about him staying with me would definitely be the view.

"You ready?" I asked my smitten daughter.

"Where Seb?" she asked, watching the entry to the living room.

"Just getting ready so we can pick Luca up."

After more coaxing, I got her to put on one shoe. The other one was apparently too yellow.

She took the one she was already wearing off again and tried on another pair. But by then she'd decided she wanted her yellow shoes after all. This was a familiar dance, and I'd discovered it was best to just go with it.

After ten minutes of back-and-forth, we settled on her sparkly unicorn sneaker on one foot and her yellow shoe on the other. I looked up and saw Sebastian leaning against the wall, watching us.

"You coming as well?" I asked.

"Of course," he grunted and followed us to Luca's preschool.

Lena chattered the whole way, including Sebastian in all her conversations.

We drew a lot of attention when we walked to the pickup area. Delilah, one of the moms I usually avoided at all costs, came straight over. She eyed Sebastian like he was her next meal.

"Moira, who's your friend?" she asked, never taking her eyes off Sebastian.

I rolled my eyes at her. I didn't think she'd gotten my name right once in the three times we'd talked. She was a snob, enjoyed showing off her money, and thought I didn't fit into her neighborhood.

She wasn't wrong. I couldn't afford the house I was currently living in. But my friend's boyfriend owned it and had rented it to me at a ridiculously low price. I'd have been stupid not to accept. So here I was in the fanciest neighborhood our small town had to offer, sticking out like a pink flamingo in a flock of geese.

But as long as I could pay tuition, she had to put up with me.

"Sebastian." I waved in her direction. "This is Callie."

Delilah huffed when I used the wrong name, and I fought hard not to snicker. She started it.

"It's Delilah," she introduced herself, holding out her manicured hand to Sebastian.

Not once did I look at either of them. I was sick of her pettiness. And besides, when I saw Luca come out, I had no reason to waste more time on one of Humptulips' desperate housewives.

I waved, and Lena ran up to hug him. I joined their little huddle, raining kisses all over his face.

He was on the verge of not letting me kiss him in public anymore. But until he told me to cut it out, I would continue doing it.

So far all I got was an eye roll or exasperated breath. Which I chose to ignore.

"How was preschool?" I asked, taking his hand. Lena grabbed his other one, and we made our way down the sidewalk.

I refused to look in Sebastian's direction. There was no way I could watch Delilah sink her claws into him. She was on husband number three and clearly working on number four. Maybe I should have told her he was in a motorcycle club. She wouldn't be salivating all over him then. I knew her standards, and anything less than a doctor or lawyer just wouldn't do.

"Why did you walk away?" Sebastian growled next to me, and I jumped. How could someone that big be that silent?

Luca gave him the side eye, not quite sure yet what to think of him. I told him about our new roommate as soon as we started walking.

"I was just giving you two some privacy," I snapped, eying him in my periphery.

He was moody and looked like he wanted to be anywhere but here. I'd built him up so much in my head that it was hard to see my dreams get squashed by his size who-knew-what feet.

"What the fuck would I need privacy for?" he grunted.

"Language," I hissed, making sure the kids didn't hear him.

"They didn't hear me," he pointed out.

I gave him the side-eye. "That's the only reason I haven't hurt you yet."

"You think you could take me?" he asked, amusement lacing his voice.

I shrugged. "If I had to."

He made a noise that could loosely be interpreted as a laugh. "Do you even know any self-defense?"

"I have moves," I said, concentrating on the sidewalk.

"Okay, show me."

I stopped and looked up at him. "Show you?"

"Yes, show me what you got."

I nodded and continued walking. "Okay. Just remember, you asked for it."

We made it to the house a few minutes later and went into the backyard. The kids ran up to the sand pit, leaving me with Sebastian.

"Let's do this," I said, wringing my hands. Truth was I had no idea about self-defense. I didn't know why I'd said it. Actually, I did. Sebastian had made me mad, and I'd just said the first thing that came to mind. Hopefully I wouldn't regret it.

I didn't get time to wallow in my stupidity before he was behind me. He put his arms around me and pulled me to him.

"Try to get out of my hold," he said, his body plastered to mine.

My senses were suddenly on overload. My body tingled from the tips of my toes to my earlobes from being this close to him. I'd dreamed about being in this position for over a year and didn't know how to react to the sensations overtaking my body.

The thought of him holding me so close. Caressing me. Protecting me. Worshipping at my feet.

Okay, enough, Nora. He's pretending to attack you, not fondle you.

"You're not moving. Why are you not moving?" Sebastian asked, his voice low.

I snapped out of my daydream and stepped on his foot. He loosened his hold, and I elbowed him in the stomach.

He grunted but didn't let go. "Nice try, but you're too small and weak for a move like that."

Small and weak? Really? I lifted my foot again and kicked his shin with my heel. It helped that I was wearing wedges, and they dug right in.

This time his hold went slack, and I dropped down and turned around to knee him in the balls. He went down with a loud groan.

I stood over him with my hands on my hips, smirking and not feeling an ounce of remorse. "Small and weak enough for you?"

The kids came running when they saw Sebastian on the ground, and we all watched him as he lay on the grass, curled into a ball. Guess I hit him harder than I meant to. Whoops.

"Is his tummy hurting?" Luca asked.

Lena leaned down and patted his arm. "Seb sleepy?"

"He'll be fine," I told them. "Let's get you guys ready for Stella."

Stella had become one of my closest friends in the last year. We met in the apartment building where I used to live and had an instant connection. She lived there for a short while in her friend Willa's apartment.

Sebastian heaved himself back up, swaying on his feet. I didn't think I could stop him from toppling over if he couldn't stand up on his own.

He was a six-foot-three giant, and I was a five-foot-two shortcake.

My dad was Swedish and huge. The only thing I'd inherited from him were his green eyes. I only knew a few Swedish words; my favorite was *Sötnos*, a term of endearment he used to call me, the direct translation of which was "sweet nose." I got my height and looks from my Japanese mom. She never taught me a word of Japanese and refused to teach me anything about Japanese culture, except how to cook traditional food.

I never understood why tradition wasn't important to either of them. They also didn't care much about family and disowned me when they found out I was pregnant with Luca.

I hadn't heard from them since they told me I had to choose between family or the baby. I obviously chose the baby.

Sebastian stayed on his feet and shot daggers at me when he limped past me. I rushed the kids inside behind him, running late as usual. Stella would be here soon.

The kids adored Stella, and the feeling was mutual. She was their fun aunt who provided endless entertainment.

We ate dinner, Sebastian having three servings and not saying a word the whole time we sat at the table. Afterward, the kids asked a million questions why Sebastian was staying over before finally having their bath. I was terrible at making things up so all I told them was that he was a friend who would be sleeping on our couch.

A knock on the door made me smile, and then a key turned in the lock. Stella walked inside, greeting me with a hug.

She froze when she embraced me, and I leaned back to see what was going on. Her eyes were stuck to a spot behind me, and I released her and turned. Sebastian was standing there with a scowl on his face.

"Does she always just walk inside?" he asked, nodding at Stella.

"She's got a key. So yes," I answered, daring him to continue arguing with me.

Sebastian narrowed his eyes, and I ignored him. I had to get changed or I'd be late again.

"Stella, this is my new roommate, Sebastian. Sebastian, this is one of my best friends, Stella. She watches the kids for me when I have to work."

The kids raced up to Stella to greet her like they hadn't seen her in weeks, and I went in search of my shoes and bag.

When I came back a few minutes later, Stella was waiting for me.

"Who is Sebastian, and why is he staying with you?" she asked, arms crossed over her chest, her foot tapping impatiently.

"He's just a friend who needed a place to stay. And I'm late for work," I said, wanting to avoid an inquisition but was also running late. "We'll talk later, okay?"

"Fine," she huffed.

I shot her a grateful smile and put my shoes on.

"I'm ready," I said, walking up to Sebastian.

The kids squeezed in next to Stella, who had taken a seat on the couch.

"We're running late," he said. He didn't really look put out by it, making it sound more like an observation than an accusation.

"We're taking the bike. I'm not trying to fold myself into your car again," Sebastian said when we were outside after I said goodbye to the kids and Stella.

"Where did the bike come from?" I asked,

frowning at the shiny motorcycle sitting in my driveway behind my rusty car.

"Chains dropped it off when he picked up his bike. Now get on."

He held out a purple helmet that I refused to take. "No way am I getting on that death trap. I have kids to live for. And maybe one day I'll be rich enough to find out what lobster tastes like. I'm not ready to die before that happens."

"Put on the helmet," Sebastian instructed, not impressed.

I nearly burst out laughing at the sight of him dangling the girly helmet in front of me. I wondered where he'd gotten one in my size from this quickly. And a purple one at that. I had to admit, if I had to wear any helmet, I'd choose one just like it.

I crossed my arms over my chest and shook my head. "No way."

"I see you once again choose the hard way."

He put the helmet on my head himself and had it strapped on before I could rip it off again. Then he picked me up and sat me on the bike. Before I could . figure out how to get off again, he'd climbed on in front of me and we were taking off.

I let out a very undignified scream, and my arms instinctively wound around his middle. It automatically moved my body closer to him, and I found myself plastered to his back.

My lady bits were doing a happy dance, and my

boobs tried to rub up against him like they hadn't been let out in years. Which admittedly they hadn't, but they should really have a bit more self-control at this stage.

Guess this isn't so bad.

The ride was depressingly short, and when we stopped in front of the club, I had to peel myself off Sebastian.

Once back on solid ground, I fumbled to pull the helmet off with little success. *The little sucker might have to stay on.*

Sebastian batted my hands away and undid the strap for me. He held my gaze the whole time. He had the smolder down to a fine art.

I really had to get over this annoying little crush of mine. He was a rude and ignorant brute who was a member of the gang that kidnapped me. I needed to remember that.

He walked next to me to the back entrance, and my steps slowed the closer we got. I hadn't done my required time outside yet. I wasn't ready to go in and stopped next to the door, leaning my back against the wall.

"You go on ahead. I'll be there soon," I said, waving Sebastian off.

I tilted my head up until I hit brick and closed my eyes. I just needed a minute. The ride had taken my mind off my impending shift, but as soon as we were in front of the building, it all came crashing back, suffocating me.

"What are you doing?" Sebastian asked, making me lose my count.

"I just need a minute," I said, not opening my eyes. "I'll meet you inside."

"Are you feeling sick?"

"No. Go away."

"You're my responsibility until Prez says otherwise. So no, I'm not going away. Now what's going on?"

I opened my eyes with a sigh and was met with Sebastian's deep frown.

"I can't go in yet," I responded.

He tilted his head, looking adorably confused. "Why not? Your shift starts in five minutes."

"That gives me four more to waste," I said.

Sebastian studied me for a moment, his eyes roaming my body, seemingly cataloguing every inch. When he was satisfied I looked healthy enough, he stepped to the side and crossed his arms.

Guess he's going to stay outside with me.

I sighed and closed my eyes again. When I made it to four hundred, I felt better, and by five hundred I had myself back under control.

I straightened and took a deep breath. "I'm ready."

"You're also late."

I checked my phone and saw my shift started one minute ago. *Jiminy Crickets.*

I hastened my steps and rushed through to the dressing room, dumping my purse and coat on my chair. The girls called out greetings when I came inside. I pulled on my uniform, tying my hair into a high ponytail. I'd just have to go without makeup today.

Sebastian had disappeared somewhere on the way inside. When I came out of the dressing room, I rushed to the bar, smiling at Stephen, who was mixing drinks.

"Sorry I'm late," I said, taking one of the tablets out of its holder to take orders.

Stephen waved me off with his trademark grin. "It's two minutes. Besides, nobody noticed you weren't here yet."

"Thank you," I said and smiled at him.

"You won't be so grateful when you find out you're in the VIP section tonight. Sorry, honey."

I groaned. I hated working in the VIP room. Hands liked to roam when in enclosed spaces, and the tips did not make up for being groped every two steps.

The night was as depressing as I'd feared. When I finally got a chance to take a break, I stumbled into the small staff kitchen, desperate to eat something.

I had taken one bite of my sandwich when the door opened and Clive, one of the bouncers, came in. He was the last person I wanted to run into during my short break.

"Beautiful, there you are. I haven't seen you in a

week. Are you avoiding me?" he asked, stopping too close to me. When I felt his breath on my face, it took everything in me not to scrunch up my nose and step back.

I'd learned early on that it didn't end well if I pissed him off. So far I'd managed to evade him, but he was relentless. We'd gone out once when I first started. I thought he was a good guy. But what was meant to be a chance for me to spread my wings and dip my toes into the dating pool again had ended in disaster.

And now I had to work with him, since I needed my job.

"Of course not. I've just been busy. You know how it is," I said, putting my sandwich down. I'd lost my appetite, my thoughts on getting out of the deserted kitchen.

"Are you free this weekend? There's a great Italian place that just opened in Butler."

I forced a smile on my face and stepped to the side, closer to the door. "I have the kids."

He was a big guy but bulky. I could probably outrun him. If he didn't catch me before I could get far enough away.

"Can't your friend babysit?" he asked.

I shook my head. "Not this weekend. I'm sorry."

Not waiting for him to reply, I rushed to the door and threw it open. I stepped outside and collided with a warm body. The relief at someone else being there was short-lived when I lifted my head to apologize and locked eyes with Sebastian.

I opened my mouth but decided it was better to just make a quick escape instead of saying anything and rushed back to the safety of the bar.

When it was finally time to go home, I nearly ran out of the building. Sebastian followed at a slower pace, but since his legs were a lot longer than mine, he made it outside at the same time I did.

I couldn't even enjoy the ride home; my skin was crawling, and the need to take a shower made me restless.

When we walked back inside, Stella was watching a reality show, her favorite pastime.

"A delivery came for you while you were out. I put it in the kitchen," she said, then took a closer look at me before waving me off. "Go do your thing. We'll talk when you feel human again."

"Thanks, Stella," I called out, already heading to the bathroom, dropping my purse along the way.

Chapter Four

I stared at the flowers and tried to get rid of the lump in my throat. I knew who they were from. He always sent me red roses. Exactly eleven of them. He was obsessed with numbers and their meaning, and I knew eleven signified change and destiny since I'd looked it up. At least it didn't signify murder and mayhem.

I pulled the cardigan I'd put on after my shower tighter around me.

"Who sent you the flowers?" Stella came into the kitchen where I was staring at said flowers on my counter. "You didn't tell me you were seeing anyone. Is it—"

She stopped in her tracks when she saw the look on my face. "Oh shit, what's going on?"

I looked up and knew it was time to fess up. Stella could smell a lie a mile away. And I just didn't have it in me to make something up. Not tonight.

"They're from Clive."

"What the fuck?" Stella hissed and stalked past me. She took the flowers, stomped to the front door, opened it, and threw them outside, vase and all. They landed with a loud crash, the vase shattering into a thousand pieces on my walkway. I had to make sure to clean the front yard before the kids went out there.

"What's going on?" Sebastian asked, joining us in the kitchen. His hair was wet, and he was only wearing jeans, water droplets glistening on his chest. We must have interrupted his shower, because he was still holding a towel in his hand.

All I could see were abs. And abs. And did I mention abs? He was a sculpted work of art.

Stella snapped her fingers in front of my face, and my eyes refocused on my friend.

"Okay, now that we have you back, it's time you tell me what's going on," she demanded, closing the door.

Sebastian leaned against the wall, settling in for the show-and-tell. I would have rather done this without him. I didn't want him to know how pathetic I was.

Stella snapped her fingers again when my gaze dipped down to the perfect V leading to Sebastian's jeans.

"Please tell me you're not still talking to that psycho," she said.

I recoiled at the thought and glared at her. "Of course not. The flowers started showing up the day after our date. How stupid do you think I am?"

"I don't know. Pretty stupid since you failed to mention any of this shit to me."

"What shit?" Sebastian chimed in.

Stella glanced at him, and I knew by her drawn eyebrows that she meant business. "Nora had *one* date with this guy, and he became obsessed with her. And I'm not talking the sweet, caring, 'I would do anything for you' obsessed. I'm talking the creepy, stalkerish, 'I want to impregnate you with my babies right before I lock you away in my dungeon' obsessed."

Did she have to put it that way? She made things sound a lot worse than they were. Clive just had a little impulse control issue. And he also thought I was his soul mate. A feeling I didn't return.

"Name?" Sebastian barked, dropping his towel on the floor and grabbing a T-shirt from his bag that was still sitting in the hallway. My inner hussy sighed when he was once again covered in clothes.

"Clive Miller. He works with Nora," my traitorous friend replied.

Sebastian stilled, locking eyes with me. "Clive? And you didn't think to mention this?"

Hang on, what's going on here? I felt like I'd missed an important part of this conversation.

"Why would I have mentioned it to you?" I asked, frowning.

He narrowed his eyes, something I was getting used to. "I'll be back."

Sebastian gave us a chin lift and turned to the door. "Gears is just across the street. Stay inside."

With that barked instruction, he grabbed his keys off the table and left.

God, he was confusing.

I turned to Stella and sniffed. "I'm sorry I didn't tell you."

She sighed as she walked over to the couch and sat down. "Who's Gears?"

"A guy who's currently across the street, watching the house," I said and followed, perching on the edge of the couch next to Stella.

"I'll let that one go for now. What I really want to know is what tall, dark, and hot is doing in your house."

Stella pointedly looked at Sebastian's open duffel bag.

"It's only temporary," I said.

I mean, what else could I really tell her? That Sebastian was here to make sure I didn't disappear? That he was waiting for my loser ex to show up again?

"Mm-hmm," she murmured, her tone telling me she wasn't buying my story.

We stayed on the couch, Stella relentless in her pursuit to get me to tell her about Sebastian. When I wouldn't budge, she turned the TV on, keeping me company. When she finally left three hours later, I stayed on the couch, too scared to go to bed yet by myself. It was pathetic to admit, but I'd let Jim screw me around for so long because I was petrified of being alone. And now I was paying the price for being so weak.

A door closing pulled me out of a dream that involved talking frogs, a gold stamp, and a pink llama. It was a great dream, and I didn't want to wake up. Next thing I knew, someone lifted me off the couch.

I opened my eyes when I was gently laid down on a bed. Sebastian pulled a blanket over my body and looked up when I turned over to watch him.

"Where did you go?" I asked, my voice sleepy.

"Just had something to take care of," he said, brushing a strand of hair out of my face, then left.

I fell back asleep a few minutes later, dreaming of talking knives and purring dolphins.

"Did you just put chocolate in the cutlery drawer?" Malena asked, startling me.

I slammed the drawer in question shut and whipped around to face her. "Don't sneak up on me like that or your key privileges will be revoked."

She handed me a coffee she'd picked up on the way over. "Are you hiding chocolate from your kids again?"

I cradled my coffee; I was grateful she'd stopped at Sweet Dreams on her way over. "Maybe. Desperate times and all that. They're not supposed to eat that much chocolate anyway. I'm keeping them sugar free by sacrificing myself and eating it."

"Of course you are."

"Hey, no judging."

"I wouldn't dare." She snickered and looked around. "Where's your new roomie?"

I'd told her about Sebastian when she called last night to tell me she'd drop in this morning. I'd put off telling her as long as I could but had to fess up. To say she was intrigued would be an understatement.

"On the phone."

He was on the phone a lot. The thing rang constantly.

"How are things going?" she asked.

"Splendid."

"Interesting choice of words."

"Shut up."

She raised her perfect brows. "Is that all you got?"

I stuck my tongue out at her, and she chuckled.

"Did you message that Peter guy back?"

I groaned from where I was sitting on the counter, one of my favorite places. "Why would I? We both know it would never go anywhere."

"I think you should give him a chance. He sounded nice."

"So did Clive."

We both sipped our coffee in silence, remembering the mess I'd gotten myself into. Clive was the first guy I'd dated after Jim, and he'd turned out to be a deranged stalker. And while Peter looked good on paper, I had no intention of messaging him.

He was one of the single dads at Luca's preschool and had asked me out a few times. He messaged me again a few days ago, and I was running out of excuses not to catch up with him. I thought he'd give up, but apparently he just thought I was playing hard to get.

"Maybe I'll go out with him tonight," I said, surprising not only Malena but myself.

"Really? Don't tease me like that, because that would just be cruel."

I laughed and jumped off the counter when Luca and Lena came running back into the kitchen, Luca wearing his sweatshirt inside out.

And that's how it would remain since I didn't have the energy to get him to put it the right way around.

"Five minutes, buddy. Then we have to go."

"I don't wanna goes," he complained, not looking up.

"Sorry, Sötnos, but I have to work."

And watching both of them while trying to work would just about kill me.

Malena left after another whispered conversation about my possible date. *Maybe I should just go. He could be a really nice guy.*

But to find out if he was, I had to give him a chance.

Mind made up, I grabbed my phone and texted him back.

Me: Hi, Peter, dinner sounds great. What night is best for you?

He responded right away.

Peter: How about tonight?

Me: I'll see if I can get a babysitter.

Peter: Sounds good.

I was staring at the message when Sebastian came into the hallway. "Ready?"

I startled and dropped my phone. We both bent down to pick it up, and Sebastian saw the message.

"You're not going out tonight," he announced, his voice gruffer than usual.

"Why not? It's not like I'm going to run away while my kids are still at home."

He pulled up to his full height. "I'm supposed to watch you. If I tell you to stay at home, you stay at home."

I threw my arms up, ready for battle. Now I would go on this date out of principle. "This is ridiculous. You can't keep me in the house all the time. I have a life."

Even if it was a small and pathetic one.

"You aren't a prisoner in your house. You go outside to drop off Luca. And yesterday you went to the supermarket."

My eyebrows shot up my forehead. "Are you serious right now? I need to go out and see people. Otherwise, I'll go crazy."

"Malena was literally just here. That should tide you over for a few days."

I stepped closer, my eyes narrowed. "That's different and you know it."

"If you go on the date, then I'm going with you."

Excuse me, what?

I scoffed. "Don't be ridiculous."

"Dead serious. That's the only way you're going on that date."

"Fine," I growled.

"Fine," he growled back, his arms crossed over his chest, his stupidly perfect face distorted into a scowl.

We dropped Luca off, and then I worked for the

rest of the day. Stella agreed to watch the kids, so after I put them to bed and made sure they were asleep, she came over.

I was already dressed in my favorite skintight black jeans, a silky green top with thin straps that dipped low down my back and black heels. I loved heels, needing the extra height. I'd also gone heavier with the makeup than I normally would—as much as my skills allowed, at least.

I didn't know who I was trying to prove a point to, Sebastian or myself. We hadn't spoken a word to each other for the rest of the day. First, he was busy on his phone, and then he was gone for a couple hours in the afternoon, so he obviously didn't need to keep an eye on me all the time, especially not on a date.

Besides, there was a guy watching the house all the time. I didn't see the need for Sebastian to be there as well.

"Stella," I greeted her when she showed up at eight. "Thank you so much for watching the kids for a few hours."

She waved me off. "You know I don't mind. Mason is busy patching up holes in the wall that I accidentally put there when I tried to help him. Better if I'm not there while he fixes them."

"I won't be late," I said and grabbed my bag.

"You finally have a date. Be as late as you want. Just let me know if you want me to stay over," she said, grinning at me like a madwoman. At least one of us was excited about tonight.

I was weighing up the consequences of leaving Sebastian behind when he came around the corner, looking like all my fantasies rolled into one.

Dark shirt, worn jeans, and a scowl on his face. I could do without the obvious displeasure, but he did this to himself. I didn't even feel a little bad about it.

The thought of being stuck in a car with Sebastian and Peter was giving me hives, so I'd arranged for us to meet at the restaurant.

"Let's go," Sebastian ordered, nodding at Stella on his way past.

Her eyes went wide, and she fanned herself after he'd passed her. I shrugged and she waggled her eyebrows at me before disappearing into the living room.

I followed Sebastian outside, and we walked to his motorcycle. Of course he wouldn't take my car. But since I loved riding on his bike—or, more specifically, being pressed against him—I didn't complain. Besides, I was wearing pants, so it didn't matter anyway.

The second time on his bike was just as good as I remembered, and I wished the restaurant was farther away.

When we got close, I saw Peter already standing outside. Sebastian parked just around the corner, helping me off the bike and taking my helmet off for me. I'd figured out how to undo the buckle, but I still didn't stop him when he did it for me.

He walked next to me to the restaurant, and it looked like we were the ones going on a date. I entertained the idea for two-point-five seconds before dismissing it as ridiculous. He'd made it clear that he had absolutely no interest in me.

"Hey," I greeted my actual date, and he leaned in. I leaned back and stuck out my hand, my back hitting Sebastian, who didn't move out of the way.

Peter stared at my hand for a second, then shook it. We'd never hugged before, and I just didn't want to give him the wrong impression. The only purpose of this date was to get him to lose interest in me and to get Malena off my back. And maybe to piss Sebastian off, since I guessed he felt as uncomfortable about this date as he looked.

Peter glanced behind me, and I stepped to the side. "Peter, this is Sebastian. He's my, um, chaperone for tonight."

Peter looked taken aback, and who could blame him? This was ridiculous.

"I'm sorry, did you just say he's your *chaperone*?"

"Just ignore he's even there," I said and led the way into the restaurant. The sooner we had dinner, the sooner I could go home.

The hostess looked up when we walked through the door, and once her gaze hit Sebastian, it stayed there.

"Welcome to Rosie's," she greeted him, her voice perky. "Do you have a reservation?"

Peter cleared his throat. "We do. But it's only for two. Is there any chance you could seat us at a table for three instead?"

"What name is it under?" she asked, clicking away on the computer in front of her.

"Peter Saunders."

She clicked away for a few seconds before turning her attention to Peter. "Ah yes, I see your reservation, Mr. Saunders. We can just add a third chair."

"Great, thanks," Peter said, sounding anything but happy that she was able to accommodate us.

"Please follow me," our cheerful hostess said and winked at Sebastian.

He smiled at her, and this time I did roll my eyes. Guess I just found out what his type was: tall and perky college girls.

We arrived at our table, and Peter sat down first. Sebastian looked around the restaurant and pulled my seat out of for me before he took his own.

"So, Sebastian," Peter said, "are you our Nora's brother? Cousin? Family friend?"

"Roommate," Sebastian responded absently, still looking around the crowded space.

Peter turned to me with a frown. "You have a roommate?"

Guess now I have to go with that one. "I sure do. He's a keeper, this one."

Desperate to make the night less awkward, I waded into safer territory and asked him about his daughter.

"How's Lilly?"

Peter's eyes lit up at the mention of her. She'd been living with him since his divorce and visited her mother every other weekend. "She's great. Such a smart kid. Must take after me, because she certainly didn't get it from her mother."

He boomed out a laugh, and I cringed. I really hoped this wasn't going to turn into a trash-talk-your-ex kind of night. As much as I hated Jim, the only people I complained about him to were Malena and Stella.

"Did you see the notice about the zoo trip?" I asked, hoping to change the topic again.

"I don't know why they keep doing those trips. They cost money, and the kids don't learn anything when they go to the zoo."

"I think it's a great way for them to learn more about animals they wouldn't otherwise see. They might not be inside a classroom, but trips like that are invaluable for their development," I said, swallowing down the rest of my lecture.

He boomed another laugh. "Of course you'd say that. My wife was the same. Always telling me that kids don't just get their education at school."

Time to change the subject again. "How is your job going?"

He was a used car salesman and loved to talk about his job. And surely that was a safe topic. And it was. Unfortunately, it was also the only thing we talked about for the rest of the night. Who knew there were so many different ways to sell a car?

Sebastian sat next to me, his knee brushing mine whenever he moved. I'd moved to the side the first few times it happened but eventually stopped leaning away.

"You should try the lemon pie. You'll love it," Peter suggested when it was time for dessert.

"She doesn't like lemon," Sebastian said, his eyes on me.

"That's okay, I'll try it," I said, wondering how Sebastian knew I didn't like lemon.

Peter nodded and closed his menu. "Great, let's share one."

I also didn't share unless it was with my kids. When the waitress came back, she leaned close to Sebastian, giving us both a clear view down her top.

"Are you guys ready to order?" she asked, only looking at Sebastian.

What was it with that guy? Had he bathed in sugar and slapped on some pheromones to make all the women within a five-foot radius crazy?

"Chocolate lava cake," Sebastian ordered, and neither his gruff tone nor lack of manners put a chink in the waitress's rose-colored glasses.

"We'll have the lemon pie," Peter said, handing the menu back.

Awkward silence encased the table once the waitress was gone. I was surprised it took that long to reach this stage in our three-person date. Peter had been handling it fairly well, considering the grumpy chaperone he had to put up with.

"So, Peter, do you still ride your mountain bike?" I asked, remembering he'd mentioned going for a ride when we were waiting to pick up the kids once.

"Sure do. There's nothing better than racing down the mountain. You'll have to come with me," he said, pulling out his phone.

"I'd love to," I said, 100 percent not intending to follow through on my promise. If there was anything I hated more than lemon, it was mountain bikes. I owned one for a brief period when I was trying to find myself; I sold that incarnation of evil a week after I bought it.

Sebastian snorted and typed on his phone. He'd barely lifted his head all night, his device keeping him occupied.

"You don't like riding a bike without a motor," Sebastian said under his breath.

How in the world he knew that was a mystery I'd solve another day.

"I have photos from my last trips to Coldstream," Peter said, oblivious to our exchange.

And this was when the longest ten minutes of my life commenced. I didn't know there were so many angles you could take a photo of your bike. I chugged my wine and signaled for another glass. I'd need it to get through the rest of this date.

It was a sure bet that I'd not be going on another one. When the waitress came back with my wine and the dessert, I nearly groaned in relief. But I had better manners than that, and instead I only let out a little sigh.

Sebastian chuckled next to me, and I elbowed him when I turned around. He grunted but didn't comment.

Peter pushed the lemon pie to the middle of the table, cutting a piece off with his fork. I crinkled my nose at the smell. I just felt like lemon should stick to what it was good at, like lemonade.

Sebastian pushed his plate in front of me with one hand, his attention on his phone. Peter didn't notice I wasn't eating the tart, too engrossed in scarfing it down himself.

Never one to pass on anything to do with chocolate, I stuck my fork—or rather Sebastian's fork—into the cake and took a huge chunk out of it. As soon as the sweet taste of heaven hit my mouth, I groaned. The velvety cake melted on my tongue, and my mouth experienced chocolate overload.

I chanced a look at Sebastian to see if he would demand the return of his cake, but he was still engrossed in his phone.

I finished the treat in a few minutes, wishing there was more. I vowed to make a trip to Sweet Dreams soon for their chocolate cupcakes.

"Did you like the lemon pie?" Peter asked, not realizing he'd finished the whole piece off by himself.

"It was great," I said, licking the remnants of chocolate off my fork.

We'd finished dinner, and I was busy chugging wine when Peter turned back to Sebastian. He'd been trying to engage him in conversation all night, but since my chaperone only gave one-word answers, all his endeavors so far had failed.

"You gonna follow us home to my place?" Peter asked.

My head snapped around. "Your place?"

"Unless you want to go to yours," he said. "But my house is kid free at the moment."

Is he delusional?

"That's okay. I'd rather just go home. I'm really tired," I said.

I got up and opened my bag, pulling out what I guessed would cover mine and Sebastian's bill. I put the money on the table.

"Hopefully this will be enough for dinner," I said, hoping future run-ins at preschool wouldn't be awkward.

Sebastian picked my money up and handed it back to me. I automatically took it and watched him get out a stack of bills and throw them on the table.

Peter stared at us with a frown. But at least he was smart enough not to say anything. Sebastian put his hand on my lower back, and we walked out of the restaurant in silence.

Once I burst through the doors, I took a deep inhale. Sebastian dropped his hand and turned in my direction.

I put up a hand, not in the mood to talk about what just happened. "Not a word. I just want to go home."

For once he didn't argue and instead nodded before we got on his bike and rode home.

Chapter Five

"I didn't bite him, I only squeezed him with my teeth," Luca said, his little face scrunched up.

"We don't bite other people," I explained, watching his expressive eyes. He wasn't sorry at all, and I didn't know how to make him understand that what he did was wrong.

"But Karl said you're a stippster. And I said you're not. And then he pushed me. He's stupid."

"Don't call him stupid. And what's a stippster?"

Luca looked at me earnestly and folded his hands on his lap. He was sitting next to me on the front step of our house. Lena was playing with her dolls on the porch, giving us a rare moment to talk.

"A stippster takes off clothes. That's what Karl said."

My heart stopped and my breath hitched.

While it wasn't exactly what I did, it wasn't far off.

The clothes I wore at work barely covered all my bits. And my coworkers took their clothes off for money. But I thought I had time left before my job would embarrass my kids.

I had no hope of finding another job in a town as small as Humptulips. I'd tried. And was still trying. My day job wouldn't be enough to keep a roof over our heads and food on the table.

I'd been slowly building a cushion, but it wouldn't last long. And it definitely wouldn't allow me to quit one of my jobs.

"I don't take my clothes off at work. I only serve drinks," I explained, struggling to get the words out.

I didn't want Luca to have to face reality just yet. He was still so little. The thought of him thinking less of me made me want to throw up.

"He said his dad saw you. And that you're going to hell. I don't want you to go to hell. It's too hot. And you don't like the heat."

I took his hand in mine, making sure he was looking at me. "Well, his dad is a hypocritical pumpernickel. But regardless of what he said, you're not allowed to bite people, okay?"

Luca seemed to think about it for a moment and then turned his innocent gaze back to me. "What if I just did it a little bit? Just until he stopped talking?"

"No, not even a little bit. Just stay away from him. He doesn't sound like he's making good choices. And if he keeps listening to his dad, he's going to end up a middle-aged divorced man with a bald patch and no friends."

He got up, clearly done with this conversation. "Can I go play now?"

"Sure," I said and pulled him close for a hug. "But stay where I can see you."

Luca ran off, and I watched him collect leaves that had fallen off the big oak tree in our backyard. I felt someone behind me and sighed. The last person I wanted to witness this conversation was Sebastian, but since he'd pretty much moved in, it was hard to avoid him.

He was sleeping on my couch, only going into work when I did and not letting me go anywhere without him. I thought he was taking things a little far. He didn't agree.

That was pretty much how all our interactions went. He said left, I went right.

Since Sebastian wasn't big on talking either, I was quite certain he wouldn't start up a conversation. What I didn't expect was him taking a seat next to me.

We sat there in companionable silence, watching the kids. His phone pinged a few times, and when it wouldn't stop going off, he glanced at it and stood up with a sigh.

A single tear rolled down my cheek, the only one I'd allow. I had to grow thicker skin. And have a chat with Karl's dad.

I had to go into work tonight and needed to get myself together before then. Stella was coming over to babysit, and she would immediately know if something was wrong.

And since the best way to get my mind off my sucky life was to play with my kids, that's exactly what I did.

After digging in the sandbox for an hour and pushing the little gremlins on the swing at the playground for almost as long, I declared it was time for dinner. I also had to leave for work soon, whether I wanted to or not.

Stella arrived just as Lena and Luca were finishing their pasta. She burst into the kitchen as usual and threw her arms around me.

"I feel like I haven't seen you in ages," she declared.

"You're here almost every day. And the days you're not here we talk on the phone."

She squeezed me again and let go. "How are my little angels?"

"Luca bit someone in school today, and Lena decided she doesn't like the color red anymore. So no more red food or clothes."

Stella greeted the kids with a kiss on their heads. "You're missing out, kiddo. Your mom makes the best Bolognese sauce."

"Ready to go?" Sebastian asked, walking into the kitchen while typing on his phone.

I took a deep breath. "Ready."

"Mommy work?" Lena asked, looking at me while she continued shoveling cheesy pasta in her mouth.

"That's right, cherub, I have to go to work. And

Stella is going to stay with you."

She nodded, used to me not being there at night all the time. And it broke my heart that she was so used to it, that this was the norm, that I wasn't the one putting my kids to bed every night.

I kissed her chubby cheek, then Luca's, and reluctantly waved goodbye. We walked to Sebastian's bike and he got on, then held the purple helmet out for me.

"Is it a normal thing for you guys to have purple helmets lying around the clubhouse?" I asked, still curious as to where it had come from.

"Just put it on. We're going to be late again," he grumbled.

I sighed but put it on and took his outstretched hand. He helped me up on the bike, and once my body was flush to his and my arms were wrapped around him, we took off.

The ride was amazing, and I felt invincible once we pulled up outside the club. But as soon as I took off my helmet and handed it back to Sebastian, reality crashed in around me and my breath hitched.

"I'll be right in," I said when we were almost at the back door.

Sebastian stopped next to me when I leaned against the wall and closed my eyes. Since this had happened every time we'd gone to work together, he knew the drill. And despite me telling him to go ahead without me every time, he never did.

I did my thing, then took a deep breath and walked past him and inside the club. Sebastian was right behind me, and I could feel the heat coming off his body. *Does he have to crowd me like that?* It wasn't busy yet, so there was no need to walk so close.

I made it to the dressing rooms and looked over my shoulder. "See you later."

He grunted a reply and lifted his chin before he stalked off. I turned the other way and went through the door. All the girls were already there, getting ready for their performances.

"Hey, honey, you need a hand with your hair?" Star asked, looking at me in the mirror.

"Do you have time? I don't want to make you late," I said, pulling out my chair.

She came over, bringing her makeup with her. "I got here an hour ago. I'm as ready as I'll ever be."

I sat down, looking at her. "Trouble with Mike?"

She started braiding my hair. "There's always trouble with that man. But this time I've had enough."

This was not a new development. She kicked him out every other week. The guy wasn't the smartest bulb in the pack, but he was sweet. Unfortunately for him, he had a terrible taste in friends, and they regularly got him in trouble.

"What did he do this time?"

"He didn't come home for three days. And when he did, he stank of cheap perfume and bad choices."

"Oh no, Star, I'm so sorry."

Up until now, he'd never cheated. I knew what it felt like when someone you trusted trampled all over you. It sucked hairy balls.

"It's okay. We should have broken up years ago. I was just too stuck on what we used to be to cut the cord."

I took her hand. "You're too good for him anyway."

"Damn right she is," Elle called out from two dressing tables away. "And I can finally set you up with my cousin. You're going to love him. Just remember to name your firstborn after me."

Star laughed, and Elle winked at me.

"Who's got the bachelor party tonight?" Tia asked, flopping down in the chair beside me.

Tia was even smaller than me but looked nothing like a little girl. Her surgically enhanced boobs were barely contained by her latex top, and her pouty lips had seen one too many injections. She was as loyal as they came, and we'd gotten along from the moment we met.

She might be small, but she was freakishly strong. Guess all that pole dancing really gave her a workout.

Groaning, Star lifted her hand at Tia's question. "That would be me."

"So what's going on with you and Sebastian?" Elle asked, studying me.

"Nothing," I said, studying my chipped manicure. I had to get out my nail polish tonight before I went to bed. Pink would look great.

"I heard he was living with you. That's not nothing," Star chimed in.

"Did you know he's the only one of the guys working at Pepper's who's never tried touching any of us?" Elle said.

"He's just crashing on my couch," I said, knowing I needed to give them something or they'd hound me all night.

"Sure he is," Tia said and then got up. "Showtime, girls."

We shuffled out of the room, the girls heading to the stage while I went to the bar.

I didn't see Sebastian for the rest of the night, but one of the guys was clearly on Nora duty. He was trying to be inconspicuous, but thanks to my recently acquired paranoia, I spotted him as soon as he took up his post near the entry.

It also helped that he was wearing clothes that screamed "biker." I didn't dwell on it though, since I was busy dodging grabby hands and sleazy offers all night. When the clock hit two, I ran to the dressing room as fast as my abused feet would take me.

I used to get away with wearing sneakers and clothes that mostly covered me, but since the club changed ownership, that was a big no-no. Smitty, the new manager, ran a tight ship and didn't give handouts.

He also didn't give sick days or days off. And since I couldn't really afford to take either, I didn't complain.

Besides, none of us were here because we loved our jobs, so we just kept our heads down and moved on.

I burst into the empty dressing room, kicking my shoes off. I stopped in the door as soon as I noticed the quiet. Being by yourself was not a good idea in this place. Especially not since I had acquired my personal stalker.

Guess it was a good thing Sebastian was teaching me self-defense. One day I'd be able to kick Clive's butt. That day was not today though. I backed out of the room, taking a deep inhale when I made it without anyone jumping me.

At least I thought I made it until my back collided with another body and I felt my blood rush from my face. I jerked back and my elbow collided with something soft. There was a loud groan, and I whipped around.

Sebastian was doubled over, cursing.

I covered my mouth in horror and gawked at my handiwork.

"You must really enjoy beating me up," he coughed and straightened back up. "Why are you so jumpy?"

I moved back. "I'm not jumpy. You just surprised me."

He pinched the bridge of his nose before pinning me with his gaze. "I know when you're lying, Nora."

I threw my hands up and stepped back into the dressing room. "This place would make anyone jumpy."

I slammed the door behind me, then realized I'd left my shoes outside. I stuck my head out again, and Sebastian held the shoes up to me. I snatched them back and clutched them to my chest.

"Will you wait out here?" I asked, my voice wavering.

He gave me a chin lift, and I disappeared back inside.

Changing back into my jeans settled my nerves, and once I'd pulled my hoodie over my head, I almost felt human again.

Sebastian was leaning against the wall, watching the crowd, when I came back out. He looked up when he heard me, and his eyes traveled from the top of my head all the way to the sneakers on my feet.

I suddenly felt like I wasn't wearing any clothes at all. But where I usually got the urge to douse myself in bleach when customers gave me the once-over, this time my body heated, my pulse beat faster, and I didn't move.

Our eyes met, and I suddenly found myself unable to look away. Then one of the security guys came up to him, breaking our connection. Sebastian turned his head to speak to the guy, and I looked at my feet, shuffling uncomfortably. I hoped Sebastian would never find out the power he had over me, because rude turd or not, I couldn't fight the attraction I felt for him.

He didn't say a word to me for the rest of the night, not when we walked to his bike and not when we got home. I fell into bed, exhausted from another blipper of a day. Sleep came slowly, my thoughts stuck on the giant currently living with me.

Chapter Six

"No," I yelled, scrolling through my phone. "No. No. No. No."

My chant went on like that as I looked through my closet, finding all my savings gone. How was that possible? And why hadn't I deposited my tip money into my bank account instead of in a shoe box?

Where had the money gone? How could it just disappear?

"Banana sucker," I yelled, running my hands through my hair. *What am I going to do?*

"What happened?" Sebastian growled from the doorway.

"I'm fucked," I whispered and tunneled my shaky fingers through my hair.

There was only one person who could have possibly taken my money. And I had no idea how to find him. I couldn't even wish that I'd never met Jim, because then I wouldn't have Luca and Lena. And they were my everything.

"Nora," Sebastian said, reminding me he was still there.

"All my savings are gone," I said. It took all my strength to keep my voice even. "All this shit for nothing."

I sank to the floor, my feet unable to hold me up any longer. This really was rock bottom. I'd worked so hard to save up that money. And it was all gone. I didn't even care that I'd just told Sebastian that I had money saved up.

Didn't matter now anyway since it was gone.

He crouched down next to me, putting a hand on my knee.

"You don't—" he started but was cut off by Luca running into the room.

"Mommy, why is you on the floor?"

"Why *are* you on the floor," I corrected him automatically. "I was looking for an earring that I lost."

"Need help?" he asked, getting down on his knees next to me.

"It's okay, I'll look for it later. We don't want to be late for preschool," I said and turned to my little human. "You ready to go?"

He grinned and plonked down on his butt, holding his feet up. "I puts on my own shoes."

There was so much pride in his voice that I was reluctant to let him know they were on the wrong feet. And if we'd only gone to the playground across the street, I wouldn't have worried. But I didn't want the teachers to think I didn't pay attention.

"Well done, Sötnos. You did a really good job. The thing is just that your shoes are on the wrong feet."

He creased his brow and looked at his shoes, then at me. "But they're the only feets I got."

A smile tugged on my lips, and I was reminded once again why I would do just about anything for my kids. "Good point." I tapped his shoes. "But I meant your shoes are mixed up. We need to switch them to the other foot."

"I'll do it," he said, and I watched him change his shoes, my fingers twitching every time he struggled. But he was determined to do it himself. His lips puckered in concentration, and I didn't want to interfere.

Once he set his mind to something he wouldn't stop until he'd figured it out. He used to have a speech problem and slight stutter, but with speech therapy, you couldn't even tell anymore.

His eyes were bright and his voice animated when he did it all by himself.

"Finished," he declared, clapping his hands.

"Where's Lena?" I asked. Usually she was glued to Luca, hardly ever leaving his side.

"I've got her," Sebastian's deep baritone sounded

from behind me.

I got up and turned, my jaw slipping at the sight in front of me. Sebastian was holding a relaxed Lena on his hip like this was a normal occurrence. She was fully dressed, one of her hands resting on his cheek, her other one holding on to the fabric of his T-shirt.

"I'll take her," I said, walking up to them.

"No," Lena declared when she saw my outstretched hands.

"It's okay, I'll carry her," Sebastian said and walked out.

I followed, holding Luca's hand. We dropped him off, Lena never moving from her comfortable perch.

When we got home, I put a snack together for Lena so she'd be busy when I made a phone call I didn't want to make. Nausea churned in my stomach at the thought of what I was about to do. But I was out of options. And I just had to get over myself.

Things could always be worse. I could have no money left at all. But since I still had a bank account where my wages were paid into, I'd be okay. Just not for too long. And I needed to earn more money or forever live paycheck to paycheck. Jim taking my meager savings showed me how shaky my situation was. I had to make changes.

One wrong move and it would all blow over like a house of cards. I owed it to my kids to try harder, and that started with finding a job that earned more money.

I got Lena settled and walked into the living room. I could still see her sitting at the table, but she wouldn't be able to hear my phone call. Not that she'd understand or care anyway, but it didn't feel right to have this conversation in front of her.

Sebastian watched me pull out my phone. "I have to go out. A prospect is watching the house, but don't go anywhere without me."

I didn't even care about him telling me what to do. I had a ton of work to do. And of course there was the call I was about to make.

"Wasn't planning on going anywhere today."

He studied me for another few seconds before lifting his chin and walking out.

When I heard the front door click shut, I found the number for Pepper's.

Smitty picked up on the third ring. "Yeah?"

"Smitty, it's Nora."

He grunted. "If you're calling in sick, don't bother coming back at all."

"I'm not. I just wanted to find out if you're still short a girl," I said, sweat beading on my brows.

"Are you telling me you're interested in the position?"

I took a deep breath. "I am."

"It's yours," he said without hesitation.

"But you don't even know if I can dance."

"Don't need to. With your body and all that hair, it doesn't matter. The customers will love you."

I unsuccessfully tried to control my breathing, hoping I wouldn't pass out before I finished the call. "When do I start?"

"Monday. But come in early before your next shift so Tia can show you the ropes and help you with your routine."

Monday was only four days away. Which meant four days to get a routine right. Four days to psych myself up to take my clothes off in front of strangers.

"Okay, I'll see you tomorrow."

"Don't be late."

He hung up, and I ran to the toilet and threw up. I'd had a lot of bad ideas in my lifetime, but this one was probably the worst so far. But I couldn't go back to an empty bank account. If I just did this for a few months, I should be able to build up a small emergency fund.

I had little hope in getting the money back from Jim. It wasn't a lot, but it was most of my savings. And him taking it was only the icing on my disaster cake. *How did I not see how selfish he was when we first met?*

Once my stomach calmed down, I brushed my teeth and went back to the kitchen. Lena was still eating her dry cereal, something that usually kept her busy for a while.

I pulled out my computer and got to work. Lena had a good day, and I finally managed to work through my to-do list. The last thing I wanted was to lose the job I actually liked.

Late afternoon, my phone pinged with a message from Malena.

Malena: When are you going to invite me over for that dinner you promised me?

Me: How about this Saturday?

I was in desperate need of my friend.

Malena: It's a date. Will hunkalicious be there? That would make the night even better.

Me: Hunkalicious? Really? How old are you?

Malena: Shut up.

Malena: What would you call him? Wet dream? Walking, talking porn?

Me: How about Sebastian?

Malena: Boring.

Me: Come over any time. We'll be home most of the day. Gotta go.

Malena: K. XX

Me: Is that code for something?

Malena: HOW OLD ARE YOU? I said okay and then

sent you kisses.

Me: K. XX

I received no response to my last message and put my phone back down. I hadn't seen Sebastian all day, but my latest guard was sitting in front of my house like the well-trained lapdog he was.

I finished up with work, and there was still no sign of Sebastian by the time I had to pick up Luca, so I got Lena ready and left.

The guy jumped up when he saw me walk down the sidewalk.

"Hey," he called out and sprinted after us. "You're not supposed to leave the house."

I continued walking. "I have to pick up my son."

"You can't go anywhere without an escort."

I huffed and still didn't stop. "Good thing you're here, then. You get to escort us to preschool."

He caught up and put his hand on my arm. "Ace said you need to stay inside."

I pulled my arm free and kept walking. "He knows I have to pick up my son. If he's so worried about me going anywhere without him, he should have been here."

"Something came up that he had to take care of," the guy explained but didn't try to stop me again.

"I don't know how you think Jim is just going to

show up here with you guys around. He might be a loser, but he's not stupid."

"Ace has a plan."

"Of course he does," I muttered and picked up Lena, who'd decided it was a great idea to rip flowers out of someone else's front yard.

"Can you at least wait outside while I get my son?" I asked when we made it to the preschool.

"Sorry, can't do that. Ace said—"

I turned and walked into the building, not hearing what else he was saying. I was getting sick of being watched. Of being told what to do. Of being made to feel like I was guilty for something I had no hand in.

Luca came flying across the playground as soon as he saw me.

"Where's Seb?" he asked, looking around my shoulder.

I took his hand, and we walked inside to get his bag. "He's busy."

"Did he forgets to pick me up?"

I stopped in front of Luca's classroom and set Lena down before kneeling in front of him. "He didn't forget. But sometimes plans change. And Sebastian had an important meeting. Otherwise I'm sure he would have been here."

Sebastian had been in our lives for only a short amount of time, yet both kids were already used to him. Just thinking about the aftermath of him leaving made me want to hide in a closet. And I wasn't sure that it was a good thing my kids were getting attached to a guy who was part of a motorcycle club.

I didn't really know what the club did, but if they lent money to Jim, it couldn't be all above board. My ex had been involved in a whole lot of stuff that wasn't exactly legal.

I just wished I hadn't been so oblivious when we first met. The signs were all there, but I'd ignored them. He used to disappear at random times, day or night. He never made a call when I was in the room, and when he answered his phone, he always went far enough away so I couldn't hear him.

And there was always a lot of cash stuffed in random drawers and closets around the house. How did I never think that was weird? When they say love makes you blind, they really were speaking the truth. I was just glad I woke up, even if it was late.

Now the one thing I'd always been scared of had happened. Jim's screwups were affecting our kids and putting their lives in danger. But I was determined to survive this latest bump in the road with only minor scratches.

Besides, if I could survive Lena's poop explosions, I could handle anything.

Our escort walked us back home, and I started on dinner. The night went on as usual. The kids ate some of their food and threw the rest at each other. They flooded the bathroom, and I lost my patience and yelled at them for not listening. But at the end of the night, when we cuddled up under the blanket in Luca's room and I read to them, I hardly remembered why I'd been angry.

"Okay, kidlets, lights out," I said after the third book as Lena's eyes were closing.

Since they shared a room, bedtime could be a challenge. But usually Lena was tired enough to fall asleep after humming a few songs. Luca sometimes stayed up for a little while and played with his toys. But since he was quiet enough to not wake Lena, I didn't mind.

I was living in a tiny one–bedroom apartment when I became friends with Stella. When she offered up this place, I was desperate enough to accept, even though I knew they wouldn't be making as much money with it as they could. I didn't know what I would have done without them.

All my friends had done so much for me, there was no way I would ask anyone for money. I was a grown woman, and I needed to stand on my own two feet. What kind of example would I set for my kids if I let someone else bail me out all the time?

After dragging myself around the living area, picking up a few toys, I collapsed on the couch. At least all the small stuff was gone so nobody would step on anything. I wouldn't lie and say the thought of leaving a few strategically placed Lego around the place didn't cross my mind, but I doubted a few Lego injuries would deter Sebastian from staying on my couch.

I turned on the TV, noticing I'd made it just in time for my favorite show. *Shake That Cake* was a reality show about pastry chefs who were in competition to create the best instant cake mixes. The winner would get one hundred thousand dollars, and three of their recipes would be made into cake mixes and sold in supermarkets across the country.

One of the participants was a local baker, Rayna. She owned Sweet Dreams and made the best pastries in the state, and I hoped she would win. So far she'd made it to round three, and I loved every minute of watching her fight it out with the other contestants.

And there were a lot of disagreements. It was the perfect entertainment for my usually dull life. And once I started watching, it was impossible to stop.

Rayna told one of the participants not to call her creation a "cake shake." Not knowing why she was offended, I was busy asking the Internet what in the world it was when Sebastian walked in.

My eyes went wide, and I choked on my own spit when I read the definition. *First takeaway: I really have been living under a rock. Second takeaway: don't ever miss Sebastian invading your space when he's mad at you.*

"I told you not to leave the house without me," he thundered, taking up space in front of me.

I dropped my phone in my lap with a squeak and looked up, taking in his worn jeans that fit him just right, his thermal that was a little snug around the chest, the leather vest he was wearing over it, and finally his stubbled square jaw.

His usually full lips were now pressed into a tight line, and a muscle pulsed in his jaw. When I made it to his eyes—which I usually loved looking at—they pierced me with a glare.

I swallowed and sat up straighter. Screw him for standing over me, trying to intimidate me. I fisted my hands, the pain of my fingernails digging into my palms stopping me from jumping up and telling him where to stick his anger.

"I had to pick up my son," I ground out. "You weren't here. What should I have done? Leave him in preschool?"

"You could have told Gears to send one of the guys."

I scoffed at his ridiculous suggestion. "They don't know Luca. And he needs to be on the approved list. You can't just show up and take a kid home. It's not a pet shop."

I refused to be the first to break eye contact, even though I was beginning to get a crick in my neck.

"Are you done with your tantrum, or do you want to interrupt my TV watching for anything else?" I asked, narrowing my eyes at him.

"Do you think this is all a game?" he growled.

A sad chuckle escaped before I could hold it in. "A game? Are you serious? You kidnapped me, invaded my privacy, and now I have to live with a stranger who doesn't want to be anywhere near me. I'm scared for my life and my kids'. So no, I definitely don't think this is a game. It's my *life*, and you are doing your best to stomp all over it."

The ticking in his jaw stopped and his eyes softened. "We won't hurt you."

I scoffed and got up, leaving only a hairbreadth between us. "And I'm just supposed to trust you and your gang?"

"We're not a gang. And you have my word that nothing will happen to you or your kids."

I poked my finger in his chest, my anger getting the best of me. "Your word means nothing to me. Nothing." Another poke. "I'm sick of guys like you thinking they can walk all over me. Do you think because I work at a strip club, I'm an idiot?"

He grabbed my finger and held it. I was too caught up in my rant to care that he was now holding my hand against his chest.

"I'll have you know I had a perfect GPA in school. I had a scholarship to college," I continued to rant.

"I never once thought you were stupid," Sebastian said, his voice raspy.

"Doesn't really matter though, what you think. I'm still at your mercy."

"Listen to me and listen good. I never go back on my word. If I say I'll do something, I will. And I'm telling you now, I will do anything I can to keep you and your kids safe."

My shoulders slumped, my head drooped, and I pulled on the hand he was still holding. He didn't let go, and my head snapped back up.

My lips parted to yell at him some more—because I had nothing else left at this stage—when he silenced me with a kiss. He kissed me with a desperation that left me breathless and aching for him. It was demanding, urgent, and drugging. Simply perfect.

I leaned in, unable not to, and wound my free arm around him, holding on tight. I returned his kiss with reckless abandon, forgetting what we were even talking about to start with.

When he pulled back, dislodging my tight grip on him in the process, I nearly lost my balance. He put his hand on my arm to steady me, then let go as soon as I was standing on my own two feet again.

"This can't happen again," he said and stalked out of the living room.

The front door slammed shut, and I was left to wonder what the flying ducks had just happened.

Chapter Seven

"I'm not sure what you would call that move."

"Dying possum."

"Wet cat."

"Sloth on a pole."

"Terrified frog."

The pole slipped through my fingers and I landed on my head—for the twentieth time that day. I was at Pepper's, trying to work on a routine. Sebastian thought I'd gone in early to help go over the inventory.

I didn't correct him and was all too happy for him to disappear into the office as soon as we made it inside. He hadn't said a word to me since our kiss. I didn't know kissing someone could feel like my whole world had been tipped on its head. Too bad he didn't seem to feel the same way.

Now the girls were helping me put a routine together for Monday, and I was screwing it up with all

I had. Turned out I was useless when it came to pole dancing. I couldn't even hold the easiest pose.

So far I'd let go of the pole and fallen off every single time. And I was pretty sure I had a concussion. My head was pounding, and my hands were hurting from sliding down the pole. We'd been at it for the past hour. And as impossible as it seemed, it appeared I was getting worse.

"Maybe you shouldn't attempt any move that puts you upside down," Elle suggested.

Tia threw up her hands and came closer. "That cuts out about 90 percent of all moves. There'll only be three positions left."

I blew hair out of my face. "I'm sorry, but I was never good at dancing. Or gymnastics. Or really moving in general."

Tia guided my hands up over my head and curled them around the pole. "Hold on like that. Now lift your legs. Maybe you can do a plank."

I blinked, trying hard not to laugh. Never in my life had I been able to do a plank. Horizontal or vertical. Not that I'd tried the pole position before.

"Come on, lift those legs," Tia said, tapping my thighs. One thing I learned about three seconds after walking up on stage with the girls was that they had no boundaries.

My butt had been in their face, they'd adjusted my boobs, lifted me with one hand on each butt cheek, and Elle moved my body every which way, not caring if she was holding on to a boob or an arm.

They were lucky I'd had two kids and didn't care who might catch a glimpse of my lady cave anymore. Because I was sure I'd flashed them a time or ten since I was only wearing tiny shorts.

I tightened my grip on the pole and lifted my legs. They came a few inches off the floor before they stopped.

"That's it?" Star asked, disbelief all over her face. "Did you even lift them?"

I put my feet back on the ground and released the pole. "I had abdominal separation after Lena, and things haven't gone back the way they were supposed to. My abs are pretty sad these days."

I also hadn't had time to work on building up my abdominal muscles again. Not that it had been a priority. And the longer I left it, the less important it seemed.

"But you're so lean," Tia said, walking around me, inspecting my stomach. I was only wearing a sports bra and shorts that could double as underwear. "And no stretch marks. Are you sure things didn't go back the way they were?"

I tensed my pitiful stomach muscles and took her hand, putting her fingers in the slight gap.

"What the fresh hell is that?" she exclaimed, pushing her hand in farther.

"That's something I could fix since it's not bad enough to need surgery. But I hate exercise, I'm as coordinated as a drunk donkey, and have no need to get my body back in shape."

Elle put her fingers on my stomach once Tia dropped her hand. "Let me feel."

"Go for it. It's not like I'm self-conscious about the hole in my stomach," I said, sarcasm lacing my voice when she started probing my belly.

"I'll give you a few simple exercises. You'll be fine in a few months. It's a small separation, but you really need to sort it out."

I stared at her, brows raised. She finally stepped back and shrugged. "I'm a physiotherapist. I see this after pregnancy all the time. And it's easy to fix, but you have to put the work in."

"You're a physiotherapist?"

Her nose scrunched in annoyance. "We live in a small town. And I don't make much money but have expensive taste. I got a second job to keep my shoe closet stocked and my mortgage paid off. Stripping is perfect because I can work at night and get a good workout in at the same time."

I put my hands up. "I'm not judging. I was just surprised that you wouldn't move to Denver where you could find a better job."

"My mom had a heart attack last year. If I'm in Denver, I'm too far away to help out."

"I'm sorry, Elle," I said.

She winked at me. "Eh, don't worry, it is what it is. And I don't hate stripping. It's just another job to me. Are the customers a bit too handsy at times? Sure, but it's nothing I can't handle. Unlike you, I don't mind prancing around a stage."

"I guess I need to work on my poker face," I said.

"Nobody is going to look at your face when you're up here. No matter how much you frown or draw your eyebrows together, the customers will love you all the same. You have a bangin' body and gorgeous silky hair. Now if you just managed at least three moves, you'll be fine."

I groaned. I didn't have enough time to get ready.

"It would help if you'd done at least some exercise in the last century," Tia put in, slapping my butt. "No idea how you can look like you do but have no muscles anywhere other than in your arms."

"Hey, I have two little kids. When do you think I have time to go to the gym? And my arm muscles are hard-won from carrying said kids around."

Tia ignored me and clapped her hands. "Let's try a flying ballerina. You don't have to lift your legs or hang upside down."

She explained the move, and it seemed simple enough: hold on with one arm and leg and stretch out the other ones, making the move look like you're jumping in the air—while holding on to a pole.

I jumped up and kicked Elle right in the face.

"Oh my Jumpin' Jiminy, I'm so sorry," I cried and kneeled next to where she was now sitting on the floor. "Do you need some ice?"

Tia was one step ahead of me and appeared with a

handful of ice cubes wrapped in a dish towel.

Elle held it to her eye while we were all fussing around her. "It's okay, guys, stop worrying. Her miniature feet didn't do much damage."

"Hey, they're proportional to my body," I complained.

"Exactly," Elle said, her mouth tipping into a smile.

"Guess I didn't hit you hard enough if you can still make fun of me," I griped.

The rest of the training session didn't go much better. At least I didn't hurt anyone else. But I did fall on my butt another fifty times.

I didn't know how I was supposed to get through my shift tonight. My head and butt were throbbing, and my arms ached from attempting to hold up my body weight.

When we got back to the dressing room, I changed into my work uniform and then collapsed onto the floor with a pained groan. "I don't know how you guys do this every night."

"I'll write up a Pilates routine for you that will help," Elle announced, sitting down next to me. "But for now, turn over and I'll give you a quick massage."

I turned around faster than I thought I had the energy for. But the promise of a massage was too good to pass up.

"Hopefully this will loosen your muscles a little. We only have five minutes, but it's better than nothing."

There was a knock at the door, and then someone called out. "Is it safe to come inside?"

I looked up from where I was stretched out on the floor.

Most of the guys just barged in, so the person outside could only be Sebastian. Tia fanned herself and replied, "Come in, gorgeous."

Sebastian stuck his head through the half-open door. "Can you get—"

He stopped talking, his attention snapping to where I was lying on the floor, Elle sitting on my lower back, giving me the best massage of my life.

When he didn't finish his sentence, I dropped my forehead back on my crossed arms and let out a moan. Elle was a master.

The door slammed shut, and when the normal chatter didn't start up again, I grudgingly lifted my head again. This time all eyes were on me. And then they all started talking at once, making me sit up.

"What did you do to him?"

"Tell me your secrets."

"Did you see the way he looked at her?"

"Was that Sebastian?"

"There goes another one of the good ones."

I narrowed my eyes at anyone who dared look at me with wide eyes. "Stop it, everyone. I didn't do anything. I told you he's just crashing on my couch.

Nothing more."

My words were lost amid another wave of chatter, directed at me.

"Liar."

"I thought we agreed we'd be honest in here."

"What's said in the dressing rooms stays in the dressing rooms."

"Talk."

The last was barked and brought the chatter to an end. Tia was standing in front of me, her arms crossed over her ample cleavage, her foot tapping impatiently.

Elle let me go, and I stood up to be in a better position to run in case they decided to lynch me.

"I think there's been a misunderstanding. Sebastian has no interest in me. You guys got it all wrong."

Elle put her hands around my shoulders, pulling me close. "I never thought you were slow, but I see we have to spell it out for you. That delectable piece of male perfection has been looking at you like you're a juicy steak since he first saw you strut your fine ass into the club."

"That's not true," I protested. "He—"

"Have you never wondered why he's always been at the club when you are from day one? Shifts don't usually line up every single time for a whole year," Elle said.

I scoffed and pulled my clothes into place, thinking

they'd all gone insane. Sebastian didn't like me. Or did he? Maybe the kiss wasn't an accident like I thought.

"You're all delusional. Stop looking for something that's not there."

Tia slapped my butt so hard I jumped. "Stop being so blind. And anyone in here who isn't attached has tried to get it on with him. He's declined every single invitation. And, honey, I hate to tell you this, but he's in an MC, and those guys like their women."

I didn't know what to do with that information. He'd been nothing but short with me. I was sure he hated every minute of living with me. What was wrong with everyone today? Maybe I wasn't the only one who'd given herself a concussion during practice.

"You've all lost your mind. Have you ever considered that maybe he's gay, and that's why he's never taken any of you up on your offer?"

The whole room burst into laughter. I flipped them the bird and stalked out.

I kept glancing at Sebastian during my whole shift. He didn't once look in my direction, confirming my suspicions that the girls had lost their minds. Sure, we'd kissed, but he seemed to have regretted it afterward.

The night was slow, turning to its lowest point when I delivered a round of drinks to my least favorite table.

The guys were regulars, and things always became uncomfortable after they'd had a few drinks. Smitty never kicked them out because they spent a lot of money at the club. None of us liked serving them, so we rotated them between us. Tonight was my turn.

I hustled to put all the drinks down at their table, but when I bent over slightly to put a drink at the other end of the round booth, I felt a hand on my butt.

I sighed and stood up straight. "Jack, we've been over this. I don't like to be groped, and no, I'm not going to give you a lap dance."

"Come on, Nora, you won't regret it. I'll pay you double."

I pried his hand off my butt cheek and stepped back. I wouldn't get up close and personal until I had to. And today I definitely didn't.

"Thank you for the offer. Maybe next time."

He sat up from his slouch, his eyes dulled from the alcohol. "Really?"

I didn't respond, just turned and sprinted back to the safety of the bar.

"Table twelve at it again?" Stephen asked, with a sympathetic wince on his face.

"Just the usual stuff. Can I get two Coronas, three—"

I was interrupted when one of the bouncers pushed his way past me, muttering, "Here we go again."

Not knowing what he was talking about, I turned around and noticed a commotion at the table I'd just come from. I recognized Sebastian, who was dragging Jack out of the club. I watched with a slack jaw and a lot of confusion. Smitty would have a coronary.

Once Sebastian and Jack were out of sight, everyone went back to their drinks and watching the girls like nothing had happened. I delivered my orders and did another round to make sure everyone had a drink.

Table twelve always needed more drinks, and I reluctantly walked over.

"You guys need a refill?" I asked, trying hard to keep the reluctance out of my voice. When nobody answered, even though I saw at least two beers that were almost empty, I said, "Another round?"

They all nodded in unison, and I left to fill their order. Not once had they simply placed an order. There was always a suggestive comment, a leer, a gesture. What was happening? I must have hit my head harder than I thought, because everyone was acting strange tonight.

After delivering their order, I took a quick break and made my way to the back alley, hoping it was clear. I needed fresh air and a minute to sit down. My muscles were sore, and despite taking painkillers, my head was throbbing.

I pushed the door open but stopped when I heard angry voices coming from outside.

"Stop fucking scaring away the customers. Especially if they're regulars."

That was Smitty, his nasally voice easy to recognize.

"I don't appreciate your tone," Sebastian's deep timbre replied.

I strained to hear more, at the same time mourning my lost opportunity for a moment of peace.

"Maybe I don't appreciate your attitude," Smitty sneered. "You can't beat up anyone who touches the girls. It happens. Get over it."

"I think you forget who works for whom here. We own your ass, you stupid little fuck. If I want someone out of Pepper's, they're out of Pepper's."

"You hired me to take care of business. And you're bad for business."

"Get out of my face before I decide I don't want you taking care of business anymore."

Smitty didn't reply, but footsteps came closer. I eased the door shut and sprinted to the bathrooms just down the hall. I stumbled inside as the door to the alley opened.

Deciding to stay in the employee bathroom for the few minutes I had left of my break, I leaned against the wall, my back against the cold tiles. Did Sebastian beat someone up tonight? And why wasn't I more worried at what he'd done?

I went back out and finished my shift. I was glad the rest of the night was business as usual and groaned in relief when it was time to go home. My body ached, and I was dragging my feet.

Sebastian met me at the bar, where I was stacking clean glasses. "You ready to head home?"

I put the dish towel down and nodded. "God, yes."

I changed back into my own clothes, the dressing room empty. It had been a busy night, and the girls were all out on the floor. I was still nervous being in here by myself, but I didn't really have a choice.

The door opened, and I looked up with a smile on my face, hoping it was Elle. I really wanted to find out more about that Pilates routine she talked about earlier.

Instead of one of the girls, Clive came through the door. The smile froze on my face, and I fumbled for my jacket. I always felt exposed when he was close, and the more clothes I had on the better.

"Clive. What are you doing in the girls' dressing room?" I asked, picking up my bag.

If I played this smart, I could get past him and outside before he could stop me. I just had to move him farther into the room while at the same time inching my way to the door.

"I wanted to see you," he said, walking closer. I evaded him by stepping to the side.

"Well, here I am. But I need to go home and relieve the babysitter."

He came closer again. "She won't mind if you stay a little longer."

I swallowed, hoping today wasn't the day he snapped. His actions were starting to scare me. I always thought he was harmless, but cornering me all the time and pushing for another date was not exactly giving me the warm and fuzzies. And not to forget the flowers he kept sending me that didn't exactly make it look like he'd take no for an answer.

"Sebastian is waiting for me," I said, glad at least that part was true. "I should really go back out there."

Clive watched me with hungry eyes, and I suppressed the gag that worked its way up my throat.

"What's going on with you two?" he asked, cocking his head and reminding me of a bird with the way he moved and blinked at me. "Don't fall for his bullshit, Nora. He's bad news."

A knock sounded on the door, and I called out, "Come in."

Sebastian stuck his head in, his eyes narrowing when he saw Clive. "Let's go."

I sprinted past Clive and nearly collided with Sebastian in my haste. He took my hand and held it all the way out to his bike.

"See you tomorrow," Sebastian called out on his way past the bar. I waved goodbye, not trusting my voice to say anything yet.

While I had an unhealthy obsession with riding on Sebastian's bike, tonight I wished we'd taken my car. But the ride would be short, and I just had to hold on enough not to fall off. I grumbled under my breath when I swung my leg over the seat, the movement awkward and stiff thanks to my earlier workout.

"Are you hurt?" Sebastian asked, turning his head back to where I was getting comfortable on the seat.

"Just sore. Long night."

He did his broody hot guy stare for another few seconds before turning around and starting the engine. I wound my arms around him and sank against his back. I usually sat close, but tonight I fused myself to him.

He tensed for a moment but relaxed once it became clear that was how I intended to stay for the ride home. I treasured each time I was on the bike with him. I wasn't thinking about anything except how much I loved feeling his abs under my hands and how content I was, laying my head against his back and letting the wind take away my worries.

I really needed to get my head checked, because this was turning into a case of Stockholm syndrome.

Chapter Eight

"There's a hole in my donut," Luca wailed, staring at the donut on his plate.

We were eating dinner, and the kids had moved on to dessert. Malena and Felix had come over, and I was grateful for the distraction.

I grabbed a banana and broke off a piece big enough to fit in the hole. I pulled Luca's plate over and stuffed the banana in it, making sure it was somewhat even with the donut, and pushed the plate back in front of him.

He looked at it for a second before taking a tentative bite.

"I take it this has happened before?" Malena asked, holding a hand over her mouth, covering up a laugh.

"Didn't you think there was a reason I told you not to get donuts?" I said, shooting laser beams at her. When she'd asked me what to bring for dessert, I'd told her anything but donuts.

"I just thought you were on some diet. It seemed like a good idea to get the one thing you didn't want."

I face-palmed with my middle finger out. "You are a cruel, cruel friend."

She grinned and took another bite of her udon. "The food is amazing as usual," she said, grinning at me, not sorry at all for causing Luca's meltdown.

Making those dishes brought up memories of my mother. She'd been tireless in her efforts of teaching me how to cook traditional Japanese food. For some reasons only known to her it was the one thing she taught me.

Food had been our way of connecting. We had nothing else in common but our love for cooking. The memories were bittersweet since cooking with her was something I'd always looked forward to when I was younger. At the same time, thinking of my mom reminded me how quickly she cut ties when I was pregnant with Luca.

My mother was a proud woman, and she didn't accept anything less than perfection. My pregnancy had brought shame to the family.

I hadn't seen them since before Luca was born. And I had little hope that my kids would ever meet their grandparents. But thinking about the past wasn't going to fix my present. My personal motto was to look forward and concentrate on the things in life I had control over.

"I also made toscakaka," I said. It was the one thing I could make that was Swedish. The almond caramel cake was my father's favorite dish, and I'd made it my mission to perfect it when I was still living at home. The kids didn't like it which was why I'd asked Malena to bring dessert with her as well since the only reason I made the cake in the first place was because she loved it so much.

Her face lit up when I mentioned the cake. "I knew you loved me."

"Of course I do, you fool. BFFs until the bitter end."

We ate our cake while the kids played. As soon as we put our spoons down, Malena asked, "So you gonna tell me why you've been fidgeting all night?"

"I'm not fidgeting," I said, knowing full well that my limbs had been moving the whole time.

"You want to tell me something but don't know how," she correctly assumed.

"Stop thinking you know what's in my head."

She rolled her eyes. "But I do. And now I know something's going on. And you just confirmed my suspicions when you got defensive."

"Cheese and rice. I'm not defensive. Now shut up."

She laughed and cleared our plates while I remained at the table. I still hadn't come up with a good way to tell her that I'd officially be a stripper come Monday. And she was almost ready to leave.

"Does it have to do with Sebastian?" she asked when she came back to the table.

"What? No, of course not. Why would you think that?"

"He's not here tonight. And he's always around. Did you two have a fight?"

I got up and started pacing. "It has nothing to do with my roommate. This is something about my work."

I looked at the ceiling and shook out my hands. "I'm going to start stripping."

There. That wasn't so hard. Just out with it.

Malena froze, her arms still suspended over the table where she'd picked up plastic cups the kids had used. "Say what?"

"It's better money."

"Do you need money? I can give you money. I have money. I don't need it. And I live at home. I have hardly any expenses and a life insurance payout I don't know what to do with," she said, the sentences flowing into each other, her voice getting higher and higher.

"I appreciate the offer. I really do. But I just can't take you up on it."

"You and your misplaced pride," she ground out, eying the kids to make sure they didn't witness our argument. "You'd rather strip than accept a loan from a friend."

I shot up, my chair scraping back at the sudden movement. "It's not like that. I just can't keep depending on everyone else."

Malena put the cups back down and ran a hand through her hair. "But that's what friends do. They help each other out."

"Stripping isn't all that bad."

"I'm not worried about the stripping. But I know you. This is the last thing you want to do. You can't even take your top off in front of me."

I glared at her. "Hey, that's not true."

She braced her hands on the table, leaning forward. "Definitely true. Remember when we went to the mall and there were no other changing rooms and we decided to share one? You made me turn around before you took your top off."

I did do that. And I really didn't like taking my clothes off in front of other people.

"I'll be fine. I need to face my fear eventually."

"I have to get Felix home, but this conversation isn't over yet, *chiquita*," Malena said and pulled on her coat.

I followed her around the room as she first collected Felix's jacket and then Felix. He didn't want to leave and tried running away. When she caught him, he screamed, and she had to carry him out.

"It's going to be fine," I said, not sure who I was trying to convince, her or myself. "It's just a job."

"I'll be back in a few days to talk some sense into you," she called over her shoulder, a struggling Felix under her arm.

"I love you," I yelled.

"Love you too," she returned.

Well, that went better than expected. There was no yelling. Although it wasn't the kind of advice I hoped for. I wanted to talk it over with her. Maybe get her to tell me I could do this.

Instead, I was left to wonder if I was making a huge mistake.

I put the kids to bed early, reading the same sentence to them three times before Luca complained.

I was stress cleaning while crying and listening to the Backstreet Boys when the front door opened. Someone banged against the wall, and then Sebastian stumbled into the kitchen. His hair was disheveled, his shirt ripped, and he had a busted lip.

My eyes widened as I rushed up to him. "What happened? Do you need to go to the hospital?"

"I'm fine. Just need some ice and a shower," he said and dropped into one of the chairs.

I went back to the kitchen and put ice in a dish towel. He was hunched over by the time I came back, his elbows on his thighs.

"Where do you want it?" I asked, holding out the ice, trying hard not to gasp at the sight of him. I scrunched up my nose at the smell of whiskey wafting off him. *Where has he been?*

He sat up, his bloodshot eyes taking me in. "Why are you crying?"

"No reason. Sometimes I just cry."

Worst excuse ever, but all I had at the moment.

Sebastian raised a brow at me and took the ice. Guess my poker face really needed some work.

"I'm going to clean up," he announced and pulled himself back to standing with the help of the dining table.

I watched him limp out of the kitchen and wondered what kind of man was living in my house.

The shower turned on, and I was still standing in the same spot when it shut off again. Since I really didn't want him to pass out in the bathroom, I decided I should check on him.

I stood outside the door, unsure if I should knock or call out to Sebastian. Or maybe this was a terrible idea and I shouldn't do anything except go back to the kitchen.

My hand made the decision for me when it lifted and knocked on the door.

A muffled curse came through the door and then it opened, showing Sebastian only wearing a towel. His hair was wet, and water was dripping off his twenty-pack. I knew I was staring, but I couldn't get myself to lift my gaze.

And what self-respecting woman would when faced with all that's currently in my line of sight?

"Do you need the bathroom?" he asked, his voice scratchy.

I lifted my head and took in his face. For the first time I noticed the circles under his eyes, the slump in his shoulders.

"Just making sure you didn't pass out," I said, keeping my eyes above his neck. It took every ounce of self-control I had not to let them wander again.

"I'm fine." He turned back around, dismissing me. "It takes more than a little beating to make me pass out."

There was a long cut along his back, and he had a big purple bruise on his side.

"You can't clean your back by yourself. Now move. I'm helping." I pushed my way into the bathroom, closing the door behind me.

"What are you—" he started to say, but I brushed past him and went to the medicine cabinet.

I had everything I'd need to clean his cuts, but I wasn't sure if he needed stitches.

"Did you fall off your bike?" I asked, taking out cotton pads, gauze, disinfectant, and dressings.

"That question is insulting," he growled.

I ignored his mood and arranged all my supplies on the vanity. "Turn around."

When he didn't move, I lifted my gaze and met his angry glare. "Turn. Around."

He still didn't move. Unfortunately for him, I was feeling like pissing someone off after my talk with Malena. I ignored his death glare and grabbed the disinfectant and a few cotton pads, then stepped around him, facing his back.

The gasp I was trying to hold in earlier finally escaped.

"It's not as bad as it looks," he said, not moving away like I expected him to.

"You just keep telling yourself that," I said and got to work. "This might sting."

He didn't so much as flinch when I doused his back in antiseptic. The wound wasn't as deep as I first thought. It looked like someone had dragged a knife across his back but didn't get a chance to go very deep.

"Almost done. Can you pass me the dressing?" I said, holding out my hand.

Another sigh, but he leaned forward and handed it to me. Our fingers brushed, and a very inconvenient tingle shot through my body.

I finished in silence. Once I was done, I paused to admire my work.

"You finished or you want to stare at it for a bit longer?" Sebastian asked, his eyes meeting mine in the mirror when I looked up.

"I'm good. Just had to make sure I remembered how long it took to patch you up. You know, for next time I feel like hurting you. This image will stop me from so much as stepping on your toe."

"Noted," he said, not sounding angry for once.

I stepped back, wringing my hands in front of me.

"Guess I'll leave you to it, then."

"Yeah, I guess so," he responded, his hungry gaze eating me up.

I stumbled back, overwhelmed by the intensity of his attention.

Besides, there was still some cleaning to be done, so I scurried back to the kitchen. It was just after eleven, but I wasn't tired thanks to the adrenaline swirling through my blood following the bathroom encounter.

Sebastian came in a few minutes later wearing tracksuit pants and no shirt. There were only a few bruises on his chest, and if I hadn't seen his back, I'd think he was fine. Don't judge; I only looked to make sure he was okay. Well, mostly.

"Why are you cleaning in the middle of the night?" he asked, getting a glass of water out of the freshly scrubbed cupboard.

"The house was dirty," I said, eloquent as ever.

"Right."

"How's the water?" I asked.

He frowned but flinched when it pulled on a cut on his eyebrow that I hadn't noticed before.

"That doesn't look like you cleaned it," I said, pointing to his face. "And you should put something on it to hold it together."

"I'll do it tomorrow."

"Stay there. I'll get the disinfectant," I said, ignoring his growl.

He was leaning against the kitchen island when I came back, his arms crossed, his jaw tight.

I stopped in front of him and reached up to his face. I couldn't stretch up enough to reach his brow without falling against him. And he wasn't helping at all, making my task much harder.

"Do you mind leaning down?" I asked through gritted teeth after he only stared at me.

He didn't move. "I told you it doesn't need cleaning."

"And I told you it does."

Reading my determined expression correctly, he sighed and walked to a kitchen chair, pulling it out. I followed him, and when he sat with his legs wide, I took the opportunity and stepped between them.

My brain started screaming at me to retreat, but my body wouldn't cooperate. Instead, it swayed even closer. He leaned forward so I could reach, his gaze on me. I took longer than necessary to clean and glue the cut, but the stubble on his face felt too good under my hand to hurry up, and his eyes felt too amazing when looking at me.

I smiled triumphantly when I was done. "Looks as good as new. You can thank me later when you find out that it'll hardly leave a scar because of my awesome nursing skills."

He didn't respond, and I took that as my cue

to leave. But Sebastian had other ideas, his hands shooting out to hold me in place.

"Do you have another injury?" I asked, blinking at him.

Instead of answering he pulled me closer. In an effort to not fall into him, my hands went to his chest to steady myself, dropping everything I was holding to the floor.

One of his arms wound around my body while the other went to my head. He pulled me close, and before I could say holy hotness, his lips covered mine.

My brain stalled, my hands held on, and my mouth opened for him. As with the last kiss, I got completely lost in him.

When he pulled back, I heard a mewled protest that seemed to be coming from me. I didn't think I'd ever sounded more desperate.

"You're too tempting to resist, and I don't know how much longer I can stay away from you," he rasped.

I was too dazed to do anything but stare when he stood up, the move making me take a step back. I was breathing hard, and my heart was beating out of my chest. I think I had a mini orgasm just from kissing him.

"Nora?" he asked.

"Yes?"

"Go to bed."

"Yes, bed. Splendid idea. Sleep tight, don't let the bed bugs bite," I said, escaping to the safety of my bedroom, wishing for once that I'd been smoother. Because there were just some things you couldn't come back from. And talking about bed bugs was one of them.

Chapter Nine

"Are you throwing up again?" Elle called through the bathroom door.

"Go away," I replied between dry heaves.

It was Monday, five minutes before I was supposed to go onstage, and I was hanging my head in a toilet.

"If you don't come out right now, there won't be time left to fix your hair and makeup," Elle tried again.

"I don't care," I groaned. Another dry heave followed, and I slumped back on the ground. I shuddered at the thought of what was on the bathroom floor. The toilets were gross, and I never planned on getting this up close and personal with them.

"I'm coming in," Tia announced before the cubicle door opened and two arms lifted me up.

Once I was upright again, Tia took my hand and led me in front of the bathroom mirrors. She handed me a bottle of disinfectant and a bottle of mouthwash and started brushing my hair. "Disinfect anything that came into contact with the toilet, and then wash out your mouth with the mouthwash."

As soon as I finished cleaning up, Elle powdered my face and reapplied my makeup.

"Just leave the hair," Star said, joining us in the bathroom. "Nobody will notice. It'll get all tangled anyway once she starts dancing."

I watched my face blanch in the mirror as my eyes widened.

"We don't have time for more upchucking. You need to move or you'll be fired before you even have your first performance," Elle said, blocking my way back to the toilets.

"You can do this," Tia encouraged, taking my hand and walking with me.

"I don't think I can," I muttered, tightening my hold on her.

"Just remember, no upside-down stuff."

I nodded, my steps slowing the closer we got to the stage. The music from the previous act was so loud, it made it impossible to say anything else.

Tia stayed by my side and waited for me to go on. As soon as Becca came through the curtain, it was my turn.

Becca gave me a thumbs-up on her way past, and I froze in front of the entrance. I'd find another way to make money. There had to be something else. Maybe I just hadn't looked hard enough. This so wasn't for me. I couldn't—

My rant was rudely interrupted when Tia pushed me and I stumbled out onto the stage. I blinked into the lights, grateful I couldn't see anything besides the stage.

I could just pretend this was another practice. The music was already playing, and I nearly missed my cue to start moving.

Luckily Tia was on it, and when something hit me in the back, I snapped out of it and started to dance. And after a few awkward movements, I began my routine. It all went well until I got to the pole.

I'd lost half my clothes along the way, like we'd planned. I had no hope of undressing myself while anywhere near the pole. The girls said once I wasn't wearing much, nobody would care if I fell on my head. I was about to do my first move, the front hook spin. It was one of the few moves I could halfway master.

I was holding the pole with one hand when there was a commotion near the stage. I wasn't sure if I should stop, but since nobody shut off the music, I kept going. There were fights at the club all the time.

I was just about to spin myself around the pole, my legs at an awkward angle, ensuring I would screw up the move. But if nothing else, I saw things through. And even though it was a certainty that tonight would be an epic failure, I was determined to give it my all since I was already onstage.

And the urge to vomit had disappeared as well. Now I felt like I would pass out from the lack of oxygen instead.

But better to faint than throw up in front of people.

I didn't get a chance to show off my newly acquired move because someone grabbed me from behind and I found myself slung over a shoulder. I screamed, kicking my legs and pounding on the person's back.

And there was the urge to vomit again. The sounds faded the farther away from the stage we got, and I lifted my head, trying to see through the curtain of hair covering my face. I struggled to free myself, not sure if I was being kidnapped again or if this was an initiation to stripping.

This better not have anything to do with Jim.

"Guess you won't be a stripper after all," Elle said when I passed her. She didn't seem concerned over my current situation, so I decided not to panic. Yet.

"Put me down," I said to whoever was carrying me.

"Fuck no," a familiar voice responded.

"Sebastian? What are you doing?" I asked, feeling a lot less worried about being manhandled.

I was really questioning my sanity about not being scared when a member of a motorcycle club carried me off the stage. Half dressed, mind you.

"Don't talk," he growled.

Okay, then. Someone was grumpy. Guess my dancing was worse than I thought.

"Incoming," he said and then knocked on a door before opening it. Shortly after, I found myself back on safe ground. I brushed my hair out of the way and locked eyes with a red-faced Sebastian.

I opened my mouth to ask him again what was going on, but when I saw his dark, angry expression, I wisely shut up. I forced a demure smile on my face instead, hoping he'd either let go of the strong and angry routine or explain what just happened.

He did neither. Instead, he stalked to my dressing table and collected my clothes. I followed, confused.

"What do you think you're doing?" I yelled at him. "You have no right to manhandle me like that."

"Get dressed," he barked and held out my clothes.

There were still a few girls left, all of them staring at us. This was sure to get back to Smitty, and suddenly the only thing that mattered was that I couldn't lose my job.

If I couldn't strip, I had to at least keep my waitressing gig. And Sebastian had just made sure I didn't have either.

"Do you have any idea what you've just done? I need this job. My kids need me to have this job," I yelled, waving my arms around. "You ruined everything."

When he didn't respond, I jerkily pulled my clothes on, the anger making my hands shake. Once my clothes were back in place and I was wearing sneakers instead of the sky-high heels I could barely walk in, I grabbed my purse and stalked past the son of a gun.

His arm shot out and stopped me. "I hope you're on your way to my bike."

I pulled free and stepped back. "Definitely not," I spat out. "I need to fix what you just broke."

He reached out for me again, but I turned and sprinted down the hallway to Smitty's office. Once there, I knocked just as Sebastian reached my side.

"We're going home," he ground out between clenched teeth.

"You can go home. I'm going to talk to Smitty and pray I still have a job."

He didn't get a chance to answer when Smitty called out from behind the closed door for me to enter.

I did so without delay, and once inside, I pushed the door shut behind me. Sebastian followed, stopping the door from closing when his big body collided with it.

Instead of an apology, I shot him a glare. Head held high, I walked up to Smitty's desk.

"What the hell is so important that you need to interrupt me?" he asked, his eyes never leaving the papers on his desk.

"Please don't fire me," I pleaded, deciding to skip reasoning and go straight to begging.

Smitty looked up, his beady eyes landing first on me, then moving to Sebastian and widening slightly.

"Why would I fire you?" he asked.

The gossip hadn't reached him yet. I still had time to tell my side of the story. Which was probably not much better than the reality, but I had to try. Losing this job would be a colossal hit to my income.

"There was an incident," I began.

"As long as you stay off the stage, you're not fired," Sebastian cut in, his voice barely controlled.

I turned to him. "Since when is that your decision?"

"It's always been my decision," he said, turning to my boss. "Smitty, tell her she's not fired so we can all get on with our night."

"You're not fired," he said, then looked at Sebastian. "But I wish you'd reconsider letting her on the stage."

Sebastian took my hand in a tight hold and pulled. "Nonnegotiable. And you have to find a replacement for her tonight."

"On such short notice? Are you insane?" Smitty sputtered.

Sebastian shot him a look that shut him up immediately, and he put his hands up in surrender. "Of course. No problem."

Next thing I knew, I was getting dragged down the hallway by an enraged hot guy who thought he had the right to tell me what to do.

His hold wasn't painful, but it was strong enough that there was no escaping. And instead of looking at me with concern, everyone we passed had a smirk on their face.

"Where are we going?" I huffed, my short legs working hard to keep up with Sebastian's angry strides.

"Home."

"But I could still help out at the bar. They could swap me and Crystal. She sometimes goes onstage. In turn, I could cover her shift."

Instead of a response, he dragged me through the door, nodding at Kai, who was manning the entrance tonight.

"I'm off for the rest of the night. You're in charge," Sebastian barked on his way past.

"You got it," Kai called to our backs.

Well, tonight could have gone worse. And I thought I did a pretty good job up on that stage, right up until I got dragged off it. I didn't even get to show off my favorite move where I swung around the pole. Shame.

I'd debrief with the girls tomorrow. I was sure they'd let me practice a bit more with them.

Sebastian got on his bike and helped me up. I strapped the helmet on and slid forward, winding my arms around him. And despite his jerkiness tonight, sitting behind him on his bike was still my happy place.

And I hated myself for it.

At least this way we couldn't talk to each other. Less chance of one of us getting pissed off.

One thing the short ride back to my house did manage was to give me time to think. And the more I thought about tonight, the angrier I got.

How dare he push me around and tell me I couldn't dance onstage.

Wait, why am I trying to defend something that I didn't want to do in the first place?

But it was the principle of it. I was a grown-ass woman, and I could make my own decisions. Nobody else made them for me. And if they were terrible decisions, I would be the only one to blame.

When we got back to the house, I was fuming mad. I hopped off the bike and ripped my helmet off, needing to walk away before I did something I'd regret later. Like kick a member of a motorcycle club in the balls.

I pushed the helmet into Sebastian's stomach and stormed off. Not the most mature thing I'd ever done, but I wasn't feeling very mature right at that moment.

When I crashed through the front door, Stella came out of the living room. She saw me and stopped in her tracks, putting her hands up. "Whoa, what happened?"

"I need a drink," I growled and went to the kitchen.

I didn't drink much anymore, not since having the kids. A hangover was made much worse by little voices yelling in your ear.

But I stashed a few emergency bottles in the top cabinet. Since I was so small, I had to climb on the counter to reach them. Which was exactly what I did.

Heaving myself up on the counter, I stood up, balancing on the small area. I reached up to the cabinet, the bottle of wine within reach, when I was pulled back.

I shrieked, but no amount of wiggling got me out of being lifted off the counter and set back onto the ground.

I whirled around and glared at Sebastian, who was still standing closer than necessary.

"I'll give you a free life lesson, buster. Don't come between an angry woman and her wine," I ground out between clenched teeth.

"You won't get to drink your wine if you fall off and break your neck," he replied, raising an eyebrow at me.

"I've done this many times before and never fallen off. And if I did, it wouldn't be your problem. At least then you don't have to babysit me anymore."

He stepped closer, invading my space like nobody else's business. If he thought he could intimidate me, he had another thing coming.

"Seems to me you need someone to keep you out of trouble. Tonight being the best example of your inability to take care of yourself."

We glared at each other, our noses inches apart.

"Ahem, excuse me," Stella cut in. "Anyone care to enlighten me with what happened tonight?"

I pulled myself away from Sebastian and took three steps back to look at Stella, who was watching us with rapt attention.

"Nothing," I said.

"Nora thought it would be a good idea to become a stripper," Sebastian chimed in at the same time.

I was ready to maim him. *How dare he?*

"You did what?" Stella whispered, looking at me with an expression of pure shock.

"It doesn't matter now. Sebastian dragged me off the stage, and I nearly lost my job."

My voice was reaching high notes, and I took a deep breath to calm myself down. The thought of that possibility gave me heart palpitations and a rash.

"You nearly lost your job?" Stella gaped at me, disbelief heavy in her voice.

"Thanks to this corn nut," I said, pointing at Sebastian.

"Nora, why did you go up onstage? You hate being the center of attention."

I deflated, knowing I needed to fess up. She would find out sooner or later anyway. "I need the money."

Stella came closer and took my hand. "Why didn't you ask us to lower the rent? Mason won't mind."

I pulled back. "No way. I'm already paying way less than what this place is worth. I would never ask that of you."

"Damn it, Nora, we're your friends. Of course we would want to help out."

She sounded hurt, her face drawn tight. I knew she just wanted to help. But my money was gone because I'd been careless. I was the only person who was going to get myself out of this mess.

"It's my problem, and I'm going to take care of it," I said, crossing my arms over my chest.

"But you're so good with your money. You never buy anything you don't need. I thought you were doing well."

I sighed, deciding it was time to fess up. "I was. Until Jim cleaned me out."

Stella recoiled at my words, her face turning into a mask of fury. "He took your money?" she yelled, and I shushed her.

"Don't wake the kids. And yes, I'm pretty sure it was him. The money was gone after he'd been at the house. And it's not like this was the first time he's taken my money."

"What a dick," Stella cursed and put her arms around me, pulling me into a tight hug.

"It's okay. Shit happens," I said, my voice muffled

from being squashed against her shoulder.

She squeezed me tight, and I wheezed out a breath. "Shit like this doesn't just happen. You know you can be angry about this. Or cry. Whatever you need to deal with it."

"I was trying to drink away my problems. But someone interrupted my date with wine," I said into her shoulder.

Next thing I knew, Stella pushed me onto a chair.

"We need wine," she instructed, and to my surprise, Sebastian pulled it down for us. He even got out the glasses and filled them. Why was he still there? I would have thought by now he'd have disappeared to do whatever he did late at night.

He was never at home after the kids went to bed. I wondered if he thought this might lead him to Jim. But since my ex had already gotten what he wanted, there was no way he'd contact me again anytime soon.

I gulped half the wine and exhaled. Things would be fine. Nothing to worry about. I'd put my head down, continue to work, and maybe I'd be able to build my savings up again in this century. At least I knew I wouldn't get kicked out of the house if I couldn't pay the rent.

"You got her?" Sebastian asked, his back to me as he looked at Stella, who was grinning.

"Of course. Go forth and do your thing. We'll be fine."

We both got a chin lift, and then he walked out.

"I'm right here, you know," I yelled after him. "And I don't need a keeper."

He ignored me, and the front door slammed shut. God, he was infuriating. As if I needed someone at the house all the time. Even if he seemed to think otherwise.

I turned my glare at Stella, who put up her hand, a smirk on her face. "Hey, don't direct your misplaced anger at me. I'm just here to help you drink wine."

My head dropped on the table with a loud bang. "Ouch, that hurt."

"Just drink your wine and tell me how I can help." She put her hand out when I started to protest. "And stop being such a martyr and instead tell me what's going on. Not sure if you still remember this, but we're friends."

I didn't lift my head; instead I talked into the tabletop. "I'm sorry. I'm a terrible friend. And I don't mean to make you feel like you're not good enough. You're the bestest friend a woman could wish for."

"Then get over your issues and tell me what I can do to help."

My head left the haven of the tabletop, and I sat up straight. "You're already doing it. Offering to lower rent is unnecessary, but it's reassuring to know I won't have to live in my car if things go downhill. And don't even get me started on how much I depend on you when it comes to babysitting. I'll never be able to repay you for—"

"And I'll stop you right there. I've told you a

million times that it doesn't matter to anyone if I study at home or here."

"Not sure if Mason feels the same way."

"He started renovating the rest of the house. He's knee-deep in drywall and sawdust as soon as he gets home. He thinks he has to finish the house by the end of the year. Don't ask me why."

I got up and held my arms out. "As your friend, can I ask for a hug?"

Stella chuckled and got up, walking into my outstretched arms. "Always. Now, do you need more wine, or is it time for something else? Chocolate? Ice cream? Or do you have any of that delicious cake left?"

The last thing was said with a hopeful lilt to her voice, and it was my turn to laugh. "As a matter of fact, I do have cake left. Always keep some in the freezer."

I defrosted a piece of cake and handed it to a drooling Stella.

"Come to Momma," she said and devoured it in less than a minute.

"You good?" she asked when I finally managed to usher her to the front door.

"I am. Thank you so much."

"Anytime. And now that I know where you keep that cake, you better start baking more," she said, grinning.

"Noted. Now go home or Mason will worry."

"Doubt it. He'll still be debating whether we need an extra living area or if we should convert it into a guest room."

I embraced her in a long hug, reluctant to let go.

"Message when you get home," I instructed when she walked to her car.

"I will, Mom. Don't forget you have some cake to bake tomorrow."

I closed the door once she was in her car and had pulled out of my driveway. After cleaning up the kitchen and then myself, I went to bed. I lay there until I heard the front door at two in the morning and then Sebastian's grunt when he ran into the hallway table.

Only then did I fall asleep with a smirk on my face, making sure to move the little table to another spot again tomorrow.

Chapter Ten

"I was standing there," Luca screamed.

"No, me," Lena responded and pushed him out of the way.

I watched my kids standing in the middle of the living room, pushing each other off a random spot on the carpet they both wanted to stand on.

There was nothing special about the spot. And no reason why either of them had to stand there. Yet they were fighting over this coveted spot like it was a piece of chocolate.

Time to distract them before someone loses a finger.

"Okay, guys, how about we go outside? Maybe the playground?"

Their attention diverted to me, and they forgot all about their fight.

"Can I goes on the swing?" Luca asked, pulling his shoes on.

"Definitely," I said, then turned to Lena. "What do you want to do at the park, gorgeous?"

"Swing," she cried and grinned at me.

Once we were ready, I made sure to grab my keys and opened the door. And wished I hadn't. There was a huge bouquet sitting in front of my door. The only difference to previous deliveries was this time I spotted a card as well.

"Flowers," Lena yelled and sprinted out.

"Lena, no," I called and caught her around her middle. She thought it was a game and giggled.

"Again," she yelled, kicking her little legs.

"Luca, stop," I said when he moved toward the flowers as well.

"But I wants to sees them too," he wailed, going into meltdown mode.

I caught his arm and took a step back, my retreat slowed down by my uncooperative children.

"What's going on?" Gears asked, walking up to my front door. He must have been the unlucky one tasked with watching me today.

His attention snapped to the flowers, and he stopped. "Who sent you flowers?"

"If you get rid of them for me, I'll bake you whatever cake you want," I said, still wrangling my kids back into the house.

He tilted his head, not removing the flowers. "Why

do you want to get rid of them?"

"I don't want them," I wheezed, getting a good workout from holding my kids.

He looked at me like I'd gone insane. "You don't even know who they're from."

"I'm sure I know who sent them. And I don't want them."

He took a step closer, still not taking care of the flippity-flip flowers. "I think I should call Ace."

"I don't care what you do as long as you remove them."

When the kids refused to go back inside, I walked around the flowers instead, careful not to touch anything.

"We're going to the playground," I said and marched across the street to the park.

At least we didn't have to go far. It also meant I could keep an eye on my front door—which I hadn't locked despite my best intention—and make sure the flowers were gone before I returned.

There was no use getting upset. I'd decided this required a case of "ignorance is bliss." If I just pretended there were no flowers, then there also wasn't a stalker. Easy.

We hadn't been at the park for long when the roar of motorcycle pipes rang through the neighborhood. I watched three bikes pull into my driveway and sighed. Looked like ignorance wasn't going to work this time.

Sebastian's head snapped in my direction as soon as Gears snitched on me.

"Let's go back home," I said to the kids, deflated. I didn't want to go anywhere near those flowers. Or anywhere near Sebastian, who was standing in my driveway, arms crossed, sunglasses on his gorgeous face. He belonged on a magazine cover with his high cheekbones and full lips.

Neither Lena nor Luca was happy about only getting to play for such a short time. But I knew if I ignored the angry hulk standing in front of my house for too long, I'd make things worse for myself.

It took a few more minutes until I was able to pick up Lena and take Luca by the hand and walk back.

Sebastian hadn't moved, his face hard, his jaw muscles tight. Why in the world would he even be angry? Wasn't my fault Gears pulled him away from whatever he was doing.

"Inside. Now," he barked once my foot hit the driveway.

"Stop bossing me around. I'm not a dog," I hissed, my nerves already frayed.

He put his hand on my lower back, and I tensed. The light touch caused my whole body to lock up. If he noticed my response, he didn't say. Instead, he led us inside, not once breaking contact. My steps hastened when we walked past the flowers, and I eyed them from my periphery.

"Pack a bag," he said as soon as we made it inside. "We're staying at the clubhouse."

I stopped, flowers forgotten. "What? Why? No way am I bringing my kids there."

"Did you read the card?" he asked.

My blood turned to ice, and I clutched Lena to me while at the same time squeezing Luca's hand. I knew the card wasn't a good sign.

"No," I haltingly replied. "I thought it was just another way for him to screw with me."

"Show it to her," Sebastian said.

Gears stepped forward and handed me the card in question. I didn't take it since I was still holding on to both my kids. Sebastian didn't make me choose who I was going to let go. Instead, he breached the distance between us and pulled Lena out of my arms.

She didn't mind at all and instead settled right in. My mind on the card instead of my daughter, I took it and looked at the image on the front. It was Salvador Dali's painting of melting clocks. I'd never liked it and thought it was disturbing.

When I flipped it over, there were words on the back.

Ticktock. Time has run out.

A jolt of panic shot through me and took hold, digging deep. He'd officially lost his mind. What a creeptastic attempt to freak me out. It was time I went to the police, because flowers were one thing, scary messages another.

"You'll stay at the clubhouse. There's always people

around, and nobody will get in or out without us knowing," Sebastian said, ignoring Lena, who was singing into his ear.

I gaped at him, words trapped in my throat. I didn't want to stay at the clubhouse with scary bikers. And I certainly didn't want my kids there.

That thought finally snapped me out of it. "I'm fine staying here. I'll tell the police, and they'll keep an eye out."

Sebastian nodded at Gears, who started collecting toys from the living room.

I glared at both men, not in the mood to be ignored. "Hey, what are you doing?"

"He's helping you pack. Now, if you don't want him to go through your clothes, you better start packing," Sebastian said.

I stalked past him, making sure to stomp extra hard. "You're infuriating."

I felt helpless. Nothing in my life seemed to be in my control anymore. My stalker was escalating, and a biker was running my life.

It was safe to say my life had gone down the drain.

Luca climbed on top of the bed once we were in my room and started bouncing.

"Luca, no jumping on the bed," I muttered and jerkily pulled clothes out of drawers and my closet.

I packed light, not needing much. I had clothes for work in my locker at Pepper's, and I usually wore jeans and a T-shirt at home.

The kids' room was next, and I stuffed their bags as full as I could. Who knew if I they even had a washing machine at the clubhouse. I needed to pack as many options as I could since I had to change them at least once every day, often more than that.

The bathroom was next, and I shoved our toiletries in a plastic bag, the only thing I could find on short notice.

Gears showed up when I squeezed the bags shut and forced the zipper closed. "It's not so bad there. You might even like it," he said and shrugged when I narrowed my eyes at him.

He took the bags and walked out of the room. Luca had been following me around the house, and I could hear Lena's voice in the living room, telling Sebastian a story about a unicorn and a ball that made no sense. My girl had an active imagination and a vast vocabulary for a two-year-old.

I stalked back to Sebastian, my nostrils flaring. I was sure I looked like an angry bull, ready to charge. Which was exactly how I felt. I didn't get riled up very often, but once I got to this stage, it was hard to talk me off the ledge.

"Let's go," he said, turning on his heel and carrying Lena out with him. I had no choice but to follow, Luca skipping along next to me.

"This is ridiculous," I argued.

"You'll get over it. Now move. I've got shit to do."

"Language," I ground out.

As usual, he ignored me. He put Lena in her seat, even buckled her in. I didn't want to be impressed that he'd figured out the car seat so fast, but I was.

Once the kids were safely in the car, I walked around to the driver side. Sebastian stopped me as I was about to get in. "I'm going first. Gears and the guys will take up the rear. Stay close."

I stifled the urge to flip him off and got in the car, slamming my door with enough force to rattle my teeth.

I took deep breaths the whole way there, putting every ounce of energy I had into calming down. There was no point in pissing off a bunch of bikers.

The thought finally got my emotions under control and stopped my head from exploding. I'd sit this out just like I had so many other things that came before. This was another bump in the road. Nothing more, nothing less. A bump that came with a building full of bikers. Easy. I could do this.

My newfound confidence evaporated when we drove through the big entry gate and stopped in front of the massive warehouse. There were a few people outside, standing in groups and talking.

They all turned as one when my little car gave off the backfire to end all backfires, making me jump. It didn't help that the squeal of the brakes was loud enough to wake people three miles away. I took one last deep breath for good luck and turned the motor off.

Guess this is it. A glance in the rearview mirror confirmed my kids looked as happy as they did when we got in the car. I hoped they would stay that way.

"To the bikers' den we go," I said, opening my door.

Sebastian opened Luca's door, and I got Lena out. Luca wasn't good with new people, especially not with so many guys at one time. I didn't blame him. There was a lot of muscle, a lot of hair, and a lot of leather.

"Hey, everyone," I said and waved at the bikers closest to us.

"Hey, darling," an older guy with a long Santa beard said.

I gave him a wobbly smile, and his expression told me he saw right through my false bravado. Oh well, couldn't win them all over.

Lena wiggled in my hold, but this time I refused to let her go. I needed her right now. She was something else to concentrate on instead of all the people staring at me.

I looked around for Luca and saw him hiding behind Sebastian's leg. Poor buddy.

"Sötnos," I called out to him, but he didn't move from his spot. "Do you want me to carry you?"

I still received no answer, and Sebastian put his hand on my son's head. "Buddy, you good?"

His deep voice was low, and I appreciated his effort to not freak Luca out more than he already was.

"Wanna hold my hand?" Sebastian tried again.

I saw Luca's little head peek out from behind Sebastian's leg, and to my surprise, he took the outstretched hand.

"I'll show you to your room," Sebastian said, and I followed him into the warehouse.

I was just as impressed with the inside as the first time I was there. This time there were more people here, making the space feel more lived in.

"Who's this?" a giant of a man asked, coming up to us.

I stepped closer to Sebastian while Luca hid on his other side.

"This guy here is Luca," Sebastian said, nodding down at the human currently attached to his leg. "And this is Lena." He nodded to my girl, then lifted his chin in my direction. "And Nora."

Our eyes locked, and I couldn't read the soft expression on his face. He was usually all hard angles and tight mouth, but if I hadn't known him, I would say he almost looked proud to introduce me.

But that was just crazy talk.

"This is Grim," Sebastian said, looking at the big guy. "If you need anything and I'm not around, you go to him."

"I finally get to meet your girl," Grim said, his eyes crinkling at the corners with what must have been a smile under his beard. "We've barely seen this guy lately. You've kept him busy."

My face went hot, and I was glad for my olive complexion to hide the worst of my blush. Sebastian cut in before I had a chance to answer.

"She's staying here for a few days," he said, ignoring the comment.

"She got trouble?" Grim asked, one brow raised.

Sebastian clapped him on the back on his way past. "I'll fill you in at the meeting later."

"Let me know if you need anything," Grim said when I walked by.

I managed another wobbly smile and passed more people who gave me a myriad of chin nods, winks, and smiles. Not one of them looked like the limb-cutting type. Well, except the guy brooding in a corner, arms crossed, staring at me. He was the one who'd dragged me from my house and slammed the door on my head. He seemed to have had a close encounter with a wall. His nose was taped up, and he sported two black eyes and a cut lip.

Karma is a bitch.

I made a note to stay far away from him. Not that I would leave my room much. Not with so many people around.

Sebastian led us upstairs, and I marveled at the intricate metalwork of the stairs and railing. There were little motorbikes and vines on the railing, and the stairs had tire marks etched into them to give them more grip.

The view from the top was impressive. I could see all of the downstairs area, and since it wasn't that high, I could also make out every detail from bald patches to tattoos. The rooms spanned around three sides of the vast warehouse, and I guessed there were enough of them to house almost everyone.

The railing on top gave me nightmares since the gaps were big enough for kids to slip through. Good thing I wasn't planning on letting them out of my sight.

Sebastian stopped a few doors away from the stairs and swiped his watch across a pad. The door opened with a beep.

He pushed it all the way open and stepped back, motioning me in. Luca was still at his side, watching everything with big eyes. I walked inside and took in the spacious room. There was a king bed on the far side and a big four-seater couch to the right, facing a large TV.

There was a door to the left that was open, and I saw tiles and a sink, guessing it led to the bathroom. The room was clean. The only thing indicating that anyone lived there was the messy bed; there was nothing on the floor, the coffee table was clear, and there were no photos on the wall.

A second door led to a walk-in closet the size of my bathroom. One chest of drawers along the wall to the left made up the only other piece of furniture in the big space besides the bed.

"Is this a spare room?" I asked, wondering if I should ask for fresh sheets or a washing machine. I didn't want to insult anyone, but I also didn't want to sleep on sheets that held someone else's DNA.

Sebastian studied me. "It's my room. We're at capacity at the moment, and it's the only one available."

The door snapped shut, blocking out all noise. We'd gone from music, laughter, and chatter to gaping silence. The room must have been soundproofed to drown out the noise like that.

Lena decided she'd had enough and pushed her chubby hands against my collarbone, determined to make her escape successful this time.

Since it felt safe to let her go inside the room, I did. She was delighted with her new surroundings, walking straight to the drawers and opening them, pulling out T-shirts.

I cringed and hoped Sebastian wasn't particular about his clothes. This wouldn't be the only time she'd be doing this while we were here.

"Sorry," I mumbled and kneeled down next to her. "She's made it her life goal to empty every drawer within her reach."

Sebastian looked down at me with an intensity that caused my hands to shake and my eyes to widen. Was he really this mad at his clothes being disturbed?

"Don't worry about it. She can empty whatever she likes in here," he said, his words contradicting his expression.

Luca climbed up on the couch, and Sebastian

turned the TV on. "What's your favorite show?"

"*Paw Patrol*," Luca exclaimed, hopping up and down.

Sebastian put the series on and left the remote on the coffee table. I figured by now he should know that Lena would go straight for it. Any resulting bite marks would be on him.

"I have to go," Sebastian said, turning for the door. "The kitchen is downstairs, big red door, can't miss it. Help yourself to whatever you need."

He put a keycard on the coffee table. "This is for the door to the room. It's yours while you're here."

He was gone before I could do more than mumble a "Thanks." And why would I even thank him? I wasn't here because I asked to be. I was here because he once again decided I needed to be semi-kidnapped.

My bags were sitting next to the bed, and I pulled out all the toys and books I'd packed. Looking around the empty space that was to be our home for the next few days, I regretted not packing more.

We hung out in the room for a total of forty minutes before the kids were trying to put holes in the walls and Lena had the meltdown to end all meltdowns.

"Okay, okay, let's go find something to eat," I said, thinking an early dinner might be the best idea at this stage.

I picked Lena up and took Luca's hand. They were excited to get out of the room.

The trip down the stairs was slow since Luca was busy watching everything but his feet and tripped every second step. I had to half carry him down as well as holding Lena. The stairway wasn't long—my only saving grace—and I released the breath I was holding once we made it to the bottom.

"Now where is the kitchen?" I said, looking around the room, searching for a red door.

I spotted it on the other end and took a fortifying breath before making my way through the leather-clad bikers.

Lena threw her little body around, not wanting to be carried. I held on tight, and she clocked me in the face with her tiny fists a few times thanks to my efforts. But if I let her go now, we'd never eat tonight because I would be busy chasing her.

Luca was too intimidated to do much more than clutch my hand and stumble along behind me.

I once again received a few nods and waves that I returned. It wouldn't be smart to piss people off on our first day here.

The kitchen was empty except for the big guy Sebastian introduced as Grim and one barely dressed woman.

"There you are," Grim greeted me. "I was wondering when you'd be brave enough to leave your room."

"The kids were hungry," I said, my tone apologetic.

"There's plenty of food, so you should be able to

find what you need."

Luca didn't leave my side when I rummaged through the fridge, finding it well stocked. I decided on hot dogs. They were quick and easy to make, and the kids loved them.

I grabbed the buns and sausages and got to work. Luca was holding on to my leg, and Lena was still trying to get down.

"Baby girl, stop trying to dive onto the floor. You have to wait until I'm done cooking," I said, placing a kiss on her head, barely missing another head butt.

"I'll take her," Grim said, holding out his hands.

He read my hesitation and said, "I've got eight grandkids. Haven't dropped a single one. Your little one is safe with me."

Lena stared at him wide-eyed when I handed her over, surprising me by not screaming at the stranger who'd picked her up.

Grim sat down with her on his lap, letting her play with his beard and leather vest. I finished dinner, keeping an eye on Lena to make sure she wasn't scared or turning into a turd and annoying the big guy.

"Do you want hot dogs?" I asked Grim, wanting to do something to repay the favor. He was really good with my little tornado, stopping her from sliding off the bench they were sitting on and keeping her entertained.

Luca had fused himself to my leg, but I had no intention of removing him. I understood his feelings well, since I also wanted to hide behind someone's leg.

"That would be great, darling," Grim said.

I put everything on plates, making sure to give him three hot dogs.

Once we were all settled around the table, Lena went straight for Grim's food.

He didn't stop her, and we both watched her pull off a piece of his sausage and stuff it in her mouth. And spit it out again immediately.

"Hot," she cried and put the regurgitated meat back on Grim's plate.

My eyes went wide, and I jumped up. "I'm so sorry. I'll get you a new plate."

"Do I look like I'm scared of a bit of saliva? Sit back down and eat your dinner."

I plopped back onto my seat and watched with not a small amount of horror as he continued shoveling food into his mouth, the half-chewed sausage getting caught up in the process. "This is amazing," he mumbled between bites.

"It's all about the right ketchup-to-mustard ratio," I said, blinking at him when he finished the last bite of his food before I'd even gotten through half of my hot dog.

I'd settled in and stopped checking over my shoulder when about four guys burst into the kitchen.

Luca immediately dropped underneath the table, and Lena stood up, leaning on Grim's arm.

"You made food and didn't make us any?" one of the guys asked Grim.

"Wasn't me who made it," he responded and pointed his fork at me. "Ace's girl did."

"Do you want some?" I asked, getting up.

"Eat first. And if you still feel like cooking up a little more after you're finished, I won't say no," he said and pulled out the chair next to me.

The guy looked to be in his thirties, with dark tousled hair and a body that saw a lot of gym time. Must have been one of the requirements to join their gang: big and muscly, facial hair preferred.

He only sported stubble and his eyes crinkled around the corners, making me hope he was a happy guy who wasn't planning on damaging a hair on mine or my kids' heads.

"I'm Talon," he introduced himself with a wink.

"I'm Nora. This is Lena," I said, pointing to my girl, then underneath the table. "And this is Luca."

Talon leaned to the side so he could look underneath the table. "Hey, buddy. Looks like a good spot down there. Mind if I join you?"

Before I could tell him that he was the reason Luca was down there, he'd pushed his chair back and crawled under the table.

I shoved the rest of my food in my mouth, not really tasting anything, watching Talon talk to my son.

After five minutes, Luca chuckled. After ten he was

talking to his new friend.

I decided it was safe to leave them to it and put more sausages in the pan. More people joined us, and soon I was making dinner for at least twenty bikers. The kitchen was big enough to house everyone, and the table was a long monstrosity with a bench attached to the wall and chairs on the other side.

Every seat was taken, and I couldn't keep up. It wasn't hard to fry up a sausage, but you'd think I'd made a three-course meal by the way the guys held out their plates.

Luca had come out of his hiding spot somewhere between sausage forty and fifty and was sitting on a chair next to Talon, eating his food.

Lena was done with her bun and climbing all over Grim, who didn't seem to mind. He let her go wild, holding on to her shirt so she wouldn't fall off.

I was beginning to think I might have judged these guys a little too soon. So far no bodily harm had been threatened, and everyone seemed welcoming.

"Blade, man, you gotta try this," Talon called to the guy who'd just walked in. They'd called him Prez last time I was here.

Two girls followed in his wake, and they looked less than pleased to be in the kitchen. Guess they weren't big on carbs. Couldn't win them all.

"There's plenty there," I said, nodding at the mountains of hot dogs I'd made.

I turned the stove off once everyone had had at

least two servings. If they wanted more, they could make it themselves.

A glance at the time confirmed we'd been in the kitchen for nearly two hours and it was time for bed for my little ones.

"Okay, I'm off," I announced, drying my hands on a dish towel. "Food's on the plate on the counter. I have to put my kids to bed."

There were a lot of groans, and a few guys jumped up to get more. Chuckling when they pushed each other out of the way, I went to collect my kids.

"Come on, baby girl," I said and tried taking Lena from Grim.

She wasn't having it and went from giggling to piercing screams.

"I've got her," Grim said and got up.

Lena quieted down, and I looked at the table, the tips of my ears burning. "Sorry, guys."

They all waved me off and didn't seem to care that their eardrums had nearly been shattered a few seconds ago.

"Luca, time for bed," I said to my son, who was playing a card game with Talon.

He could barely hold the cards but was having the time of his life. The tip of his tongue was sticking out in concentration as he studied the cards on the table.

I tapped him on the shoulder when he didn't respond. "Come on, Sötnos."

"No, Momma, I'm playing Go Fish with Talon."

I blinked at my four-year-old, then at Talon. He shrugged, grinning at me. The big biker was playing Go Fish with my son. Who would have thought that would ever happen?

"It's a great game. And he wanted to play, so one of the guys went out and bought the cards since all we usually play is poker," Talon said, like he had to defend himself for playing a kids' game.

"Hey, I'm not judging," I said and put my hand on Luca's arm. "Time to finish your game."

"But, Mom," he whined, looking at Talon with big eyes.

"We can play again tomorrow, but you have to go with your mom now," Talon said.

Luca huffed but put the cards down. "You promise?"

Talon put a hand to his heart. "Promise."

Luca studied him for a moment, then seemed to come to the conclusion that Talon could be trusted with his promise. He got up and took my hand.

"Say goodnight to everyone," I said, and Luca and Lena both called out to everyone. They were delighted when they received a loud chorus of goodnights back.

"You coming back down?" Talon asked. "We're having a few drinks tonight. Nothing big."

"Maybe," I said, having no intention of doing anything but sleeping tonight.

We walked back to the room, Grim following me with a tired Lena. I opened the door to Sebastian's room with the keycard he'd given me and ushered Luca inside. Lena let me take her this time, her eyes drooping.

"Thank you so much," I said once both kids were inside.

"It's no problem at all. And you should really come down. You'll go crazy if you stay in the room the whole time you're here."

I forced out a smile, hoping I hadn't been too obvious about my thoughts on my temporary accommodations. "I'll think about it."

He waved to the kids. "Good night, munchkins. See you tomorrow."

The kids went to bed easier than anticipated, and I soon found myself sitting in the dark, trying not to make too much noise so I wouldn't wake them up.

I didn't want to turn the TV on, and there was only so much online poker I could play on my phone before I got bored. After an hour, I still wasn't tired enough to go to bed.

I plugged the child monitor in, making sure it faced the bed, and grabbed the other monitor.

Guess I was joining the party downstairs.

Chapter Eleven

"Why are you looking under the table? Your kids are still fast asleep upstairs," Talon asked, watching me stick my head under the table.

"Just checking," I muttered, my face feeling numb.

I'd had too much to drink. Five shots were too much for me. I hated tequila. But the guys looked so hopeful when I came back down. And then they offered me alcohol, and it felt rude to say no.

"Checking for what?" he asked, looking under the table as well.

"The orgies?" I said and slapped a hand over my mouth. That thought was supposed to stay in my head.

"Orgies? We don't have orgies in the main room. And definitely not under the table. Not enough space," Talon said and then broke out into roaring laughter.

I pushed him, his tall frame not moving an inch. "That's not... I meant... it was just..."

"I think you've got bad reception. You're cutting out," Talon said, watching me with a twinkle in his eyes.

"You really thought we'd just all get down to business right here?" Gears asked, amusement evident on his face.

"I read books," I said, blinking to clear my vision.

"Books of what? Orgies?"

"Bikers."

Talon shook his head, his eyes still beaming with mirth. "You might see someone's naked ass by the end of the night, but we keep the rest in our rooms. Sorry to disappoint."

I'd come to realize that everyone was really easygoing. They all seemed to care about each other, liked to joke around, and welcomed me like I was their long-lost sister.

Being part of something meant a lot to me. Being part of a family, even if it wasn't by blood, meant even more, especially since my own had discarded me so easily.

"I love you guys," I declared, throwing my arms around Talon's shoulders and my body into his arms, orgies forgotten.

He caught me, squeezing me around my middle. "How are you this drunk already?"

After hugging the other guys in the group that consisted of Gears, Grim, and a man they called

Smoke, I settled back in my seat. I had a permanent smile attached to my face, my cheeks aching.

"I'm not drunk, you are," I said, crossing my arms over my chest.

"You've had five shots over three hours and you can't even figure out how to cross your arms. That's the definition of a lightweight," Gears said, taking a drink of his beer.

I looked down and noticed I hadn't crossed my arms but instead was holding my own hand over my chest. *Huh, I really thought I'd crossed them.*

I squinted at the monitor sitting on the table. The image was grainy, but when I saw Luca and Lena still fast asleep, I relaxed back into the couch.

"So how did you meet Ace?" Gears asked. "You don't seem like his type."

"You mean he doesn't like a woman with a brain? Or is it the kids? The half-Asian thing? You gotta be more specific here, dude."

Grim smacked Gears over the head and murmured something to him, causing his face to blanch.

"Sorry, Nora, that's not what I meant. Forget I said anything," Gears said, his eyes shifting from me to Grim and back.

I waved him off, too drunk and happy to be offended by the comment. "Don't worry about it. I know I'm not exactly a catch."

Grim heaved himself up and squeezed in next to

me. "Girl, if I was twenty years younger, I'd ask you to marry me today. You are the full package. You can cook, you're beautiful, you're funny and smart, and did I mention you're beautiful?"

I leaned my head on his shoulder. "Thanks, Grim. That's a really nice thing to say."

"Don't let Ace hear you," Talon said from Grim's other side. "He'll make you disappear faster than you can say 'wedding.'"

Grim grunted in agreement and patted my hand that was holding on to his bicep. "I don't fear many things, but that man's wrath is one of them. Sorry, girly, no marriage for us."

"Shame. I was looking forward to it. I've never been married before."

There was silence on the table and I sat up, brushing my hair out of my eyes. "What? I bet none of you have been either."

"You didn't marry the kids' father?" Talon asked.

"Nope. We were together eight years, had two kids, and he always said it wasn't the right time. Should have known something was up. But I guess I like to learn my life lessons the hard way. Anyway, it all worked out for the best, because there's no way I could afford an attorney to get a divorce."

"That deserves another drink," Grim announced and got up.

He poured as much tequila in each shot glass as he could fit and handed me mine. "Drink up."

We clinked glasses, and I chugged the vile liquid, holding my breath the whole time. I took a large gulp of water to chase it down, taking a deep breath once it was done.

"Isn't there something else we can drink?" I asked, my voice croaky from the alcohol.

"Nope. If you want to sit at the big boys' table, you have to drink tequila," Talon said and winked at me. "If you prefer a girly drink, you're welcome to sit at the bar."

I eyed the bar and suppressed the grimace that wanted to escape. Most of the girls were gathered along the metal bar, spanning almost one whole side of the warehouse. I looked at my sweats and T-shirt and knew I'd rather drink a whole bottle of tequila than go over there.

It was safe to say that the club didn't attract shy girls. Or girls who wore clothes.

I poked my tongue out at Talon. "Hard pass. How about a round of poker?"

Talon's face lit up, and he looked like a kid who just got the key to a candy store. He pulled a deck of cards from somewhere and shuffled them.

"Who's in?" he asked.

Everyone murmured their assent, and he started dealing the cards.

Lucky for me, I wasn't drunk enough that I couldn't read the numbers on the cards anymore. Poker was also something my dad taught me when I was ten years old.

The guys were loud and boisterous while playing. Every time I beat them, they made such a ruckus that soon we were surrounded by a wall of bikers who watched in fascination as I wiped the floor with my new besties. I couldn't lie if my life depended on it, my facial expressions always giving me away. But when it came to poker, I somehow managed to keep a straight face. Now if only I could transfer that skill.

"Are you cheating?" Talon asked for the third time.

"Maybe you're just bad at this game," I said, putting my full house down.

Gears shot up, throwing his cards on the table. "Where are you hiding the extra cards to pull this off?"

I didn't get a chance to respond before he was on me. He pinned me under his arm and stuck his hands in my sweatpants pockets. I giggled, fighting him off with little success since he was about twice my size.

And that's when all hell broke loose.

Gears was ripped off me, and I stumbled to my knees from the sudden loss of contact. When I looked up, I saw Sebastian, face contorted into a furious mask, throwing a punch at him.

Sebastian looked ready to kill Gears, who was already bleeding from a cut on his lip. He wasn't defending himself, his face slack in shock. I jumped up and in between them before my brain had time to catch up with my terrible decision.

Sebastian released Gears and turned his crazy eyes my way.

"Are you insane stepping in front of me? You could have caught a fist to the face," Sebastian yelled, his eyes spitting fire.

"Am *I* insane? I should be asking you that question. What is wrong with you?" I yelled right back, the alcohol giving me courage.

"Nobody touches you. They all know it. I'm not big on repeating myself," Sebastian ground out. "He broke the rules. He has to pay."

"You don't own me," I yelled. The music had shut off, and it looked like the whole room was waiting to see what would happen next. "And you definitely can't ignore me one minute only to be a possessive caveman the next."

I turned on my heel and sprinted to the staircase. Heavy footsteps followed, and I raced up the steps, hoping that for once my short legs wouldn't fail me. Tears were brimming in my eyes, and one wrong blink would send them tumbling down my face. The last person I wanted to witness my humiliation was Sebastian.

That hope was dashed when I opened the door to his room and he pushed in behind me.

I whipped around, ready to shove him back out. But anyone who'd ever tried pushing a six-foot-three giant out the door would know it was impossible. He had about a foot on me and weighed twice as much as I did.

"If you wake up the kids, I'm going to chop off your balls and throw them over the balcony," I hissed, glancing over my shoulder to make sure the kids were still sleeping.

Sebastian looked at the bed, then took my arm and pulled me back out, shutting the door behind him.

"Talon, keep an eye on the kids," he called out over the railing.

"You got it," Talon called back.

Good thing I left the baby monitor downstairs. Not such a good thing was Sebastian dragging me past the long row of rooms. He stopped halfway down the hall at a wooden door that had seen better days.

There was no lock, and he banged the door open and pulled me inside behind him. He turned us so he was between me and the door and shut it.

The room went pitch black once the light from the hallway was gone, and I let out an undignified squeak. "If you have to cut anything off, take my small toe. I figured I don't really need it and it's easier to hide a missing toe than, say, a finger."

The light turned on, and I blinked the black spots in my vision away.

"I'm not cutting anything off. What is it with your fear of losing body parts? I told you we don't do that. Especially not to women."

"You dragged me into a dark room and closed the door. What else was I going to think?"

He seemed taken aback for a moment before roaring with laughter.

I watched the beautiful display and sighed. He was a work of art. And when he laughed and all the tight lines on his face softened, there was nobody who came even close to him.

"You really have no idea, do you?" he asked, taking a step forward, all rage drained out of him.

I took a step back and bumped into a shelf, knocking a bucket off. Guess we were in the cleaning closet. But better to do this here than in his room and risk waking up the kids.

"Idea about what?"

The shock of not only fighting with him but getting pushed into a dark room sobered me up a lot, but I still couldn't make sense of what he was saying.

Turned out I didn't have to, because while I was busy thinking of what was going on, he'd breached the distance between us.

Stunned, I looked up as his mouth took mine in a claiming kiss. He pulled me close, holding me against him. His hands roamed to my ass, and he lifted me. My legs went around his waist and my arms around his shoulders.

His kiss felt like a branding. Like he couldn't go another moment without his lips on mine. Like he was breathing me in and fusing us together at the same time.

Our tongues clashed, and I whimpered. The sound

must have snapped him out of whatever temporary insanity had overtaken him because he released me, making me stumble back onto the ground.

And I'd had enough. This was getting ridiculous. He kissed me; he pushed me away. He kissed me; he pushed me away. Rinse and repeat. My head was spinning—and not from the alcohol—and I was angry.

"Why do you keep kissing me?" I yelled, all the frustration that had been building over the last few days bubbling over.

"Because I can't fucking stay away from you no matter how hard I try," he roared, running a hand through his hair.

"Then stop trying," I yelled again, my breath coming out in heavy pants.

He was on me again in the next instant, his arms caging me against the shelf, his lips claiming me in the kiss to end all kisses.

I found myself wrapped around him, meeting his kisses with my own. We broke apart when he pulled my top over my head. Sebastian stilled, his eyes drinking me in. He looked like a man starved. I watched him swallow visibly, then lick his lips. My breathing became shallow, and I squirmed under his perusal.

He didn't waste any more time and was on me in the next instant, his lips blazing a path down my neck, over my collarbone, stopping when they reached my breasts. He undid my bra, and it fluttered to the ground, forgotten.

His kisses made me act like a brazen hussy, thrusting my boobs in his face and panting like I was running a marathon.

I was overwhelmed with all I was feeling. His kisses lit up my body, the caress of his hands ensuring I was turning into an incoherent mess.

"Please," I begged, wanting him so much in that moment that everything else faded in comparison.

He pushed my pants and panties down in one move, his mouth following his hands. He whispered more kisses on the insides of my legs and I shivered.

I plunged my hands in his hair and tugged, burning up with need for him.

He placed one last kiss on my thigh before standing up and lifting me onto something wobbly. I didn't check what it was. The only thing I saw was Sebastian and his dilated eyes and jerky movements when he pulled his shirt over his head and pushed his pants down.

He somehow put a condom on while I was trying to catch my breath.

"You want this?" he asked, standing in front of me, studying my face. "And you're not too drunk?"

"Ducks yes to the first, mother puffin no to the second," I said, my voice coming out strangled.

There was nothing I wanted more in this moment than Sebastian. I didn't think it was healthy to feel such a desperate need for another person. But here I was, a quivering mess who took her clothes off in a cleaning closet and didn't even care she was sitting on something wet.

His mouth tipped up in a half-smile. "Still not swearing, I see."

I ran my hands over his chest, my eyes following the movement. "It's second nature by now not to. And I'm bad at turning it on and off. Either I don't swear at all or I go all out. I have no middle ground."

He brushed a strand of hair out of my face, and I shivered when his finger traced the shell of my ear. "It's just one of the things that makes you who you are."

He didn't elaborate, and I didn't ask because I was done talking. I wanted him. Now. No more waiting, no more hesitation.

As if he knew what I was thinking, he pushed between my legs and our eyes locked. He never looked away, not when he entered me with aching slowness and not when he started to move.

He looked more relaxed than I'd ever seen him, the harsh lines on his face gone. If I didn't know any better, he looked at peace. A soft expression I couldn't read replaced the scowl I'd gotten used to.

Warmth spread through my chest, and I gave myself over to him. His hands roamed every inch of my body they could reach. All my nerve endings were on fire, my body a pliable mess in his arms.

The wave of heat slamming through me took me by surprise, as did my orgasm. I felt like I'd found a unicorn, never once having come so fast, the feeling building and building until it exploded into a crescendo of fireworks.

His movements became faster and deeper, causing another surge of pleasure to overtake my body. He planted himself deep and came with a loud groan, his face buried in my neck.

We stayed connected, breathing hard. I expected a quick exit on his part, but instead he peppered soft kisses all over my face. His lips caressed mine, the kiss more intimate than our lovemaking.

When we separated, the feeling of loss was immediate.

He chucked the condom in a bin near the door and pulled his clothes back on, his eyes on me the whole time. I jumped down from what I found out was a cleaning cart that had lost nearly all its contents and got dressed as well.

The wet thing I was sitting on turned out to be a sponge.

As soon as I was finished, he ushered us back outside. The noise smacked me in the face as soon as the door opened. It would have cost a fortune to soundproof all the rooms, but I was grateful they did.

I glanced at Sebastian when he walked me back to his room. His hand was at the bottom of my back, his fingers grazing my butt. If it hadn't been for that touch, I would have thought nothing had happened between us.

If he was going to pretend he'd never shown me his banana and ignore anything had ever happened between us, I would show him what I could do when I was really angry.

"You can turn the monitor off," Sebastian called down to Talon, who lifted his hand in acknowledgment. I was slightly mortified at the thought that everyone knew what we'd been doing. But maybe they thought we just needed a moment to talk. Maybe.

I relaxed slightly when he followed me inside his room and closed the door. I stood near the entry, unsure of how to proceed. Sebastian didn't seem to have the same hang-up.

He pulled me close, brushing his lips against mine in a gentle caress. "Let's sleep. It's late."

That sounded like a good idea. And the promise of a talk tomorrow and the fact that he was there with me with set my mind at ease.

"Okay," I whispered and went to the bathroom to clean up. When I came back out, Sebastian was lying on the couch, shirtless. He'd found a pillow and extra blanket as well.

At least the couch was huge and he could stretch out.

I walked to the bed, moving Lena to the middle and crawling in behind her.

"Thanks for bringing me here," I whispered, looking at the outline of his body in the dark. "The guys are awesome. And they're going to show me how to ride a bike tomorrow."

"Baby, if anyone is showing you how to ride a bike, it'll be me," he growled.

I fell asleep with a smile on my face.

Chapter Twelve

"We don't lick people," I said, crouching in front of Lena.

"Don't we?" Sebastian asked, and winked at me before taking another bite of his eggs.

We were in the kitchen, eating the breakfast Sebastian had made. Lena had taken it upon herself to lick first my cheek, then Sebastian's arm. Every time I told her off, she hid her face in Sebastian's neck, giggling.

He wasn't helping the situation when he chuckled along with her, holding her to him whenever she burrowed in. It took a while to separate them, but when I finally did, I sat her on her own chair and squatted down in front of her.

She put her hand on my head in response and rubbed my hair, something she'd seen Sebastian doing earlier. I brushed my hair out of my face and shot him another glare that he responded to with a wink.

"Do you want more bread, or are you finished?" I asked when it became clear she didn't care that she wasn't supposed to lick people. I hoped it was only a phase and that the licking was confined to her family.

"Finished," she sang and jumped off the chair when she saw Talon walk into the kitchen.

He scooped her up as soon as she was in front of him, throwing her up into the air. I didn't think I'd ever get used to seeing the tattooed bikers play with my kids. But to my surprise, most of them didn't mind the children being in their space.

There were a few people in the kitchen, eating the eggs and bacon Sebastian had made for everyone earlier. Luca was sitting next to him, copying his every move. Sebastian took a sip of his coffee and Luca took a sip from his own cup filled with orange juice. When Sebastian leaned back in the booth, Luca dropped his cutlery and did the same. Seeing my kids so relaxed and having fun brought my emotions to the surface.

Sebastian had woken up with us this morning, helping me with the kids. Whenever we didn't have little eyes watching, he'd pull me close and kiss me. He never missed an opportunity to tell me how much the night before meant to him.

I couldn't remember the last time I'd felt this happy and settled. What I thought would be a nightmare stay had so far turned into one of the best times I'd ever had.

"Whoa, buddy, no throwing that thing until I teach you how to," Talon said, directing my attention from Sebastian to my son, who was currently wielding a knife in front of his body, narrowly missing Talon's arm.

Lena had thankfully moved to sit on Grim's lap a few minutes ago, keeping her far away from the lunatic throwing knives.

"Luca," I called out, making my way over. "Knives are for cutting food, not people."

Laughter rang out around the table, and I rolled my eyes. *They better not tell my son that knives are handy for all sorts of things.*

"And you're not allowed to use knives yet," I said and took the knife off him once I stood next to his chair.

"Sorry, Nora, my fault," Talon chimed in. "I showed him how to throw up a knife and catch it by the handle."

Of course he did. I mean, it was perfectly safe for a four-year old to learn how to throw knives. Not.

I put my hands on my hips and put on my best teacher's voice. "He's not old enough to even cut his own bread. For now, knife throwing is out of the question."

"I'll show him once he's a few years older," Talon said, winking at my son.

"I'll be big next year," Luca said, beaming at me.

My heart flipped in my chest at the thought that we'd be around long enough for him to be old enough to throw knives.

"That would still be a no to the knife throwing," I said, raising a brow, waiting for another response that might encourage Luca.

His bottom lip curled outward, and he looked at me, his eyes pleading. "But, Mom, I'm a big boy," he said, sticking out his leg from under the table. "Look how long my legs are."

"I know you are. But not big enough for knives."

I left Luca to pout while hopefully finishing his breakfast and sat back down in my chair. Lena was still busy climbing all over Grim, and I seized the child-free moment to take a bite of my eggs.

Sebastian, who was sitting next to me, leaned forward, looking at Talon. "He won't need to learn how to throw knives. Once he's old enough, I'll show him how to shoot a gun. Less messy."

Talon saluted him, his face splitting into a big grin.

I stopped chewing, staring at Sebastian's profile.

There would be no shooting guns. Or wielding knives. They were delusional if they thought my child needed to learn any of those skills.

And did he say what I think he just said? Would he be around long enough? I didn't want my son to know how to throw a knife or shoot a gun, but the thought of Sebastian still being around in a few years filled me with warmth.

A familiar hand settled on my thigh, wrapping my body in a warm blanket. Sebastian kissed my head, then looked across the table.

"Hey, Grim, you mind watching the kids for an hour?" he asked.

"Of course not," Grim said between pretending to bite Lena's fingers.

"Why didn't you ask me? I'm a great babysitter," Talon said, sticking out his bottom lip much like Luca had earlier.

Sebastian raised his brows at him. "You tried teaching Luca how to throw knives."

"And? I wouldn't have just left him to it. I'd have been there the whole time."

I giggled, causing Sebastian to lean in, his lips brushing my ear. "Don't encourage him."

"I would never," I said, turning so our lips were only inches apart. "Are you sure the kids are okay? I don't like leaving them with strangers."

Sebastian put his hand on my cheek and I leaned in. "I know this situation is unusual. But these guys are my brothers. I'd lay down my life for them and they'd do the same for me. The kids will be safe with them."

I took in the sincerity in his gaze and nodded. I trusted him. As crazy as it seemed after such a short amount of time.

"I'm helping Grim, and there's nothing you can do about it," Talon said, then picked up Luca and flipped him upside down, holding on to his ankles.

Luca shrieked in delight, and I was worried his breakfast would make a reappearance.

"Let's go. I'm teaching you how to ride a motorcycle," Sebastian said, pulling me out of my chair.

"Bye, babies," I called out, waving at Luca and Lena, who couldn't have cared less that I was leaving.

Talon blew me exaggerated kisses. "Bye, Momma."

I took in the scene in front of me, my kids giggling, the guys laughing, before Sebastian dragged me out of the kitchen.

"Ease off instead of just letting go," Sebastian explained when I released the clutch too fast and stalled the bike again.

Despite my apparent lack of skills, I had the time of my life. The kids were cheering me on from their position near the warehouse, and I grinned at them.

I started the bike up again and released the clutch slower. It was picking up speed, and I cheered.

"Look where you're going," Sebastian called out when I drove off the side of the driveway because I was too busy watching him.

He was by my side as soon as the bike stalled again, holding me upright, placing one hand over mine on the handle, the other on my leg.

"Sorry, but I'm thinking I'm not made to ride a bike," I said, blowing out a big breath.

This was harder than it looked. I had fun, but only because Sebastian was a handsy teacher who showed me how to ride a bike by directing me in the positions he wanted.

My body felt like one raging inferno, ready to combust thanks to his frequent touches and lip brushes.

"Slow and steady," he rasped, and I swallowed hard. "Treat the bike like one of your kids—gentle and with patience."

"Okay, I can do that," I said, my voice croaky.

"You on my bike is the hottest thing I've ever seen," Sebastian said, his hands wandering up my thigh.

"Nope, I can't do it," I squeaked and pointed to the side of the building where a vast forest started. "I'll never learn how to ride a bike if you don't move at least a mile that way."

His finger traced a path up my side. I swayed into him, closing my eyes.

"But if I'm that far away, I can't watch you. Or touch you."

"Exactly the point," I said, licking my lips.

Sebastian's eyes zeroed in on the movement and went molten.

Uh-oh. I know that look.

"The kids," I said, hoping he'd understand.

"Grim and Talon took them inside," Sebastian said, leaning in and taking off my helmet.

Our lips met in a soft caress, and I sank into him. He took my weight and held the bike steady, kissing me like we had all the time in the world.

When I was a hot and wanting mess, he pulled back, resting his forehead on mine. "I don't want to leave you, but I have to go."

That dumped a bucket of cold water over my head. "Of course."

"Nothing could have stopped me from being the one to teach you how to ride," he said, placing a gentle kiss on my lips and pulled back. I got off the bike, and he pushed it back into the driveway.

"I'll be back tonight to take you to work. Don't leave the compound," he said.

And there's the bossy biker I've come to care so much about.

"Okay, boss," I said, turning to go back inside.

A hand on my arm stopped me, pulling me back against a hard thigh. "I'll see you tonight," he growled and placed a whisper of a kiss on my neck.

I shivered and my legs didn't move right away after he released me.

I turned around to wave at him, earning a wink in return.

Once he was gone, I made my way back into the compound. Grim and Talon were easy to find since they were entertaining two giggling and shrieking children.

"Okay, kidlets, time to go back to the room. I have to work," I said.

I hoped if I confined them to the room, I could bribe them with food and TV so I could do some actual work.

"You go on up. I'll hang out with them down here," Grim said, waving me off.

I turned, staring at Grim, wondering if he was serious and if I was ready to leave my kids with a stranger.

"That's okay. They can watch TV," I said, deciding it was too soon to entrust my babies with a guy I barely knew.

Grim studied me, coming to the conclusion that I wasn't going to leave my kids with him for that long. The hour he'd watched them while Sebastian taught me how to ride made me feel guilty enough. I wasn't reckless, especially not when it came to my kids.

And he understood, nodding at me. "Then work down here. I'll watch them while you do your thing."

That was an offer I'd gladly accept. "Are you sure? They can be a handful."

"Honey, as I mentioned before, I have eight grandkids," he said, his eyes dancing with mirth. "I also have three kids. And so far, I haven't killed any of them."

I bit my lip, thinking I should take this opportunity

to concentrate on work for once and maybe get ahead a little instead of always playing catchup.

"That would be amazing," I said, meaning it.

"I'll help too. I have an hour before I have to take off for work," Talon said, sitting down on the ground next to Lena. She was busy putting dresses on her dolls, and he dove right in and helped her.

After one last glance at my kids, I got my laptop, headset, and notebook from the room and set up on the bar that was currently deserted. It was huge and gave me plenty of room to spread out. The day went by in a blur of phone calls, calendar appointments, and people coming in and out of the building.

Talon came back from work after a few hours and sat with me for a bit while Lena was taking her nap and Luca was watching a movie.

"Do you like your job?" he asked, pointing at my computer.

"It pays the bills," I said, not stopping my furious typing on the keyboard.

"What would you do if you could choose anything?"

I missed a few keys and had to start over. Nobody had ever asked me that question, and I'd never thought about it because it had never been an option.

"I'd become a nurse," I said. I'd always loved listening to my mom tell us stories from the hospital she worked at. She was an ER nurse and loved her job.

"Huh," Talon said, taking a sip of his coffee.

"What does that mean? You don't think I could be a nurse?"

He leaned back, eyes wide. "That's not what I meant at all. You would be a great nurse. I just didn't think it would be what you would want to do."

Intrigued, I stopped typing and looked at him. "Why?"

"Ace said you love cooking and your food is the best he's ever eaten. And he said you're into that baking show on TV. Just thought you'd be interested in becoming a chef or something like that."

His comment startled me. Not only did Sebastian talk about me, but he also seemed to know about my secret obsession. Guess he hadn't been ignoring me as much as I thought.

"I enjoy cooking but don't want to do it for a living. It would suck the fun out of it. I'm not passionate enough," I said, having found my voice.

"Talon, what the fuck are you doing?" Blade called out from the hallway that led to his office.

I narrowed my eyes at him and huffed out a breath. "Stop using the F-word."

"Sorry, Nora," Blade called out and looked at Talon, jerking his head toward the hallway, the universal sign to get over there.

Talon got up with a groan. "I better go. Nice chatting with you, Nora."

"Tell Blade I'm putting a swear jar on the bar," I said.

"Good luck with that," Talon said, grinning. He walked to where Blade had disappeared into his office, closing the door once he was inside.

I finished work an hour later. Grim was in the kitchen feeding the kids. He was incredible with them, and for once I had time to get ready without rushing around. When Sebastian showed up just before we had to leave, I was waiting for him instead of trying to find my wayward possessions.

The kids were in their pajamas, and Grim said he would hang out with them and then put them to bed. I hadn't thought about what I would do when I was at the club. Neither Stella nor Malena could come to the compound to watch my kids, so Grim offering to watch them not only during the day but also at night was saving my bacon.

And since they'd taken to him so well during the day, I felt somewhat confident leaving them with him. Besides, there were at least ten other people in the compound. And what it all came down to was that I didn't really have a choice. Just like with everything else in my life lately.

"You sure you're okay to put them to bed? I can just call Smitty and ask to start later," I said, eyeing the kids while they fought it out over what book they wanted to read.

"They'll be fine. I'll stay with them until they're asleep, and then I'll hang out downstairs," he said for the tenth time, his deep baritone calming me down. "And I have the baby monitor and know how to turn it on."

I went up on my tippy toes and kissed his cheek. "Thank you so much. I don't know what I'd do without you."

It almost looked like he blushed under his beard. "It's no problem. I'd be here anyway. Might as well do something useful."

I squeezed his arm and went to the kids to say goodnight. "Okay babies, I'm off to work."

Lena leaned up, and I peppered her cheek with little kisses, making her giggle. Luca was next, but as soon as I made contact with his cheek, he put his hands up to ward me off.

"No, not there. Take the kiss off," he wailed, pointing at the spot where I'd kissed him.

This wasn't the first time we'd been through this, so I pretended to take my kiss off his cheek and made a throwing motion to the other side of the room, getting rid of it.

"Other cheek?" I asked.

He nodded and leaned to the side, letting me press a quick kiss there.

"Sleep tight," I said and then walked up to Sebastian, who was standing in the door, watching us with a soft expression.

We walked outside hand in hand, and for the first time I didn't feel like throwing up at the thought of going to Pepper's.

Chapter Thirteen

"Why is your face so splotchy?" Elle asked, taking in my appearance when I came into the dressing room.

I cringed when I looked in the mirror, the red spots looking worse in the bright light. "I forgot my lotion at home and used Lena's diaper rash cream instead. Which somehow gave me a rash," I replied and sat down at my change table.

I was at the club earlier than I had ever been, and I only counted to one hundred before going inside, the usual anxiety at going to work almost nonexistent. Sebastian had stood outside with me, his steady presence and warm touches calming me more than anything else ever could.

He didn't ask questions, just waited with me until I was ready. After walking me to the door of the changing room, he kissed me and went off to do whatever it was he did at the club.

I'd only noticed the rash a few minutes before I left

the compound, when it was still only a slight red tinge. I didn't think much of it since a diaper rash cream was supposed to help with rashes, wasn't it? Turned out that wasn't the case for faces. Who would have thought?

"Whoa," she said, stopping next to my chair. "You didn't sleep at home?"

"We stayed at the clubhouse," I said, looking around my small dressing table in search of my foundation. I should be able to cover most of the red splotches, and the dim lighting in the club would hide the rest.

Elle leaned forward, catching my eyes in the mirror. "You're staying at the *clubhouse?*"

"Wasn't my choice. Sebastian insisted," I said, slathering my face in foundation.

"Sebastian insisted?" she asked and took the makeup sponge out of my hand, applying it more evenly.

"Why are you repeating everything I'm saying?" I asked, following her practiced movements in the mirror.

"Because I'm trying to understand what's going on. Are you together?"

"No."

She groaned, putting the foundation away and starting with the powder. "You keep telling yourself that."

"It's the truth. We're just staying there until he sorts out…"

I trailed off when I realized what I was about to say.

"Until he sorts out what?" Tia asked, appearing at my other side.

"I kind of have a stalker," I said, tired of keeping things from my friends.

"A stalker?" Elle screeched.

"How long has this been going on?" Tia chimed in.

"Almost a year," I said, going for full honesty tonight.

Elle stopped fixing my face and stood up, wielding the brush in her hand like a sword. "And you never told us? What the hell is wrong with you?"

"I thought it wouldn't escalate. It was only little things. Nothing too crazy."

The girls stared at me like I'd lost my mind. Which I guessed I had. But I was used to taking care of things myself. And it didn't seem like a big deal at the time. Not until I got the note.

"Who's stalking you, girl?"

I twisted my hands in my lap. "It's Clive."

He wasn't exactly subtle about it either, so at least I knew who was after me.

"It's your lucky day, because Clive is gone," Elle said. "Didn't anyone tell you about last night?"

I hoped that meant he'd seen the light and moved on from his stalkerish ways. If he really was gone, I couldn't say I was upset about it.

"What happened? Did he quit?" I asked, turning in my seat.

"He was arrested," Tia said. "A dozen cops swarmed into Pepper's and took him out. It was quite the spectacle. I can't believe you haven't heard about it yet. Sebastian was here when it happened."

I stilled. Why wouldn't he tell me about that?

"What did they arrest him for?" I asked. *Does this mean I can go home again?*

"Assault," Tia said, stepping out of her dress and pulling on tiny jean shorts and a red-checkered shirt.

"Of who?" I asked, watching her tie the ends of her shirt together, leaving it unbuttoned.

She walked to her table next to mine and rummaged through her makeup bag. "Police officer, I think."

Elle finished with my makeup. "This is the best I can do. Did you take an antihistamine so the swelling goes down?"

I shook my head. "I didn't think to bring any with me when I packed for our sleepover."

"I think I've got some," Tia said, rummaging through her bag, coming out with a case full of pills.

"That's a lot of pills," I said and pulled my clothes into place.

But just like every other time I'd worn them, they didn't magically lengthen or cover my butt just by tugging on them.

"It's just painkillers, antihistamines, and Viagra. Don't worry, I'm well aware of Pepper's policy on drugs. Besides, I'd never do them. I've seen too many of my friends get dragged into the dumpster."

I wasn't even going to ask why she had Viagra in there.

"I'll start with one, and if it doesn't make me too sleepy, I'll take another one," I said.

Tia pulled out a packet and pushed a pill into my outstretched hand. I swallowed it and stood up.

"I better go or Smitty is going to dock my pay." I waved at the girls. "See you out there."

The night was slow. I searched the floor for Sebastian but couldn't see him. He was usually near the stage, but he'd disappeared almost an hour ago, leaving Gears to stand in his spot.

"I'm done for the night. Can you cash me out?" I asked Stephen an hour later. I finished my shift early tonight because it was quiet, something that didn't happen very often. But since I was tired, I didn't even care about the hit to my paycheck.

"Of course, doll, just give me a minute."

I leaned against the counter, easing the pressure on my feet.

"There you go," Stephen said, handing me my tips.

I went back into the dressing room and slipped my comfortable jeans and sweater back on. There was still no sign of Sebastian when I came out, and I was starting to get worried. *Should I call a taxi or wait?* It was earlier than I was meant to finish, but he didn't say he was going to leave the club. Maybe he was in the office.

I went to the long hallway leading to the office, toilet, and staff room. Smitty's door wasn't closed all the way, and I could hear voices.

When I recognized Sebastian's growl, I stopped, curiosity getting the better of me. His back was blocking my view, and the opening was too small to make out who he was talking to.

"It's your call. If you want to bust them now, we'll bust them now," an unfamiliar voice said.

"We have enough on them to put them away for a while," Sebastian's familiar timbre rang through the room. "But I want Jim Turner. We're not making a move unless he's there."

"You shouldn't have put so much pressure on him. He ran like the spineless little weasel he is as soon as he knew we were on to him. He's only a small cog in a big machine. And we finally have enough on his boss. I'm not going to hold off much longer."

Feet shuffled on the ground, and then the unfamiliar voice asked, "Did you get anything out of his woman?"

There was a loud growl, then a crash. "She's not his woman," Sebastian said, his voice icy. "And she's not involved."

"Then why are you still wasting your time with her?"

I ground my teeth, hoping the man would trip and fall into a toilet.

The blood in my veins turned to ice. Had Sebastian been playing me this whole time? It all made so much more sense now. That would explain why he'd suddenly shown so much interest in me after ignoring me for the past year. Nobody who looked like him and could have his pick of girls would choose someone like me.

There was another crash and a few shouts.

"Let him go," Blaze said, sounding like he was on a Sunday brunch date instead of in an office in a strip club. Guess it made sense for Sebastian's boss or president or whatever he was to be there as well.

I suppressed the gasp that wanted to escape. Jim's betrayal didn't hurt. It was an annoyance I could do without. What caused a stabbing pain to shoot through my chest was the thought of Sebastian using me to get to my ex.

I stepped back, running into one of the bouncers coming out of the storeroom. "Oh, sorry," I mumbled, ready to go home.

I adjusted the strap of my bag and shot the guy a tight smile. I didn't know his name, but he was part of the regular rotation. He nodded at me and turned back to the main area when the door behind me opened.

Sebastian came out, looking like a bull ready to charge. He stopped, his face going soft when he saw me. "Nora. You finished already?"

Bastard. How dare he talk to me like nothing happened. And he made me swear on top of lying to me. Double bastard.

"Just on my way out," I replied, my voice wavering.

I couldn't seem to take a proper breath; the only thing on my mind was putting as much space between us as I could.

"Let's go," he said, taking a step forward.

My hand shot up, and he frowned. "That's okay. You look like you're busy. I'll call a cab."

"You're not taking a taxi," he said, not giving me a chance to reply before taking my hand and leading me outside.

I found myself on the back of his bike before I could protest. He put a helmet on my head and untangled a strand of hair that had gotten caught up in the strap. His fingers whispered across my cheek, the gentle caress making my chest feel like it would cave under the pressure of my emotions.

And I hated him a little in that moment. How dare he make me fall for him and then turn out to be my biggest downfall?

We drove back to the compound, and I jumped off the bike as soon as he'd come to a stop, the engine still running.

I was halfway to the front door when he caught up with me. "Nora, wait."

There was no way I could pretend everything was

okay. I wore my emotions on my face like a billboard advert.

"What?" I asked, my voice low, not turning around.

"Something happened," he said. It wasn't a question but a statement.

No shit, Sherlock.

I clenched my jaw to hold in the sob working its way up my throat. "It's nothing. I'm fine. Just tired."

"Hey," he said, his voice raspy. "Talk to me."

I struggled to get the next words out. "There's nothing to talk about. Now can I please go to bed?"

He stiffened as if I'd told him his bike had a scratch. His hand dropped from my arm, and I shivered at the sudden loss.

"This conversation isn't over," he said, never taking his eyes off me. "But there's something I have to take care of. If I could stay, I would."

With one last glance at me, he got back on the bike. "We'll talk tomorrow, okay?"

I didn't respond, and he didn't wait around. Instead, he started his bike back up and left.

I went inside, dragging my feet. The temptation to lie down on one of the couches downstairs instead of hauling myself up to bed was great.

"Sweetheart," Grim greeted me as soon as I took the first step inside.

"Hey, Grim," I said, taking a seat on the barstool

next to him. The baby monitor was in front of him, the image showing my sleeping babies. "What are you still doing up?"

"I don't sleep much. Usually don't go to bed before five," he said.

The room was still busy, everyone except Grim glassy-eyed and most of them swaying on their feet. I guess everyone but me had had a good night.

"Thanks so much for watching the kids," I said, getting back up. "You're the best."

"Anytime. And I mean it."

He tilted his head, our eyes meeting.

"Whatever happened, happened. You can only move forward," he said, making an accurate interpretation of my defeated expression.

"If only it was that easy," I said and yawned.

He got up and opened the giant tree limbs he called arms. I didn't even pretend to think about it before I fell into him, winding my arms around his big body. He held me close, and I felt like I was in a biker cocoon. He smelled of leather and oil, and I took a big breath.

"If you ever need anything, you know where to find me," he said, pressing a kiss to my head.

I nodded into his chest and let go, deciding that was as much of a pity party as I would throw for myself. "Thank you. Again."

I gave him one last half-hearted smile and went

to Sebastian's room. Even though I could barely walk because I was so tired, I went into the bathroom to shower the smell of Pepper's from my skin, slathering myself with soap and shampoo.

My pajamas were an old ratty T-shirt and sweatpants. I didn't bother drying my hair since that required turning on the hair dryer, which would in turn wake the kids.

And I needed at least a few hours of sleep before I could function.

Chapter Fourteen

"Let's wait for Sebastian to get back before you make any rash decisions," Gears said for the third time in as many minutes.

I was packing my suitcases while he stood in the doorway, his eyes following my every move.

"I'm going home. Unless I'm a prisoner, there's nothing you can do about it," I said, stuffing the last of our clothes in the bag.

Sebastian still hadn't gotten back, and I was sick of waiting around for him. It would be much easier to do this without him here anyway, so I decided to move out while the moving was good.

Gears looked from me to the suitcase and back, conflicted. Well, he could be as conflicted as he wanted to be, but I was going home. I wouldn't spend another minute living in the same building Sebastian was in.

Since they'd arrested Clive, I didn't get cold sweats anymore at the thought of going home. I was 99.4

percent sure I would be safe there.

"But Sebastian said—"

I ignored him and kept looking under the bed and couch, making sure we didn't leave anything behind. Luca and Lena were busy turning the tap in the bathroom on and off, getting soaked in the process. But I had no time to lose, so I let them go crazy until we were ready to leave.

"You want me to put them in the car?" Grim asked, pushing past Gears and pointing at my bags.

"You have impeccable timing," I said.

He grinned and grabbed my three bags with ease.

"What the fuck are you doing, man?" Gears whined when Grim pushed past him.

"Letting her go home. Which is what she wants and what she'll get."

And that was that, apparently.

Grim put all my bags in the car and then helped me with the kids while Gears looked like he was about to pass out. Not sure how he survived being part of a motorcycle club with the way he was wringing his hands.

He needed to relax. I was leaving their compound, not stealing their silver.

"Whatever happens, you remember to call me if you need anything," Grim said, stopping me from getting into the car.

I put my arms around him for a short but tight hug and nodded. "I know."

He closed my door for me once I was safely buckled in, and I started the car. The motor purred to life, and there wasn't a single warning light flashing at me.

I checked the dashboard, wondering if maybe the lights broke as well. And where was the angry beeping? I wound my window down, and Grim leaned in.

"Did you do something to my car?" I asked.

"I can't believe you were driving that health hazard," he said. "Sebastian fixed it."

I stared at him, giving him my best impression of an owl. "He fixed it? All of it?"

"The guys helped since there was quite a bit to do. Can't believe the thing was still running."

"Wow, thanks so much," I said, words not adequate to describe how grateful I was. Buying a new car would have been impossible. Someone fixing my rust bucket meant everything to me, even if it was Sebastian who'd done it.

"That was all Sebastian," he said with a wink. "Don't be a stranger."

I rolled the window back up and waved to him on my way out of the compound.

When we drove through the gates and hit the road, I didn't feel free like I thought I would. There was no weight off my chest, no happy dance. Instead, I felt like I'd left a piece of me at the compound.

I drove straight home, leaving our bags in the car and only taking the blankies and stuffed animals out that couldn't be left there for the night. The kids were happy to be home and went straight into the backyard.

Luca let out a shriek as soon as he was through the door, and I raced after them. There was a fence around the backyard, and there wasn't much in it except a few trees and a small sandbox. I wondered if he'd tripped.

"Mom, look," Luca shrieked, racing Lena to a swing set that wasn't there when we'd left.

Something else that hadn't been there was the playhouse nestled underneath the big oak tree.

"A swing," Luca called out, doing his best to help Lena.

"Swing, swing, swing," Lena chanted, hanging off the seat with one leg, Luca pushing her up.

I blinked a few times, making sure I wasn't having a mental breakdown and hallucinating. After the ninth blink, everything was still there, and I followed the happy shrieks to help my kids.

We spent the next hour outside, exploring the additions to our yard. I had no explanation for where they'd come from. I couldn't afford anything this big and shiny. And everything was brand-new, putting it further out of my reach.

I had some investigating to do and started with

Stella since she liked grand gestures. This would be right up her alley.

She picked up right away, her phone an extension of her arm.

"You guys back home yet?" she asked.

I'd only told her that we were spending a few days with Sebastian. She thought we were together anyway and didn't need an explanation.

"Got back an hour ago," I replied, watching Luca open and close the shutters on the playhouse three million times. Lena was busy rearranging the fully stocked interior that included a kitchen, chairs, a table, and a shelf with papers and pens.

"You working tonight?" Stella asked.

"No, but I have to go in tomorrow. I know it's short notice, but can you watch the kids by any chance?"

"Of course I can. Mason has now decided that he needs to finish the house within the next few months, so I have plenty of time. I barely see him anymore."

Oh no, that didn't sound like the bubbly Stella I knew. "What's going on?"

"Nothing. I'm just being a big baby. Since Mason has a full-time job, renovating a house this big on top of it takes a while and a lot of his time. And I know I shouldn't complain because he's doing it for us, but I just don't understand what the rush is. Ever since we came back from our trip, he's been on a mission."

"He won't be tied up with the house forever. Have you tried helping him?"

Stella had a big heart but no real life skills. She grew up with a butler and maid, and sometimes it showed.

"Of course I did. I might be spoiled, but I'm not lazy. The stubborn mule won't even let me touch a paintbrush. Apparently he doesn't trust me because last time I tried to help, I set the house on fire."

"While you used a paintbrush?" I asked, wondering how she managed to start a fire with paint.

"No, while I was making dinner. I burned the eggs."

Luca had now moved on to taking everything Lena threw out the window back inside the playhouse. He was getting more and more agitated when she wouldn't stop, and I knew I had only about thirty seconds left before they would start fighting.

"How do you start a fire when you burn eggs?"

"Forgot they were on the stove and they burned to a crisp. Then the pan got really hot and started catching fire."

Wow. I had nothing. Absolutely nothing. "I'm impressed. That's quite the feat."

"Mason didn't think so. And now I'm not allowed to do anything anymore."

"Maybe that's for the best," I said, snickering.

"Shut up. Some friend you are."

I remembered why I called and asked, "You didn't happen to leave a few things in my yard, did you?"

"I haven't been there since I watched the kids last time. Why?"

"Nothing, all good."

Luca was shouting at Lena to stop messing up his house, and I made my way over. "Honey, I have to go. But we'll talk tomorrow, okay?"

"See you then," she said.

"Bye," I said and took the small pot off Luca, who was lifting it to throw at his sister.

I herded the kids back inside, our progress resembling a zigzag rather than the straight line I was hoping for. "Let's see what we can find for dinner."

When Lena started wailing whenever Luca got too close to her, I knew I needed a distraction while I made dinner.

"How about you guys hide, and I'll find you," I said, pulling pasta out of the cupboard.

The kids ran off to hide, and I counted to forty before I looked for them. It gave me enough time to put the water on and start the sauce.

It only took four times of hiding before dinner was almost ready. As long as I continued counting, they usually stayed hidden. Not my finest parenting moment, but it worked.

Dinner was quiet compared to how we'd spent the last two nights. How could I miss the guys after only having met them a few days ago?

The kids kept asking why the guys weren't eating dinner with us. When they were finally in bed, I went to the kitchen, ready to take some time and wallow in self-pity. Tomorrow I'd pick myself back up and pretend I was fine. But I'd allow myself one night of ice cream and chocolate liqueur debauchery.

I decided tonight was a four-scoop-and-five-shots kind of emergency situation. After adding bits of crushed chocolate to my boozy dessert, I jumped up to sit on the counter and dig in.

I was only three spoonfuls into my pity parade when a key turned in the front door and it opened.

Sebastian appeared in the entry to the kitchen, looking like an angry god with his stormy eyes and wild hair. "Is this how you're going to play this? Have your fun, take a walk on the wild side, and then disappear without a word once you got what you wanted?"

"How dare you say that to me, you… you… you banana-sucking turd," I said, my voice barely controlled, my body shaking. I wasn't the one who'd done something wrong.

I took measured breaths in and out, willing my hands to stop shaking and my heart rate to return to normal. I braced my hands on the sink and hung my head.

"Why did you leave without a word?" he asked, his big boots appearing in my line of sight.

I didn't lift my head, worried I'd do something

embarrassing if I looked at him, like drizzle him in the rest of my chocolate liqueur and then slowly lick it off.

"Was everything a lie?" I asked his shoes.

He shifted his weight but didn't step closer. "What do you mean?"

His voice was hesitant, all the earlier anger gone.

"Did I ever mean anything more to you than a way to get closer to Jim?" I asked, my voice steady despite my inner turmoil.

"Baby, what happened between the time I left you last night to this morning?" he said, his voice soft.

It took everything in me to lift my head and meet his eyes. The intensity of all that was Sebastian hit me and sucked all the anger out of me, leaving only devastation behind. A fist took hold of my heart and squeezed.

I sucked in a breath and studied his masculine features, drinking them in like it would be the last time I'd ever look at him. "It's okay, you don't have to answer the question. I know I was only a means to an end."

His hand came around my neck and turned me around so we were facing each other. "That's bullshit and you know it."

I shook him off and put space between us. "I heard you."

His face blanched. "What do you mean?"

Not wanting to go back and forth, I tried a

different line. "You lied to me."

One of his hands went to his hip, and he looked down at the ground before focusing his attention back at me. "I never lied. I might not have told you everything, but I never lied."

The fist around my heart tightened. "Lying by omission is as bad as the actual lie. You made me believe you liked me." My voice broke, and I studied my nails. I'd painted them a dark maroon last night, a color I usually loved but right now couldn't stand to look at. "I heard you at Pepper's."

"Let me explain. Please," Sebastian said, his tone wavering. For the first time since I'd met him, he sounded unsure. "I don't know what you think you heard, but you got it all wrong."

"There's nothing to explain. I got the message loud and clear," I said, then turned on my heel and ran. A strangled shout for me to stop sounded from behind, but I didn't stop until I was in my bedroom with the door shut.

We never even had the chance to become anything before it all fell apart.

Chapter Fifteen

"You look like shit," Malena said, sweeping her eyes over my face. "Please tell me that's not actual shit on your brow."

I glanced at my reflection in the hallway mirror and swiped a finger across my eyebrow. A closer look confirmed it was only applesauce.

"Not poo, just the food Lena threw at me this morning," I said.

After washing my hands, I joined Malena at the kitchen table. Lena was currently asleep, and Malena was spending her lunch break at my house.

Sebastian had been gone when I got up this morning, avoiding any awkward encounters. Gears was back in his post across the street, and things were as they were before.

Well, almost.

So far there was no sign of Jim or my stalker, but it

was still early in the morning. Who knew what the day would bring?

Malena raised a brow at me, linking her fingers on top of the table. "Start talking. I only have twenty minutes before I have to go back to the office."

I sighed but had already decided to tell her everything. "Jim screwed up and pissed off the wrong people. They want the money he owes them and think I'm the way to get it. Sebastian is part of the people he screwed over, and he's responsible for watching me."

I stopped, gauging her reaction so far. She was staring at me slack-jawed, unblinking.

I forged on, the dam now open and the words flowing. "We hooked up. For him it was just a way to get off, but for me it was so much more. He made me feel special, like I was important to him. It was stupid, and I should have known it would never lead to anything. But I did it anyway because no matter what, I couldn't shake the attraction I felt for him. I've never felt this way for anyone. Not even Jim."

"Oh, chiquita," Malena said, getting up.

I met her halfway and fell into her arms, giving a choked laugh. "I'm so stupid."

"You're naïve, not stupid. And it's nothing to be ashamed of. It's what makes you so special. Despite all the shit life has piled on you, you're still optimistic and—most of all—happy."

My heart ached with sorrow, and I closed my eyes in an attempt to ward off the misery that was building inside. I wasn't feeling very happy in that moment.

"What do I do now?" I asked, holding her tight.

"You dust yourself off and move the fuck on. Nobody who treats you like that is worth your pain."

I shook my head, not moving out of the safety of her embrace. Closing my eyes seemed like a solid strategy to cope with life.

Malena had other ideas, taking my arms and moving me a step back. "*Querida*, you're stronger than this."

"But I'm not."

She leaned closer, making sure I was paying attention. "Yes you are."

We stayed like that, eyes locked, both waiting for the other one to say something.

"Mom," Lena's sleepy voice interrupted us.

She was walking into the kitchen, her feet shuffling along the floor.

"Hey, baby girl," I said, picking her up and cuddling her close. She snuggled into my arms, making me forget some of my heartache.

"Cute outfit. Did you dress yourself today, *guapa*?" Malena asked, eyeing Lena's pink and white striped dress and red and orange polka-dot tights.

"No, I did," I said, sticking my tongue out at Malena.

"At least you'll always be able to see her, even in the dark," Malena said and picked up her bag, winking at me. "Call me tonight?"

"I will. Thanks for coming over."

She hugged us and kissed Lena's head. "Anytime."

I worked the rest of the day, watching the clock, every passing minute bringing me closer to seeing Sebastian again. No matter how much he hurt me, the invisible connection pulling me to him was still there.

I picked Luca up with Gears trailing us. After asking where Sebastian was when he didn't come along to pick him up, Luca chattered the whole way back.

"Why do you have to works tonight?" Luca asked later that night when he was getting ready for bed. I was once again running late, but apparently so was Sebastian.

"Because I need to earn money," I said. He was a bit young to understand why people had to work, but I tried my best to explain it to him.

"Buts we got money," he said, stepping into his pajama pants.

"We do because I have a job. If I didn't go anymore, then we wouldn't have any money and would have to sleep in a tent."

I hadn't thought that through properly, because sleeping in a tent was an exciting prospect for my kids.

"I wants to sleep in a tent," Luca cried.

Lena joined him. "Me too."

"Who's going to sleep in a tent?" Stella asked,

appearing in the door.

"Me, because Mom is staying home," Luca said with a big smile.

Stella looked at me with a smirk on her face. "Is that right?"

I caught Luca and lifted him, making sure I had his attention. "Sleeping in a tent isn't really a good idea. Especially not when it's cold. I'll still have to go to work."

He slumped in my arms, and his bottom lip quivered. "But I love tents."

"How about we put one up in the living room?" Stella suggested.

"Small problem," I said, putting Luca back on his feet. "I don't have one."

Her excitement didn't falter. "I'll message Mason to drop one off. He's got about ten."

She pulled her phone out and started typing, Luca and Lena dancing around her.

I left them to it and searched for my shoes and bag. Every day I promised myself I'd put them down near the front door so I would find them again. And every day I dropped them somewhere in the house and forgot where.

My shoes were under the couch, and my bag was in the bathroom.

I opened the front door, calling across the street to Gears. "Do you know where Sebastian is? I have to go to work."

He jogged over, coming to stand in front of me. "He's on his way."

"Okay, thanks," I said, and he went back to his post across the street. They couldn't be more obvious if they tried. No way would Jim come back with a big bike and bigger dude sitting in front of my house.

When a knock sounded a few minutes later, I kissed the kids goodbye and waved to Stella. "Have fun."

I opened the door, but instead of Sebastian, it was Mason standing in front of me. "Hey, Mason. You here to drop off the tent?"

He nodded and leaned in, kissing me on the cheek.

"I was summoned," he said, holding up two bags. "I had two small tents lying around, collecting dust. The kids can have them."

"They'll love that. Just go inside. They're in the living room," I said, smiling at him.

Mason and Stella had been the most supportive friends I could have ever wished for. I shouldn't have been surprised that he not only brought two tents but ones the kids could keep.

The load roar of a motorcycle sounded, and we watched Sebastian pull into my driveway.

"That your new roommate?" Mason asked, his tone amused.

"Yup. He's also my lift to work, so I should go."

He nodded at me and looked back at Sebastian,

who was stalking up my walkway. "He looks angry."

I shrugged. *What's new?*

"What's going on?" Sebastian growled when he was only a few steps away.

I frowned at his obvious dislike of Mason, who he'd never met before. "Sebastian, this is Stella's *boyfriend* and my landlord, Mason."

As soon as the word boyfriend left my lips, Sebastian's entire demeanor changed. His posture relaxed, his fists unclenched, and he even held out his hand to Mason. "Heard a lot about you. Good to meet you."

"You too," Mason said, accepting the peace offering. After a brief handshake and a wink in my direction, he went inside.

With the latest crisis averted, I turned, ready to be on my way to work.

"Sorry I'm late," Sebastian said, following me to his bike.

I wanted to know where he'd been but didn't ask. He didn't owe me anything, after all.

I put on my purple helmet, standing far enough away that he couldn't reach out to do it for me. Sebastian got on the bike first and then held out his hand to help me up.

As soon as our palms connected, I froze, the instant tingle shooting through my body making me squirm.

He didn't release my hand once I was sitting behind him; instead, he pulled it around to his front, causing me to slide forward and into his body.

Since I would never protest about sitting this close to him, my other arm joined the one he was still holding. No matter how mad I was at him, I still craved him, and the need to touch him was ever present.

Once he was satisfied that I wasn't going to move back, he put his hands on the handlebars and started the bike.

I sat stiffly behind him, not enjoying the ride as usual. I was desperate to touch him but still too mad to let myself enjoy being this close to him.

He stayed with me while I did my thing outside Pepper's, his attention on me the whole time.

"Okay, I'm ready," I said once my racing heart settled down and I felt like I wasn't going to pass out if I walked inside.

He led me to the dressing room door, trailing his hand down my arm before leaving.

I watched him walk away, my heart wheezing out a few pathetic breaths. When I came back out and started working, I spotted him standing in his usual spot near the stage, arms crossed in front of his chest, his muscles bulging, watching me.

I messed up a few orders because all I could think about was the way he took care of me. How he'd made me feel special. The way he was with my kids. And all of it I liked. Craved more of.

But at the same time, I didn't want to lose what little dignity I had left. Been there, done that. My thoughts were all over the place, veering from planning a way to get him alone to a way to hurt him as much as he'd hurt me.

Since revenge wasn't in my repertoire, the thought fizzled out as soon as it ignited. I usually just moved on when someone had done me wrong. Guess that didn't work out so well with Jim. He deserved for me to go all *The Godfather* on him. But since I was more *Forrest Gump,* I'd never get anywhere close to making him pay.

And that was okay. I just wished he'd keep his problems away from me and the kids. If I was honest, Sebastian's betrayal hurt much more than Jim's ever had. I'd moved on after Jim, thinking I'd dodged a bullet finding out when I did instead of letting him drag me down with him.

Sebastian, on the other hand, managed to twist my stomach into knots, and the thought of never kissing him again made my body ache. He'd buried himself so deep into my heart, I didn't know how to ever get him out.

As desperate as I was not to repeat past mistakes, all I wanted was to forgive him.

"Bitch, are you deaf?" someone yelled at me, causing me to snap out of watching Sebastian.

I pasted on a weak smile and turned to the entitled cheesedick demanding my attention. I'd never understand how some people thought it was okay to treat waitresses like second-class citizens. Especially when they worked in a strip club.

"How can I help you, sir?" I asked, holding my tablet at the ready.

"We want another round," he barked at me. Their table wasn't in my section, so I didn't know what they'd all had. But it would be easy to find out, so I nodded and turned to do his bidding.

A slap to my ass made me stumble forward. My cheek stung from the harsh treatment, and tears shot to my eyes. I really needed to grow a thicker skin. I refused to look back at what I was sure would be a smirk on the guy's face, daring me to tell him off. That was how it usually worked, and I was over it.

There was a loud crash, and I turned after all. Sebastian was dragging the guy off his chair and to the exit. He threw him outside like he wasn't a middle-aged, overweight guy but a sack of potatoes.

The whole room watched in awe, and I knew it would take about three seconds for Smitty to show up. There were cameras all around the main area, and he always knew what was going on.

"You are a death sentence to my business," Smitty cried right on cue, stalking up to Sebastian.

I shuffled closer like everyone else, not wanting to miss a word.

"You mean the club's business," Sebastian corrected him, looking like he was dealing with an annoying bug he wanted to brush off his sleeve.

"Stop throwing customers out the door. You could

handle this shit more discreetly."

Sebastian raised a brow, looking down at Smitty, who was at least two heads shorter than him. "I want them to know they aren't allowed to touch the girls."

Smitty threw his hands up. "You mean they're not allowed to touch one particular girl. Never seen you handle someone like that when it was one of the other girls."

He stalked off with as much drama as he'd arrived. Sebastian glanced in my direction and only turned away when I gave him a tentative smile.

Everyone behaved for the rest of the night and Sebastian met me at the back door when it was time to go home. He opened the door for me to walk through, but I stopped in front of him and tilted my head back. "Thank you."

"You don't ever have to thank me for putting those assholes in their place. He had no right to touch you."

I put my hands on his chest and stepped closer. He was still holding the door with one hand, his other fisted at his side. "You always seem to come to my rescue."

"I don't know if you've noticed, but you're important to me," he said, his voice raspy.

I took another step forward, putting us closer together so we were almost touching. "You're important to me too."

His eyes flicked over my face, and I tipped my head back, leaning in. He didn't miss the invitation and lowered his lips to mine, the contact whisper soft but no less impactful.

I sighed into his mouth, and he deepened the kiss.

"Sorry to interrupt, but you chose the worst spot to do this," Elle said, and I jerked back. She was standing behind us with a smirk on her face. "I let you go for as long as I could take it, but that kiss nearly took my pants off."

I flushed in embarrassment, and Sebastian shook his head at her, amusement dancing in his eyes. "Sorry, Elle. Come on through."

She walked past him, giving him a wink, then turning to me, waggling her eyebrows.

Sebastian put his arm around my shoulders and walked us to his bike. He waited until Elle was in her car and pulling out of the parking lot before starting the engine.

I leaned my head against his back and enjoyed the ride, feeling lighter than I had in a while.

When we pulled back up to the house, I was reluctant to get off the bike. It was the one place we could just be. No misunderstandings, no hurt feelings. Just us.

Instead of walking up to the front door, Sebastian pulled me around the side. I followed, curious what he was up to.

We stopped at the foot of the playhouse, ushering me inside.

"Are we having a tea party?" I asked, crawling

inside. I still hadn't found out who put it there but had my suspicions it had something to do with my roommate.

He followed me, shrinking the space to about a quarter of its size.

"The last thing I have on my mind when I'm with you is a tea party," he said and leaned his back against one of the walls, pulling me into his side. I relaxed into him, my arm snaking under his shirt, caressing the soft skin of his abs.

"I want to talk to you without distractions," he said, placing a kiss on my hair. "That's why we're hiding out here."

I chuckled, my body vibrating with mirth. "You know Stella is going to show up out here in a few minutes. She'd have undoubtedly heard the bike pull up and seen us walk around to the backyard."

"I know. But I didn't want to wait a second longer to make this right. I want you—no, I need you to hear me out. If you still don't want to give me another chance, then I understand."

I sighed, the seriousness of his words sinking like a warm blanket around me. He took my silence as assent to continue.

"The initial plan was if Jim thought you'd shacked up with one of us, he'd do something stupid in response and come out of hiding. But only because that happened to be part of the plan doesn't mean my feelings for you are any less real."

I buried my head in his chest, breathing him

in, reminding myself that he wasn't pursuing any agenda right now. He didn't have to say those things to continue staying with me. It slowly sank in that maybe—just maybe—his feelings for me matched my own.

"I volunteered for this job. Blade wanted to send someone else. Said he needed someone with a clear head who wasn't obsessed with you. In a healthy way, of course."

All my movements froze, my breath stalling.

Did he just say what I think I heard? Or have I fallen asleep and this is a dream?

"But we'd never spoken a word to one another before the first time I came to the clubhouse," I said, lifting my head off his chest.

"Doesn't matter. Not to me."

"Sebastian—" I said, but he stopped me.

"My parents have loved each other their whole lives. In fact, they still love each other like they did when they first met," he said. I shuffled closer, putting my hand on his cheek, and he turned into the gentle caress. "I always wanted what they have. My dad told me it was love at first sight for him and Mom. That when I saw the one who was meant for me, I'd know. And I always laughed at him. Told him he was crazy."

His eyes held mine, showing me how much he meant every word he said. "And then I met you, and I finally understood what he was talking about."

I crushed my lips against his, clawing my way

closer, the need to feel him overwhelming. He met my tongue stroke for stroke, and soon we were panting, our hands gliding over every inch of each other's body.

"If you're trying to hide from me, you're doing a terrible job because I can see your legs. And they're way too close to each other," Stella interrupted us. "No sexy times in the playhouse. That's just wrong."

I untangled myself from Sebastian, closing my eyes. His hand whispered across my cheek, and then he shuffled out before helping me.

Stella was waiting for us, barely holding it together, vibrating with the effort it took to stop the laughter that I could see was bubbling to the surface. She lost the battle and guffawed so loud, I was worried she'd wake the kids.

"I knew you had it in you," she wheezed out once she'd calmed down.

"Shut up," I said and rolled my eyes at her.

We walked back inside, the look on Stella's face telling me I'd have to give her a word-for-word replay of tonight.

"I knew the kids loved their new play equipment, but I didn't realize you were so fond of it as well."

"It's a pretty good tree house," I said, eying Sebastian.

"Glad you like it, baby," he said.

Ha, I knew it. He was the one who'd upgraded my backyard. "Did you put all the new stuff in my yard?" I asked.

"You said you wished you could give the kids a

swing because they love it so much at the park."

I'd mentioned it once, in passing, because I was too lazy to walk across the road. And he'd gone out and put a playground in my backyard.

"Oh hell no," Stella said. "You're giving him the smoldering eyes. I'm out of here."

I waved to her, my eyes never leaving Sebastian's. As soon as the door clicked shut behind her, I lunged at him and he caught me in a tight embrace. My legs were suspended off the floor, my arms locked tight around his neck, as our mouths met in a bone-melting, spine-tingling kiss.

He dragged me to the bedroom and then spent the rest of the night making sure I knew what I'd be missing out on if I didn't give him a second chance.

Good thing he didn't know I'd already forgiven him.

Chapter Sixteen

"When I was a lizard, I climbed up the wall and sat on the roof," Luca said, his hand on my cheek to make sure I was listening.

"When were you a lizard?" I asked, my attention on my son.

"Last weekend," he said, the earnestness on his face adorable.

We were in the backyard, Lena playing with Stella in the sandpit, Luca sitting with me on the grass. We'd been playing Go Fish when he dropped his cards to tell me a story that included him being a lizard.

A loud knock sounded on the front door, interrupting our conversation. I looked at Stella, who narrowed her eyes.

"I'll have a look at what's going on," I said, getting back to my feet. "You good with the kids?"

"Of course. But maybe take the bat with you,"

she said, pointing to the baseball bat lying next to our blanket.

No way would I take a bat with me, so I waved her off and made my way inside and to the front door. A look outside made me wish I had, in fact, taken the bat with me.

I ripped the door open, interrupting Jim mid-knock.

"What are you doing here?" I asked, my lips thin, my nostrils flaring like an angry bull about to charge. The thought of doing exactly that didn't sound like a bad idea at the moment.

"I need to talk to you," he said, then pushed past me and inside the house. "You're in danger."

"No kidding," I grumbled and watched him walk into the living room. I turned back to the road, wondering where Gears was. No way would he just let Jim come up to the front door.

When I saw no sign of him, I followed my ex, who was making himself right at home. "Jim, you need to leave. You can't be here."

He was pacing, his movements jerky, his hair a mess, his clothes wrinkled and dirty. "You need to pack a bag and come with me."

I looked at the ceiling, praying for patience. "No way. I'm not going anywhere with you."

Not liking my response, he grabbed my arm, pulling hard.

"Everything okay?" Stella called out from the back door, and Jim released me.

I stuck my head in the hallway and asked her, "Can you take the kids to get ice cream? Jim is here."

Her eyes bugged out of her head and she took a step inside. I shook my head, and she nodded before going back outside.

I knew I could count on Stella to take the kids out the side gate so they wouldn't see Jim. One crisis averted, I turned back to the bane of my existence.

"Leave," I said, pointing to the door.

"Are you mad at me?" he asked, brows furrowed.

I prayed for patience and non-murderous thoughts to survive this conversation. "Of course I'm not mad. Why would I be mad about you owing a motorcycle club money and getting me caught up in your mess? And let's not forgot the money you stole from me. In case you missed it, we're not together anymore, so my money is not yours."

Surely nobody would notice if I hid his body in the backyard.

"Whoa," he said, putting his hands up. "I didn't intend for them to come after you. And looks to me like they made themselves right at home here. Maybe I should be the one who's mad."

"What did you think would happen? They would just ask nicely for their money back? And since you have no say over who I spend my time with, you also have no right to be mad."

What a selfish banana sucker.

"Of course not. But I didn't know they even knew about you. That's why I'm here now. To rescue you."

I put my hands on my hips, needing something to hold on to or risk punching him in his smug face. "You led them straight to me when you showed up at my house. Of all the stupid things you've done in your life, that one was the most selfish. The last person I need to rescue me is you."

Useless cumbubble.

"I didn't think they were still following me," he responded, showing me his annoying dimple.

"Did you ever think about how much danger you put your kids in?"

I didn't think the bumhole could sink any further in my opinion of him. But he just managed to go from a zero to a minus three thousand.

"That's why I'm here now. To get you far away from them." He put his hand out, and I flinched back.

This shitlicker can't be for real.

"So you come back weeks later? After they could have done God knows what to me?" I yelled, hands balled into fists. "Do you have any idea what you've done?"

He stepped back, eyes wide. "Whoa, why are you so angry?"

What. The. Fudge.

"Get out," I shrieked, my body vibrating with fury.

He shook his head but retreated farther. "Fine. But just for the record, I think you're being unreasonable. And I tried to help."

"Out," I screamed, my voice too shrill for my own ears. He was never good with confrontation, and I knew he'd leave.

Jim opened his mouth in a last effort to plead his case. He'd never known when it was time to quit.

He didn't get a chance to say a word, because in that moment all hell broke loose.

The front door smashed open, and men in balaclava masks appeared from all directions. "Police, get down on the floor."

I stood frozen, hoping this was all just a figment of my imagination. Jim was taken down in a full-body tackle, landing with a crunch on the ground. I watched with wide eyes as men streamed into my little house, holding guns and yelling.

When I didn't move fast enough, I found myself crushed to the ground as well, my landing somewhat softer than Jim's but still leaving me breathless from the impact. "Put your hands behind your back," someone instructed.

I complied, my brain not able to comprehend what was going on. The same person who cuffed me lifted me back to my feet and led me out of the house. I prayed Stella didn't show up with the kids and they'd see me like this.

"I don't ever want to see you again," I whisper-hissed at Jim. "This is by far the worst thing you could have done to me, you selfish twatwaffle."

What if they arrested me? I had to take care of my kids, not hang out at the police station. And I didn't even know if they would charge me with anything. Was I helping a criminal when I let him into my house?

"Ms. Lindberg?" A guy came up to us, his attention on me.

"Yes?" I answered, glad my voice sounded steady.

"I'm sorry, but you'll have to come to the station with us. You're not under arrest, but we need to talk to you."

I blinked at him, not wanting to piss him off but also not wanting to go to the station. "Can't you talk to me here?"

"We'd rather you come to the station."

I didn't think I had a choice and relented. The movies always said to cooperate or look guilty. "Fine. But I need to make a call to make sure my kids are okay first."

He took the cuffs off me and opened the door of an unmarked police car. "Of course. You can call them on the way."

"I need my cell. My friend's number's in it."

He helped me into the car and leaned down. "I'll get it for you if you tell me where it is."

"It's on the kitchen table," I said, and he closed the door.

The officer came back with my phone a few minutes later. He got into the driver seat and handed it back to me.

"Thank you," I said, pulling up Stella's number.

I prayed she had her phone with her.

"Nora, hey," she answered, breathless. "Is it safe to come back yet?"

"Not yet. Can you keep the kids for a few hours?"

There was silence before Stella came back on. "If you're in trouble, cough once. If you just want some alone time with your hot guy, make a kissing sound."

"I wish it was one of the two. But I'm on my way to the police station."

"Did you finally murder the bastard?"

"Unfortunately, he's still alive. But they want to ask me a few questions and are taking me to the station with them."

Probably shouldn't be saying that too loudly while I was in a police car.

"Do you need a lawyer?"

That was a good question. And one I didn't have an answer to yet. I didn't want to look guilty because I immediately lawyered up. But I also didn't want them to pin something on me.

"I don't know yet," I said, my voice sounding small.

"Call me if you do and I'll mobilize Malena."

My mouth curved into a half-smile. The last person I wanted to rile up over what was hopefully nothing was Malena. I didn't know anyone with half a brain who wasn't scared of her when she went into lawyer mode.

"Thank you, honey. I don't know what I ever did to deserve a friend like you."

"Call me if you need a lift."

"I will." I hung up and slid my phone in my pocket.

We made it to the station a few minutes later. When we walked inside, it hit me that I was in a police station, about to be interrogated. It didn't matter that they called it a conversation; they wanted me at the station for a reason, and I doubted it was for a casual chat.

As soon as I took one step into the interrogation room, all my earlier bravado disappeared, and I felt as if my breath had solidified in my throat. The officer hadn't spoken another word since getting my phone for me, and the silence grew tight with tension.

He led me to a chair, and after I sat down, he left. I perched on the edge, body coiled tight and ready for flight.

The door opened what seemed like hours later, and I jumped at the sound. I wiped my clammy hands on my pants and willed my pounding heart to slow down. They'd take one look at me and think I was guilty without even having talked to me.

"Ms. Lindberg," a tall, lanky guy with short-cropped dark hair greeted me.

He was wearing jeans and a T-shirt, his badge clipped to his belt. I guessed him to be in his thirties.

"My name is Agent Cody Jenkins and I work for the federal bureau of investigation." He sat down opposite me, putting a thick folder on the table.

Why is the FBI involved in this? What exactly has Jim been up to?

I watched him open the file and read over it, shifting in my chair when the silence stretched again. Maybe he was here to intimidate me after all.

"What is your relationship with Jim Turner?" he asked, and I sighed in relief. I'd been one nervous inhale from passing out.

Okay, that was an easy question I should be able to answer without making them think I was a criminal.

"We used to be in a relationship, and he's the father of my children."

More silence, the sound of more pages turning. "When did your relationship end?"

"Two years ago."

"Isn't your daughter only two?"

I clasped my hands in my lap, then released them again. "He took off before she was born."

He looked at me for the first time since coming into the room, his gray eyes wandering over my face.

"Have you spoken to him since you broke up?"

I put my hands on the table, palms down. "A few times."

"What about?"

"Child support. Visitation. The Darth Vader helmet he left at my house and I sold on eBay."

Agent Jenkins tilted his head, looking more interested than before. "Why did you break up?"

I hugged my arms around my body. "Various reasons."

"I need more than that," he said, his focus now solely on me, papers lying forgotten on the table.

"I don't see how that's relevant," I said, not wanting to dig up things I'd rather forget.

"It is very relevant since I need to know if you parted on good terms and would be willing to help him move drugs."

"Drugs? Is that what you arrested him for?"

Why am I not surprised?

"Among other things. Now, if you'd please answer the question."

I looked at my lap, hoping this would all be over soon. "He stuck his wick in someone who wasn't me on our coffee table and then took off with all our money."

Money I'd worked hard for. Money I needed so I could take a few weeks off after Lena's birth. Money that made the difference between us having a roof over our head and living on the street.

I'd been lucky I had my virtual assistant job already back then and could keep working. It was hell on earth working with a newborn and toddler in the house, but we made it out the other side. And now it had all happened again and I only had myself to blame. At least this time he didn't take all my money.

"If you think I'd ever help that sorry mother puffer, you're delusional. I hate him with the heat of a thousand suns and hope he burns in hell," I said, looking directly at Agent Jenkins.

"Is there any record of Mr. Turner moving out?" he asked, not impressed by my passionate declaration.

"My name was the only one on the lease."

Something that should have made me realize right away that he didn't plan on sticking around, even back then. But he said it was easier that way. Of course it was if he was planning on leaving all along.

"But if you want to check my story, look up his marriage certificate. He got married three weeks after he left me."

It was also three days before Lena's birth. I didn't find out until almost a year later, when I finally tracked him down and his wife answered the phone. She didn't even know I existed. They didn't last, and I couldn't say I didn't feel some sense of satisfaction when I heard she left him for someone else.

"I think that's all I need for now. Don't leave the state, and be available in case we need you to come back in."

I stood up when he did, holding back the urge to roll my eyes. Where did he think I would go? I had about a hundred dollars in my bank account and two small kids. Not exactly the ideal setup for a quick getaway.

"Of course," I said instead.

The officer from earlier was waiting outside the door and escorted me through the busy station. My eyes flitted around the space, taking in the chaos surrounding me.

My attention was diverted to the far end of the room and to three men who were involved in a scuffle.

"Let me the fuck go," a familiar voice shouted over the noise.

Every eye in the room turned to Sebastian, who was held back by two police officers who weren't going to be able to contain him for much longer.

"Sebastian," I gasped, slack-jawed, staring at him.

His head snapped up and his eyes found mine, holding me captive. My steps faltered and I stopped, not caring whose way I was blocking.

No way was he able to hear me, but as much as I was drawn to him, he seemed to know when I was in the room. He pushed at his arm, and the officer to his left lost his grip. As soon as one of his arms was free, Sebastian easily stepped out of the other officer's hold.

Not wasting any time, Sebastian rushed to where I was still standing, blinking at him like an owl. He crushed me to him in a tight embrace once I was within reach, the air in my lungs escaping in a wheeze. But I didn't care, holding him just as tightly.

"What are you doing here?" I asked once he loosened his arms. He was still holding me close, but I could look at him if I tilted my head back, which I did as soon as I was able to.

"I heard they brought you in," he growled, looking unhappy about this latest development.

"I had to answer a few questions, but they let me go again," I said, putting my hand on his cheek, needing to feel him.

He closed his eyes when I made contact, leaning into my touch. He turned his head and kissed my palm, making it tingle.

"Agent York," someone barked next to us. "Can you explain to me why one of the officers has a sprained ankle and the other what appears to be a bruise on his jaw?"

Sebastian sighed and turned to the voice, tugging me into his side.

"You didn't tell me you were going to take her in. And those two idiots had it coming. I told them to let me go," he said.

"I'm your boss. I don't have to justify my actions to you. Now unhand the girl and get your ass into my office."

I recognized that voice. It was the other guy I didn't know talking in Smitty's office when I overheard them. And Sebastian was somehow connected to him.

This day just keeps getting better and better. What's next? A unicorn taking a shit in my front yard?

"Ms. Lindberg, everything okay?" the officer accompanying me asked, watching the scene play out with interest, just like the rest of the office.

"I'm fine," I said, stepping out of Sebastian's warm hold. He seemed ready to pull me back to him but was interrupted by another reprimand.

"Agent York," angry guy hissed. "Get. Your. Ass. Into. My. Office."

And that was when it clicked. Agent York. That had to be Sebastian. He told me his last name was Jones. But I guess he couldn't have used his real name while he was undercover. I wondered if his first name was Sebastian or if that had been a lie too.

I silently said goodbye to his beautiful abs, godlike arms, and soft, full lips that I'd never touch or kiss again. Because this was worse than anything my imagination could have come up with.

"Nora, it's not what you think," Sebastian said when he saw the expression on my face.

"So you're not an FBI agent who went undercover at a motorcycle club to catch my ex and whoever he was working for?"

"Well, yes, but that has nothing to do with us."

"So you didn't use me to get to him?"

"Kind of, but it wasn't like that."

I put my hand up, stopping him from saying

anything else and making me cry in front of the whole police station. "No. I'm done. No more."

And with that I walked away, blinking more than necessary. I'd almost made it out of the police station when I heard shouts behind me.

"Agent York, come back here."

Then a hand on my arm stopped me from opening the door, turning me the other way. And I was once again facing Sebastian.

"Not how this is going to end," he growled in typical Sebastian fashion. "I'll take you home, and then we'll talk."

No way was that happening. I was all talked out. Done. Finished.

"I'll be fine. Stella said she'll pick me up." I didn't need him all up in my space.

He ignored me and instead started walking, taking me with him.

"Didn't you hear me? I already have a ride," I said, trying to free myself again.

"I know you do, because I'm your ride."

"Let me go," I called out as we made it outside and crossed the road. "I'll find my own way home."

His bike was nowhere in sight; instead, he stopped next to a huge black monstrosity. The truck was about three times the size of my little car and looked brand-new.

Opening the door for me, he helped me up. Once I was in my seat, he closed the door and climbed in on his side.

"You don't need to explain. I understand," I said, understanding nothing at all. But the last thing I wanted was to listen to lame excuses that would hurt me even more.

In response, he interlaced his fingers with mine, not giving me a chance to pull away. "I don't think you do."

I messaged Stella to let her know I was on my way home. She responded immediately and told me the kids were asleep and that they could stay with her and Mason. Instead of messaging back and forth, I called her.

"Hey," she answered. "Everything okay?"

"I'm fine. Just so mad at myself for being so stupid."

"What happened?"

"They arrested Jim, and I got caught up in the process."

"That ratbag," she cursed. "What can I do to help?"

"I just need my kids close," I said. The thought of them not being home with me made my heart hurt. "Can I pick them up?"

"I'll get their stuff ready."

"Thanks, honey. I'll see you in a few minutes." I

ended the call and turned to Sebastian. "I need to pick the kids up from Stella's."

He nodded, and we turned onto my street. "Let's swap cars, then."

I didn't protest when he went inside to get the keys to my car. When we pulled up in front of Stella and Mason's beautiful farmhouse, it was pitch dark, the stars in the sky clearer than I'd ever seen them.

The front door opened and Stella rushed out, engulfing me in a big hug that I didn't know I needed as soon as I was out of the car.

"I can't believe you had to go to the station," she cried, pulling me even closer.

"It was only to talk. They didn't arrest me," I said, untangling myself from her tight embrace.

She looked behind me to Sebastian. "Sounds like you were conveniently absent when all this happened."

"Stella," I growled, widening my eyes at her. This was not the time or place.

"I'll never forgive myself for not being there," he said, surprising me. "And if Jim hadn't knocked Gears out, I would have been."

I gasped, turning to Sebastian. "Is he okay?"

"He'll be fine. All that's damaged is his pride because Jim got the best of him."

Stella seemed mollified by his response, but she definitely wasn't welcoming his traitorous ass with open arms.

She led us inside, and Mason met us in the hallway. He hugged me close, and I sank into him. "You sure you don't want a break for tonight? We don't mind keeping the kids."

I stepped back and collided with Sebastian. He didn't move and neither did I, the contact settling my frayed nerves. "I really appreciate the offer, but I need my kids close tonight."

He nodded. "I understand. But know that the offer is there whenever you need."

We followed him and Stella upstairs to one of their spare bedrooms. Lena and Luca were sprawled out on the big guest bed, snoring up a storm.

A smile played on my lips at the sight. I picked up Lena, and without hesitating, Sebastian lifted Luca into his arms, making sure to not jostle him too much. He didn't wake up, settling in right away.

Once the kids were buckled into their seats, I closed the door with as much care as I could, praying the noise wouldn't wake them up.

"That calls for a girls' night in," Stella declared when we were standing next to my car. "You're not working tomorrow, so Malena and I will bring the wine, you make sushi, and Willa can bring dessert."

I managed a half-smile and nodded. I didn't have to work tomorrow, and hanging out with my girls was long overdue. "It's a date."

After more hugs and promises to call tomorrow from both Stella and Mason, we drove back home.

We carried the kids inside, making our way past the front door that hung off one hinge. Once we'd laid them on their beds and pulled their blankets over them, I exhaled in relief. It was a miracle neither of them woke up. At least something was going right tonight.

When we made our way back into the kitchen, Sebastian lifted me onto the kitchen counter and put his hands on either side of me. "Stay."

"But what—"

He went outside, leaving me in stunned silence. I debated if it was safe to get off the counter or not when he stalked back inside, holding a screwdriver and wooden planks.

"You only have three tools," he said on his way past.

That's because I didn't need more than a hammer, screwdriver, saw and glue. That was all I knew how to use, and as soon as something took more than one of those three tools, I had to find someone else to fix it for me.

After a few minutes I heard the door closing and figured he must have used the screwdriver to fix the planks to the door for a temporary fix. Instead of using a hammer, he'd made sure to not wake the kids and opted for the painstaking task of putting screws in with my rusty screwdriver.

He came back a few minutes later. I was still sitting where he'd left me, stunned at his thoughtfulness.

"The door is okay for tonight, but I'll get someone

out tomorrow to replace it. Since I'm staying on the couch, nobody is going to come in whether you have a door or not."

"You're not staying here," I sputtered, bracing my hands on the counter, ready to jump down. "There's no reason for you to keep up this charade. Jim is under arrest."

Sebastian dropped the screwdriver on the kitchen table and caged me in before I had a chance to hop off the counter. "No matter how our talk goes, I'm staying."

"I can tell you right now how our talk will go. With you walking out and never contacting me again," I said, incensed at his audacity.

"That will never happen," he said, leaning close enough that I could make out the gray specks in his eyes.

I hesitated, torn by conflicting emotions. My feelings for him were like a deranged fairy that just wanted to throw herself at him and forget he ever lied. And my brain wanted to find a kitchen knife and poke him a little. Only in the arm, of course. Or maybe his leg. Nothing to permanently damage him, just something to cause a little pain.

"What do you want?" I asked, tired of dancing around the real issue. Because he had to have ulterior motives for being here.

"You," he said, his voice thick with emotion, his tense jaw working overtime. He'd pull a muscle soon if he kept it up.

"I don't understand," I said, because I didn't. He had what he wanted and could move on to his next assignment. What did he still need me for?

"I know you think this was all a cover, but you couldn't be further from the truth."

I put my hand to his chest, applying pressure. He didn't move back an inch but rather leaned into my touch, closing his eyes. I sat, mesmerized by his beauty, intoxicated by his smell. If he kept this up, I would forget he ever broke my heart.

"Are you saying you didn't hook up with me because of my connection to Jim?"

He opened his eyes, stepping closer. I let out an undignified squeak, not sure my emotions would be able to withstand this conversation. He looked like he was in pain and I was his remedy.

And then I finally understood what this was all about. He was a good guy. I'd always known it; the girls at the club had said the same thing to me. And he was trying to soften the blow. Let me down easy. It was time I acted like the adult society deemed me to be instead of the heartbroken fool I really was.

"I loved our time together, and it's no secret I'm attracted to you. It's not something I can just switch off. But don't worry, I'll get over it eventually. I want you to know I forgive you and I understand. It was a job, and one you did well," I said, the words tasting like poison on my tongue.

Sebastian shook his head and lifted one hand behind my back, the other into my hair. "Nora, I—"

I couldn't stand to hear how he enjoyed our time together or something equally as painful. "Don't feel guilty. And for the love of all you hold dear, don't stick around because of it. I don't ever want to be someone's second choice. Or worse, a charity case. I have great memories I'll cherish forever. Don't turn this into something it's not."

He pulled me closer. "Nora, listen to me—"

"Stop trying to be the good guy. Not everyone gets their happily ever after, and I'm a big girl. I'll be okay. Find your person, Sebastian, and don't settle for anything less. I think—"

He put his hand over my mouth and stopped me from continuing my bullshit speech. It hurt to even say the words and to give him absolution.

"Shut up," he growled. "I'm not going anywhere. Not because I feel guilty about what happened between us but because I fucking love you. I nearly lost my mind when I found out you were connected to Jim. The only reason I never approached you until I had no choice was because I tried to keep you out of his mess."

Well, that's not what I thought he was going to say.

His hand was still over my mouth, making it impossible for me to respond.

"Do you really think I'll let you kick me out that easily? I'm a stubborn bastard and hard to get rid of when I see something I want. And newsflash, baby, you're the only thing I want."

Now he'd gone and done it. I was speechless, my

eyes wide, my hands clenching into fists on his shirt. He dropped his hand from my mouth and stepped between my legs, which automatically widened to accommodate him.

When I didn't kick him in the nuts, he must have deemed it safe to proceed, and he pressed close and his mouth found mine. I felt crippling relief at his lips on mine. I thought I would never again experience the sensation of completeness that seemed to come with his touch.

He pulled back slightly and spoke against my lips, each brush melting me further. "You are everything to me."

I leaned closer, not finding the right words, my mind going into overdrive.

"I heard about Jim being here too late to do anything about the raid," Sebastian explained. "I thought you were safe with Gears watching the house. I never thought Jim would be so ballsy as to knock him out."

"I'm not blaming you for Jim getting arrested at my house or for me getting taken to the police station," I replied, meaning it.

No matter how much I looked for more things I could blame on him so I could hang on to my anger, this wasn't one of them.

I let out a deep breath, overwhelmed with today, overwhelmed with Sebastian sitting right next to me, and really just overwhelmed with life.

"You lied to me," I said, my whisper cutting

through the heavy silence. "You used me. And worst of all, you broke my heart. I don't even know your real name."

I still couldn't believe he really wanted to be with me. Our kiss should never have happened. I was sending mixed signals and hated myself for it. I wasn't one to play games. What you saw was what you got with me. But when it came to Sebastian, I seemed to jump right onto the crazy train. Especially if he made all my dreams come true by telling me he loved me.

"Sebastian is my middle name. My first name is Lincoln. But I've grown to love it when you call me Sebastian."

I stared at him, not sure what to respond and he took it as his cue to continue.

"I'm sorry for how things went down, but I'm not sorry for what happened between us. I stayed away from you for a year. And a man only has so much self-control when everything he ever wanted is right in front of him."

Oh God, did he really just say that?

Oblivious to my inner turmoil, he took my hand. "How can I make you trust me again?"

"I don't know," I said, studying his beautiful face, wincing at the pain shining in his eyes. "But I need to think. Can you give me some time?"

He lifted my hand and pressed his lips to the back. "I can do that."

I stood up, desperate to touch him but knowing I'd

regret it if I let him back in before I had time to sort my head.

"I need to go to bed," I said, watching the hurt and longing play over his face.

"I'll be here if you need anything," he replied, pointing to the couch.

I washed my face and brushed my teeth, the routine helping to settle my heart that was beating a drum solo in my chest.

When I crawled into my cold bed, I dragged the sheets over my body, burying my head in the pillow.

A flash of loneliness tore at me, the pain so acute that I curled up into a ball and stayed awake for most of the night, replaying Sebastian's words over and over again in my head.

Chapter Seventeen

"Did you make miso soup?" Stella asked, piling her plate high with food.

I snatched the last piece of prawn sushi off the platter before she could reach it, making her pout. "I made you ramen. And sushi. Do you know how long it takes to cook all that? Especially with kids in the house?"

Stella and Malena had come over for a girls' night as promised, bringing our other friend Willa with them. I hadn't seen them in a while, and I missed them. The last member of our group, Maisie, couldn't come tonight because she was at her boyfriend's cabin. And if she wasn't hiding out with him in the middle of nowhere, she was busy with her store and pregnancy.

And the reason why I hadn't seen Willa in forever was that she wasn't only managing her aunt Rayna's café while she was participating in *Shake That Cake*, but she was also going to culinary school at the same time.

And I had two jobs, two kids, and not much free

time, making a catch-up a rarity.

The whole group of girls was not only generous and always willing to help, but each one of them was also a knockout. If I didn't love them so much I'd hate them for it.

I'd cooked more food than we could possibly eat, but leftovers were always welcome in my house. The kids had demanded pasta for dinner and refused to try any of the Japanese food I'd made. That was nothing new, but I wasn't going to give up trying.

"Fine." Stella sighed. "I guess I'll survive with all this amazing sushi instead."

Malena threw a chopstick at Stella who ducked, tipping over her wineglass.

I threw her the paper towels that were already on the table for exactly that reason. The girls were messier than my kids, especially when it came to food.

"We should start selling sushi at Sweet Dreams," Willa said, waving her chopsticks around.

She hadn't been able to pick up a single piece of food with them. Everyone else was almost finished, and Willa was still on her first plate.

"Screw this. I'm not made to eat with two sticks," she said and threw the chopsticks on the table.

Stella giggled. "I told you to use a fork."

"I wanted to use chopsticks," Willa pouted. "You guys make it look so easy."

"Okay," Malena said, looking at me and stuffing

her face while talking at the same time. "Spill. And don't think you can leave anything out again."

I knew she was still hurt that I hadn't told her about the money Jim stole. And that I didn't ask her for help when things got tight. But she knew most of what was going on, so I just needed to fill in Willa and Stella.

"How are you doing for wine? Do you want more?" I asked, eyeing her still full glass.

"Stop stalling, *chiquita*," she said around a mouthful of food.

"Urgh, Malena, I think I just saw a half-chewed piece of salmon floating around your mouth," Stella complained, refilling her own glass.

"Naw, I think that was prawn," Willa put in.

Malena shrugged and continued eating. At work, she was the picture of perfectionism and dressed like every guy's wet dream—I knew because we often had lunch together and I would pick her up from work with Lena in tow. Yet at the moment she was wearing leggings and an oversized sweater, her thick long hair bunched up in a messy bun. And there wasn't a stitch of makeup on her beautiful tanned skin. She didn't really need the makeup, but I got why she did it. Makeup was armor, and she wielded it to perfection.

"Just remember that I love you and you're a lawyer. Attempted murder and causing bodily harm are frowned upon in your circles," I said, taking another drink of my wine.

She leaned back, crossing her arms over her chest.

"I promise I'll stay on my side of the table. But I can't promise there won't be any yelling."

"Okay, so here goes nothing," I started, diving in. "You both know I noticed Sebastian over a year ago when I first started at the club."

"Noticed him?" Stella asked, chuckling. "That's a nice word for falling head over heels for someone you'd never met before. Or hadn't ever talked to."

"It wasn't like that. I just liked the way he looked."

Malena twirled her hand in the air, telling me to get on with it since she was well aware of that part of my story.

"And you also know I thought he'd never so much as looked my way in all that time," I said. "Well…" Then I told them the whole tale, from first talking to Sebastian to last night.

"Now I don't know what to do. The thought of never seeing him again breaks me in half. But he broke my trust. And he lied," I finished, looking at the girls, who were doing their best impression of blow-up dolls; their mouths formed O's, their eyes were wide, and none of them spoke.

I waved at them. "Hello? Anyone there?"

"Have you considered drawing dicks all over his bike?" Willa asked, looking at me innocently with her big doe eyes.

"He's in a motorcycle gang," Stella said, her voice a hushed whisper. "And he's an FBI agent."

"Why are you whispering?" Willa whispered. "He's not here."

"Because what if the guy outside hears you? They'll never find our bodies," Stella whispered again, her eyes comically wide.

"They're not that kind of club," I put in, my voice sounding loud after all the whispering. "And he's not really part of the MC. It was only a cover."

Malena jumped up, waving her hands around, still holding her chopsticks. "*Mi amor*, you know I love you, but right now I want to shake you until your brain pops back into the right position. How could you not tell us what was going on? A stalker? And a motorcycle club? Jim taking your money? Are you insane taking that on by yourself?"

"I know this wasn't the best way to handle it, but—"

She started walking the whole length of my kitchen and then the hallway when she had nowhere else to go. "Not the best way? It was outright stupid. Careless. After everything we've been through, you still don't think you can lean on us."

She'd stopped yelling halfway through, her voice now thick with hurt. I got up and walked up to her. "I'm sorry. So sorry. And it has nothing to do with me not trusting you. You're my best friend. I trust you with my life. My children's lives."

Stella joined our huddle. "Best friend? What about me?"

"And me?" Willa asked. "You need at least three best

258

friends. If one isn't available and the other one is too far away, you can call your third option, who will ride in like a lady in shining armor on a white horse and rescue you. FYI, that would be me. I'd make a great lady."

I chuckled and pulled her close as well, and we all huddled together in a group hug.

"And why did you not invite me to help you with your dance routine?" Malena asked, now pouting but not sounding upset anymore. "I used to do ballet."

"I didn't realize that transferred over to pole dancing."

"Dancing is dancing. If only you'd asked me, I could have put an unforgettable routine together. I always wanted to try pole dancing."

I pulled back, raising a brow at my friend. "You should give it a go. It was fun even if I was hopeless at it."

"Hell yes. I want to come too," Stella said, her eyes lighting up in excitement.

"I'm so in. Maybe Jameson can put a pole in at the apartment so I can practice," Willa said.

Oh no, Mason and Jameson wouldn't be down with that at all. The Drake brothers would cause a worse scene than Sebastian did if their girls started wrapping themselves around poles on a stage.

"You're as coordinated as I am, if not worse. Remember how you're banned from home renovations?" I said, looking at Stella, hoping she'd change her mind.

She crossed her arms over her chest, glaring at me. "What could possibly happen to me?"

"Let's see," I said, counting on my fingers. "You could fall on your head and crack it open. You could pull something. Break a leg. Arm. Your pick."

"Fine. But if Malena gets to dance, I want to be there," Stella said.

"Don't think you can leave me at home. Poles love me," Willa said, dancing around the living room.

"That doesn't even make any sense," I said, watching her attempt a pirouette and falling on her butt.

Malena nodded, and I could tell she'd be up on that stage before the week was over.

I went back to the table and started clearing the dirty dishes. Everyone pitched in, and we had everything put away within a few minutes. We decided to have a quiet night in, watching movies and drinking wine.

I'd banned the girls from bringing any alcohol that could be turned into a cocktail since that hadn't ended well last time. It was wine only from here on out.

We squeezed onto the couch, Stella topping up everyone's glass.

"Did you hear from your mom again?" I asked her.

Her mom used to be the mayor of our town. She'd controlled Stella until she finally broke free and fell in love with Mason.

"She tried threatening me a few times to get me to fulfill the contract. But my lawyers said I did everything required to break it, so I'm good."

Malena scoffed. "Where does she think she lives? And a marriage contract? Really?"

Stella shrugged. "There's a contract for everything in her world. But she's moving to DC, so I hope I'll never have to talk to her again."

Sounded harsh, but I'd met her mother once and didn't care to repeat the experience. She was dismissive and cruel, and I was glad my friend was nothing like her.

"Is she still going to try and get a spot in the senate? Even after the whole mall scandal?" I asked, not surprised at her audacity.

"I guess so," Stella said, biting her bottom lip. "But can we please stop talking about her? Thinking about her gives me an ulcer. And we have more important things to discuss. Like what you're going to do now."

Malena lifted her glass. "First, we need a toast."

Stella, Willa, and I held up our glasses as well.

"What are we toasting to?" I asked.

"To women who think they're not good enough even though they are everything and more," Malena said, giving me her best side-eye.

I nudged her. "Why do I feel personally attacked by this?"

She clinked her glass to Willa's, mine, and Stella's.

"Because you are."

Stella chuckled. "She's right, you know. Sounds to me like Sebastian was caught in a shitty situation. And he didn't ghost you after the assignment was done. Now *that* would have been a dick move."

"But he lied to me," I said, already knowing I was just arguing to not look like a pathetic lovesick loser.

Stella leaned forward to look at me from behind Malena. "And that wasn't okay. Don't think we're saying it was. But it sounds to me like he wants to make up for it."

Can it really be that easy?

"If he wants you to forgive him, he won't just give up. And do you really want him to disappear?" Willa asked.

"No, I guess I don't," I said, the realization slamming into me.

I would be devastated if he left. And no matter how angry I was, I still loved him with every breath I took.

"Now what did you bring for dessert?" I asked Willa, giving my brain a break from thinking about Sebastian.

"Cupcakes," she said, getting up.

She went into the kitchen and returned with a box from Sweet Dreams.

"Gimme, gimme, gimme," Stella chanted.

Willa grinned and opened the box. "You act like you didn't go to Sweet Dreams yesterday."

Stella grabbed a cupcake and then handed the box to me before glaring at Willa.

"No pastry shaming. This town is too small for a feud between us."

Stella might have huffed about the size of the town, but I knew she loved it here. Especially since it was where Mason was. She was head over ass in love, and I didn't see that ever changing.

Mason was her person, and he treated her like a queen. After her sheltered and controlled upbringing, the free-spirited mechanic was exactly what she needed.

"Is he picking you up tonight?" I asked, knowing she wouldn't drive after having more than one drink.

"He'll be here at ten. That's usually when you throw us out. Unless there's cocktails involved. Then you wouldn't care if we stayed till the next day."

They both giggled, and I pouted. "Not true. I would never throw you out."

We spent the rest of the night laughing at Malena's stories from work. She had an ongoing feud with one of the lawyers in her firm, and neither one of them was willing to call a ceasefire.

He sent her to the wrong courthouse, gave her the worst clients, and scared away her assistant. In turn she messed with his calendar, regularly switched out his coffee orders, and made sure he had a vast supply of pens, totaling fifty boxes so far and counting.

A knock on the door signaled the end of our girls' night. Stella let Mason in, who planted a long kiss on her, making Malena widen her eyes at me.

When they came back up for air, he nodded at us in greeting. "Hey, girls."

"Hi, Mason. How have you been?" Malena asked, collecting her bag and jacket. "You still okay to give me a lift?"

"Of course," he said, pulling a beaming Stella into his side.

She leaned against him, her body molding to his. I met her dopey smile with a grin of my own.

We walked outside just as Jameson pulled up to get Willa.

After hugs and kisses and promises to call tomorrow, they took off. I watched their taillights, and only when they disappeared around a corner did I go inside.

I straightened the already clean house, waiting for Sebastian to come back.

When it was nearing midnight and it was clear that he wasn't going to show, I got ready for bed. Maybe he'd given up on us already.

I woke up what felt like five minutes later to a body sitting down on the bed. A finger whispered over my jaw and a familiar scent engulfed me.

"Sebastian," I mumbled, opening my eyes.

"Sorry to wake you. I just wanted to see you before I went to sleep. You usually sleep like a bear in hibernation, and I didn't think you'd notice if I was in here." He looked at his hands. "Wow, that sounded creepier out loud than it did in my head."

Is he embarrassed?

"Are you staying on the couch again?"

He took my hand, his thumb tracing lazy circles on my palm. "Of course."

The thought of getting to keep him close warmed me, my heart doing cartwheels in response.

"Don't you have your own place you want to go back to now that your assignment is over?"

He squeezed my hand. "I live in Chicago, so no, I'm in no rush to get back to my place."

My heart stuttered to a stop and then lay down in defeat. How did he think we would make this work? Had I been wrong to think he wanted us to be together? Was I once again acting like a lovesick fool and reading the signals wrong?

"Oh, okay. I didn't know."

"I quit the FBI today," he said, holding my hand tighter.

I sat up, bringing our faces close together. The dim night-light coming in from the hallway was enough to make out the clear-cut lines of his face and his firm and sensual lips.

But I couldn't read his expression. He almost

looked like he was holding his breath.

"Why?" I asked.

He brushed his thumb across the back of my hand. "It was time. I've known for a while that I had to get out. You can only do that sort of work for so long before it drags you down. My work used to be my life, my passion. But my priorities have changed."

I lifted my arm, putting my hand on his cheek, the need to comfort him all-consuming. My next words came out stuttered. "Does that... does it mean... I mean, are you going to... stay?"

"All I care about is in this small town. Why would I go back to my life before you walked in?"

"Lie down with me?" I asked, shuffling to the middle of the bed and pulling the blanket back.

He didn't hesitate to take off his shoes and lie down on his side, facing me. He laced his fingers through mine and rested our clasped hands between our bodies.

"I know there's a chance you won't forgive me. But I'm not willing to give up. If I have to prove to you for the rest of my life that you can trust me, I will," he said.

Tears stung my eyes, and I shuffled closer, smothering his last words with my lips. He responded with slow kisses in return, stealing my breath, the undeniable magnetism between us pulling us together.

When we broke apart, I buried my face in his throat, and he wrapped his arms around me.

"I love you," I murmured against his skin.

"I love you too," he rasped against my hair, his voice overflowing with emotion.

I fell asleep cocooned in the safety of his arms, his drugging scent surrounding me.

Chapter Eighteen

"Are we really going to a biker party?" Malena asked, eyes wide, taking in the compound. "I can't believe you talked me into this. I'm not sure it's good for business to be seen with a bunch of bikers."

Grim messaged me this morning, asking if I wanted to come to a party. I'd missed the guys and would take any excuse to see them, even if it was for a party at the compound. I wasn't exactly the partying type, despite them thinking otherwise.

Sebastian had spent all week at my house and, true to his word, made sure I knew how much I meant to him. From flowers—the non-creepy kind—to dinners in the backyard, he'd pulled out all the stops.

He was gone during the day but still drove me to Pepper's when I had a shift. He stayed with me when I stood outside the door, holding me tight and letting me do my thing without judgment. Last time, I only had to count to thirty-four before my legs agreed to carry me inside.

I knew he didn't like what he saw by his taut expression and the intense way he watched me. But just having him there made everything so much better.

He picked me up again after my shift, driving me back home.

Luca and Lena were having a sleepover at Malena's house tonight. Her parents were watching them, something they did occasionally. The kids loved it, and I felt safe leaving them there.

I couldn't remember the last time Malena and I went out together. So when Grim messaged me, I immediately asked her to come along. It took a little convincing, but she eventually gave in.

"You told them I'm coming too, right? They're not going to throw me out?" she asked, still staring at the brightly lit building. People were milling around outside, and the music was loud even from where we were standing in the street.

The taxi driver had refused to get too close and had dropped us halfway down the street. We walked up to the gates, and while I didn't recognize the guy manning them, when I told him my name, he opened it right away.

"Nobody is going to throw you out," I reassured my nervous friend. "They're all nice. You'll love it. Relax and enjoy tonight."

She huffed but kept walking next to me instead of running back into town, which seemed to be an option at this stage. "Easy for you to say. You're with one of them. I'm a nobody. And a lawyer."

I chuckled and linked arms with her. "They're not doing anything illegal in there. Maybe a little pot. But I'm sure you can ignore that."

"Have you heard from Sebastian?" she asked, frowning at a couple making out next to the entrance.

I patted the pocket of my tight jean skirt, making sure I had my phone on me in case he called. It wasn't like I expected him to tell me his every move. We'd only exchanged a few texts today, and I hadn't heard from him in a while.

"He said he was at the clubhouse. Do you think he'll be mad if I just show up? He didn't invite me."

Malena squeezed my arm, and we stepped into the huge building currently crammed with people. "Of course he wants you here. That man worships the ground you walk on."

We pushed our way through swaying bodies in search of a familiar face. Talon was one of four people pouring drinks behind the bar, pushing mostly beer into people's hands.

He winked at me when he saw us and came over. "If it isn't the little card shark coming back to the lion's den. You want a rematch?" he shouted close to my ear to be heard over the deafening music.

"No rematch. Grim invited me. Know where he is?" I yelled back, leaning up on the bar.

Talon nodded to the right, and I craned my neck until I made out Grim's huge form. He was talking to someone at the end of the bar, and I groaned at the thought of pushing my way through more people.

Turned out I didn't have to when I felt hands grip me around my waist, lifting me high in the air. I yelped in surprise and found myself standing behind the bar. I turned back around and looked at Gears, who winked at me before disappearing in the crowd.

"Much quicker this way," Talon said, tilting his chin at Malena. "She with you?"

"This is Malena," I said. "Can you keep an eye on her while I talk to Grim?"

Talon grinned and nodded. "Of course I can."

He leaned closer to Malena and said something to her. I couldn't make out what it was, but my ball-buster friend blushed and nodded.

I caught her eyes and pointed to the end of the bar. When she nodded, I gave her a thumbs-up and walked over to Grim.

My face lit up when I saw who he was talking to. Sebastian was standing next to him, and Blaze rounded out the group. I ducked under the bar at the end to get out and popped back up on the other side.

Grim saw me first, barreling past Blaze, who stumbled to the side. The big teddy bear engulfed me in a tight hug. "Sweetheart, I'm so glad you decided to come."

"Me too. You still haven't told me what the party is for though."

He put his arm around my shoulder and led me back to Sebastian and Blaze. "It's Ace's party. He's now officially a member."

The smile died on my face when I laid eyes on Sebastian. He had a black eye and a busted lip. I slid out from under Grim's arm and rushed up to Sebastian. "Oh my God, what the fork happened?"

He put his arms around me and kissed the side of my neck. I sank into him, holding him tight.

"It's nothing. Just a scratch," he said near my ear, his lips brushing my lobe.

I shivered at the small contact, gripping his T-shirt. "That doesn't look like nothing. Did you get into a fight?"

He pulled back so he could look at me and kissed the tip of my nose when he saw the expression on my face. "It was payment for lying to the club."

The look on my face must have shown my horror at the thought of at least twenty people taking a shot at him.

"Are you insane? They could have done some serious damage."

He brushed a strand of my hair out of my face, tracing his finger along my cheek in the process. "The club has become my life. It's where I belong. Blaze and a few others knew I was here undercover, but I still lied to most of my brothers. Something that required payment."

I sighed but decided to drop it. Besides, him being in the club meant he wouldn't be leaving. Maybe he really was serious when he said he wanted to stay here.

"Baby, I'm fine. I'm happier than I've ever been.

I have everything a man could need: brothers at my back and my girl by my side."

He leaned back to look at me, taking me in from top to toe, his gaze a caress that sent a tremor through my body.

"Like the skirt, beautiful. And the shoes. Especially the shoes," he said, pulling my front into his side so I could face Blaze and Grim, who were both watching us, Grim with a huge smile on his face, Blaze with a frown. The guy really needed to loosen up. Every time I saw him, he looked like he'd taken a sip of Bud instead of their treasured Stella.

I found out at the last party that they didn't allow Budweiser into their clubhouse. Nobody told me why, but even if they had, I probably wouldn't remember since I'd had a few drinks too many that night.

"Why didn't you tell me you were coming?" Sebastian asked. "I could have picked you up."

"Is it okay I'm here?" I asked, pulling back.

He didn't let me get far, tightening his arms around me as he leaned in. "It's more than okay. I didn't know how tonight would go, so I didn't want to make you go through the trouble of organizing a babysitter for what could have been nothing."

"Apparently Grim knew it would work out," I said, sinking into him. "I'm happy for you if this is what you want."

Sebastian finally did what I'd wanted him to do all day and leaned down and kissed me. I wound my arms under his leather vest—something that was called a cut, as Gears informed me, horrified when I called it a vest—the touch of his lips a delicious sensation I didn't think I'd ever tire of.

The kiss soon turned heated and my hands wandered under his shirt, the feel of his smooth skin under my palms intoxicating. There was something to be said about biker parties. They didn't care what you did. I never thought I was into public make-outs, but it turned out there wasn't much I wasn't into when it came to Sebastian.

"How much do you have your heart set on partying?" he asked when we broke apart, both breathing hard. My body was flushed, my pulse racing. His kisses were magic.

"Depends on what else you have in mind," I said, my hand still under his T-shirt.

He grinned at me, and I knew what he had in mind. "You want to take this upstairs?"

The answer to that question would always be yes. "I have to check on Malena first. She came with me, and I left her with Talon."

"I can guarantee she's in good hands," Sebastian said.

He was right. If I could pick anyone to take care of my friend, it would be Talon. "I'll text her to make sure she's okay."

"So how does it feel to finally be on the right side of the law?" Grim asked Sebastian, then laughed when he received a rude gesture as response.

I texted Malena while Sebastian drew circles on my hip with his hand, making my whole body heat up and break out in goose bumps. I had trouble concentrating and ended up sending a few messages before one made sense.

Me: Are you Ikea?

Me: What hushed to my message?

Me: Meant to say ostrich.

Me: How can it spell ostrich but not ukulele??

Me: Argh, not ukulele either!!

Me: Let's try again. Just checking in. Do you want me to come and get you?

She responded a few seconds later. I knew she would because she always had her phone in her pocket. That way if she ever lost her handbag, she could still get home. I'd started doing the same and then ditched the handbag altogether.

Bestest bestie: I'm good, but maybe I should be asking you the same question?

Me: With Sebastian.

Bestest bestie: Then you're better than good. Glad you found him. I'll be okay down here for a few hours. Let me know if you're staying the night.

Me: No can doodle. We promised to never ditch each other and go home alone. Besides, I promised the kidlets a sleepover. They'll wonder where I am if I'm not there when they wake up.

Bestest bestie: Got it. I'll let you know when I've reached my limit of badass biker party.

Sebastian leaned in, his hand traveling over my butt. "Malena okay?"

"All good," I said and turned to Grim. "Have you guys met my friend Malena yet? She's a hoot. You'd love her."

"She's a foot taller than Nora, has brown hair and hazel eyes and an attitude. Hard to miss. Feel free to find her. Now if you'll excuse us, we've got somewhere to be," Sebastian said, taking my hand and pulling me away from Blaze and Grim. Grim belted out another laugh, and Blaze frowned at us. Again.

We made it up to Sebastian's room slower than we hoped. There were a lot of people who wanted to congratulate him and stop him for a chat.

The first few times, he talked his way out of it, but then he started waving instead of stopping, and soon he was just pushing through people, not even bothering to acknowledge anyone. I thought that was kind of rude, but I wasn't complaining.

The thought that he wanted to be with me tonight and not party with the guys added another layer to my already swooning heart.

We burst through his door and he didn't waste any

time. He kicked it shut, and then his hands and mouth were on me until everything ceased to exist except the two of us.

And a man sitting on his couch.

Wait, why is there someone in his room?

My breath hitched when Sebastian kissed a trail from my neck to my collarbone. "Ahem, Sebastian, maybe you should stop."

"Mhm," he responded, continuing on his path, worshipping my body. And as much as I wanted the worshipping to happen, we needed to get rid of our audience first. I couldn't make out the guy's face, but the white of his eyes was enough to tell me all his attention was on us.

I pushed on Sebastian's shoulders, and he stopped on his quest.

"What's wrong?" he asked, his breathing ragged.

I pointed to the couch, and Sebastian's gaze followed my hand. He went stiff when he saw the stranger in his room.

"What the fuck are you doing in here?" Sebastian growled.

"Waiting for what's mine."

The voice sounded familiar, but I couldn't place it.

"Get out," Sebastian said, his eyes narrowed, his posture taut.

The guy stood up, holding what looked like a gun.

My eyes went wide when he lifted his arm. Definitely a gun.

Sebastian pushed me behind him. I slipped my phone out of my pocket while he was now blocking the guy's view. I texted Malena since her message was still up on my screen.

Me: SOS

She immediately messaged back. Thank God for mothers. She'd always check her phone if she got a message.

Malena: Let me guess. You tried out a little bondage and now you're stuck.

Me: Get Talon and Grim. Tell them be careful. Gun.

Malena: A gun?? What's going on???

Me: TALON AND GRIM

Malena: They're on their way.

Malena: I'm worried.

I didn't respond to her since I didn't want to push my luck and risk the guy seeing me text.

"You're delusional if you think you'll ever make it

out of here in one piece, Clive," Sebastian said, and the weird feeling I had about knowing him clicked into place. My harmless stalker had turned into a psycho with a gun.

"I'll walk out without a hair out of place if you want to keep her unharmed," Clive spat, waving the gun around. I hoped he knew how to handle that thing or at least kept the safety on. Accidental shootings weren't really on my night's agenda.

"Nora, come over here," Clive said, gesturing to his side.

"She stays right where she is." Sebastian's hand tightened on my arm, keeping me firmly behind him. I didn't pull away or try to step around him since I wasn't keen on going anywhere with Clive.

"You have two seconds to move or I'm putting a hole in your boyfriend." Clive pointed the gun at Sebastian, his arm shaking.

He looked high and unstable, not a good combination.

Since I liked my men without holes in them, I stepped to the side, pushing past Sebastian. "I'm not going to be responsible for you getting hurt. Let me go to him. Please."

Sebastian's hold on my arm tightened even more. "No fucking way. If he wants you, he has to go through me."

"Great, at least now we have a solution," crazy Clive said.

This was the one and only time I wished the club didn't soundproof their rooms.

"No, wait, please. I'm coming over. Don't shoot," I pleaded, holding my hand out, palm facing him.

Not sure what I was planning to accomplish going up against someone holding a gun, but all I could think was that he couldn't hurt Sebastian.

Too bad Sebastian didn't share my sentiment, and his hand was like a shackle around my wrist. I tried to twist free to no avail.

While we were distracted, Clive must have decided this was taking too long.

A shot rang out, I screamed louder than I had ever screamed in my life, and Sebastian groaned in pain, folding in on himself before dropping to his knees.

I dropped down next to him, my hands wandering over his body, looking for the injury. "Oh my God. Oh no," I cried, my breathing erratic, my hands shaking. "Where are you hurt? Show me."

Sebastian caught one of my hands in his, holding it to his chest.

Oh God, is this the point where he says his last words to me? While holding my hand?

There was still so much to do. Like go on a date. Or fight over his dirty socks on the bedroom floor. Or make him do the dishes. So many plans that would never become reality if he died.

Snap out of it, Nora. He's fine. Now shut up and try to talk the crazy psycho out of shooting you too.

"I'm okay," Sebastian said, sounding fine. But maybe he was just putting on a front.

I didn't exactly have much experience with gunshot wounds.

Before I could contemplate my next move or the right words to say to diffuse the situation, the door burst open and a guy I'd never met ran in, shooting his gun. Clive went down, and I jumped on top of Sebastian to cover his body.

"Dang rabbit, everyone needs to stop shooting," I yelled, my head buried in Sebastian's chest, my voice muffled despite my screams.

The ground shook, and Sebastian's arms around me tightened. I lifted my head, deeming it safe enough to do so. "You jumped on top of me," he said, his voice disbelieving.

My attention was diverted when I saw what caused the floor to vibrate. What must be the whole club had followed the shooting guy into the room, guns drawn.

I sat up, careful not to push on any parts of Sebastian's body since I still didn't know where his injury was. "Of course I did. You're already injured. And I still have uses for you. Like helping me wash the dishes."

He chuckled and sat up as well. Guess that was a good sign.

"I would be happy to wash your dishes for you, gorgeous," he said, his face lighting up with amusement.

"Well, that was fun," the stranger said, grinning down at Sebastian and me.

"Jacob," Sebastian said.

"Good to see you lying on the ground, waiting for someone to rescue you," Jacob said, raising a brow at Sebastian.

"I had a plan," Sebastian replied, standing up.

"What would that be? Play dead and hope he leaves? Didn't they teach you anything at that fancy police academy you went to?" Jacob asked.

Sebastian ignored him as he held out his hand and pulled me up as well, tucking me under his arm once we were both upright.

"Why the hell are you at the clubhouse? I thought you were banned from ever setting foot in here again," Sebastian said.

"That ban was lifted months ago. I was in the neighborhood and heard about you having a girl. Wanted to meet her. Things have gotten boring since Jameson stopped talking to me. And all over a little kidnapping. How could I have known Willa was his girl? He never tells me anything."

Sebastian raised a brow at Jacob before leaning down, his hand going to my cheek. "Are you okay?"

I blinked at him in disbelief. "Shouldn't I be asking you that question? You're the one who got shot."

He lifted his arm, and I could make out a rip and a dark stain on the sleeve of his T-shirt. "He's a terrible shot. We've been to the shooting range a few times together, and he barely hit the outline of the targets."

"So you *did* have a plan," I said.

"Of course I did. I'd do anything in my power to keep you safe."

Oh my God, he was willing to get hurt for little old me. There wasn't any hope left of recovering my heart.

"I was going to take his gun if he came closer. He always liked his coke, and it makes his hands shake."

"But he could have hit you. Especially if he was such a bad shot. A shaking arm might have pointed his gun in the right direction," I said, horrified that he took a chance like that with his life.

"Baby," he said, kissing my cheek, then my nose. "I knew what I was doing."

I was ready to argue about his strategy more when Malena burst into the room, eyes frantic, thick dark hair tangled around her face.

"Holy shit, are you okay?" she called out to me, pushing her way through the bikers still standing in Sebastian's room.

When she reached me, she lunged, not caring that I was still attached to Sebastian. I caught her in a tight embrace, falling into Sebastian, who had wisely let me go just before she attacked.

"You scared the shit out of me." She sniffed against my shoulder.

She turned to where Clive was detained, his hands

cuffed behind his back and one of the guys patching up his side. Shame, I was hoping they'd hit something important.

"I'm going to sue your ass until you don't even know your own mother's name. You better brace yourself, because you'll never see the world without bars again."

I put my arms around her middle when she made a move in his direction.

"He's already in a world of trouble. But I appreciate the thought," I said.

"If you're worried about paying me, don't be. I'm taking this on pro bono."

I let her go when I was sure she wouldn't turn into Rocky and patted her arm. "I know you would. But it's really not necessary."

She glared at Clive, who was being led out of the room.

That was as much as she'd relent, and I'd let it go for now. If she really wanted to take on another case on top of her insane workload, she was welcome to.

When we got back downstairs, we heard sirens coming closer, and soon the clubhouse was filled with uniformed police officers and paramedics. Sebastian refused to go to the hospital, and since it was just a graze, they patched him up and sent him on his way.

Clive was officially arrested. After they took him away, one of the officers came over to speak to us.

"I'm Officer Leland," he introduced himself. "I know this is a bad time, but I need you both to give your official statement. You can either do it tonight or come to the station tomorrow."

We both nodded, eager to get this night over and done with. The thought of having to go to the police station to give our statement tomorrow seemed too daunting, and I was glad we could do it now.

"Do we know yet how he got inside the clubhouse?" Sebastian asked once we'd both told our versions of how the night had gone down.

"I'll see if they got anything out of him at the station," Officer Leland answered, then pulled out his radio. He walked a few steps away to make his call, and Sebastian pulled me into his body, kissing my head. I sank into him, holding on, counting my lucky stars that tonight didn't have a different ending.

The officer came back, frowning. "Looks like a guy called Bullet let him in?"

He'd barely finished speaking when Sebastian charged across the room and up to a group of guys. He plucked someone out and punched him so hard he went down like a sack of bricks.

"You fucking traitor," Sebastian growled.

Officer Leland ran up to him, stepping between Sebastian and the guy on the ground. "I'm going to pretend he fell and hit his head. But that was your only free shot."

Sebastian gave him a curt nod but backed off. I joined them a few moments later, watching with big eyes as Officer Leland gave the guy a hand up. I recognized him as the same person who'd pulled me out of my house the first time I'd come to the clubhouse.

The bruises on his face had faded, but he'd be sporting another shiner soon.

Another officer joined us, and they led him away to ask him some questions.

Blade walked up to us, his face thunderous. "He the one?"

"Sure seems that way," Sebastian said, glaring at Bullet.

"Grim, get all his stuff out of his room. Don't care what you do with it as long as it's gone. Make sure everyone knows he's not allowed back here and he's lost his patch."

Grim gave me a half-smile, then saluted Blaze and walked off in the direction of the stairs.

Sebastian and Blaze were talking in hushed voices, and I decided to leave them to it and find Malena. She was sitting on a barstool, Talon keeping her company.

"Let's go home," I said and took her hand. "We can snuggle with our babies and forget how crazy our lives are just for a few hours."

The guys all hugged me when I walked past, making my heart burst with joy at the obvious affection they felt for me.

"I'm glad you're okay," Grim said when it was his

turn to hug me.

"Not as much as I am," I replied and kissed his cheek before untangling myself.

Sebastian joined as we reached the exit. "Let's get out of here," he said, slinging his arm around my shoulders.

He drove us back in his truck that was parked at the compound, and since he refused to leave me, he crashed on the couch at Malena's parents' place.

Good thing they were the most easygoing parents I knew and would be fine with him staying there. Especially once we told them what had happened. That would be an interesting conversation. But for now, I snuggled up with my kids, who were sleeping on a mattress on the floor in Felix's room. Malena crashed in her son's bed, and we fell asleep amid the snoring and sleep-talking.

Chapter Nineteen

"Don't ever let me see you do that again," I ground out, kneeling in front of Luca, who was holding the bucket he'd just used to dump water all over his sister.

"Okay, then close your eyes," Luca responded with a shrug. "I told her not to take my shovel again."

Lena was wailing next to us, her face taking on a deep shade of red. Not satisfied with my attempt to get justice on her behalf, she walked up to Luca and pushed him, causing him to start crying as well.

"What's going on?" Sebastian asked, joining us in the backyard.

"Just a little disagreement," I said, holding Luca on one side, Lena on the other.

Sebastian held out his arms for Lena, and she abandoned me for her favorite person.

"Watch out, she's wet," I called out when she threw her little body at him.

He caught her, holding her close. "A little water never hurt anyone."

It was almost a week after the psycho stalker incident, and it seemed Sebastian had moved in with us. He slept in my bed, his clothes were in my closet, and his dirty socks were getting comfortable on my bedroom floor.

"You got time to head to the compound before your shift tonight?" he asked, holding a now quiet Lena.

Luca had stopped wailing as soon as he saw Sebastian, not wanting to cry in front of his hero.

"I'll ask Stella if she can come over earlier," I said, hoping he'd take his shirt off now that it was wet.

"Great, it shouldn't take long," he said, carrying Lena inside.

"That wasn't cryptic at all," I muttered to myself and followed him, holding Luca's hand.

After taking my daughter off Sebastian, I changed her into clean clothes and then called Stella.

"Hey, Stella, any chance you can get here an hour earlier tonight?" I asked when the phone connected.

"I can probably do that."

"You're the best. See you soon."

"See you soon."

We hung up and Sebastian came back, kissing me lightly on the lips. He was now wearing a different shirt, and I regretted missing the show.

"All good?" he asked, hugging me close.

I wound my arms around him and rested my cheek on his chest. "She's coming earlier. Now, are you going to tell me what we're doing?"

"It's a surprise," he said, making me curious.

"Will you be wearing clothes for this surprise?" I asked, looking up at him.

He chuckled, and his eyes lit up in amusement. "I will. But if you ask nicely, I'll see what I can do tonight."

I pursed my lips, pretending to contemplate his offer. He leaned down, whispering kisses along my jawline and then lips.

"I think that's an acceptable offer," I said right before his lips fused themselves to mine. The kids were just in the next room, and I didn't want to chance them walking in on me humping Sebastian's leg, something I was close to doing, so I pulled back sooner than I wanted to.

"I'm glad," he said, his eyes crinkled at the corner. "Now why don't you go relax while the kids are playing by themselves and I'll start dinner?"

"Your foreplay game is strong," I said, swooning at the thought of not having to cook. It was one of my favorite things to do, but when you were always short on time and money, it wasn't as much fun anymore.

"I'm not even close to running out of moves yet,"

he said, then winked at me before I left the kitchen.

I checked on the kids, who were still playing in Luca's room, taking the bedding off and building a fort.

I left them to it and caught up on emails in the living room. The house was small enough that I could hear them from anywhere.

We had dinner together, and the kids even tried a bite of the steak Sebastian cooked. There was also pasta and Bolognese sauce on the table since he already knew my kids' eating habits well.

Stella came over just as I was getting the little hellions out of the bathtub. Sebastian was cleaning the kitchen, and I wasn't swooning anymore, I was close to throwing myself at him. Guess he was making good on his promise to do the dishes.

"You look happy," Stella said, helping out as soon as she walked through the door by wrapping a towel around Lena.

I handed Luca his towel, and we walked the kids to their bedroom.

"That's because I am," I said, pulling Lena's pajamas out of her closet.

"No, wear flowers," she cried when she saw the purple unicorn pajamas I'd chosen.

"Sötnos, the flower pajamas are dirty," I said, cursing myself for not doing a load of washing earlier today.

"I wish I had pretty unicorn pajamas like you," Stella said, taking the pants and putting her arm through one leg. "They even fit me, don't you think? Can I borrow them tonight?"

Lena giggled and pulled the pants off her arm. "They're mines."

"Of course they are. Want to show me how you put them on? I think I did it wrong."

Lena nodded, looking serious. She pulled her pants up, putting both legs in one hole. Stella tickled her and fixed her legs when she was distracted. It didn't take us long after that to get both kids dressed and sitting on the couch, ready for their stories.

I couldn't read to them tonight because of our detour, but I knew they were in good hands with Stella, even if she was a pushover and would read about twenty books before she made them go to bed.

"Love you guys," I said, kissing both kids and then Stella on their cheeks.

Sebastian took my hand and waved at them. "See you guys later."

The clubhouse was busy with a long row of bikes parked in front of the building, music and voices drifting outside.

Sebastian helped me off the bike, then took my hand to walk inside. The guys greeted us with hugs for me and back slaps for him.

But Sebastian had a destination in mind and kept walking. He led us to the office, the door already open.

Blade was sitting behind his huge wooden desk that dominated the room. Grim and a guy I didn't know by name but had seen around were standing in front of it.

They all looked at us when we entered, and Sebastian closed the door behind him, shutting out the noise.

Now this wasn't what I expected. But judging by the relaxed vibe in the room—except for Blade, who was forever frowning—it wasn't anything serious.

Sebastian nodded to the guys, and I smiled and waved at them.

"Sweetheart, good to see you," Grim said.

"You too," I responded and stood next to Sebastian, facing Blade. "So what's this about?"

"We have a proposal for you," Blade began, and I put my hand up, stopping him from saying anything else.

"Before you continue, let's make sure this is nothing illegal or involves orgies. Both are hard passes for me."

Blade's mouth twitched, and my focus narrowed on his lips.

Is it just a tic or did he almost smile?

"You're safe. It's neither of those. It's a job," Blade said, having regained his emotionless expression.

"A job? What kind of job? I should mention at this stage that organ donation is also out of the question."

Sebastian chuckled next to me and squeezed my hand. "Don't worry, I wouldn't let anyone get near you."

"We want you to be our office manager. We have a few businesses, and the paperwork is getting out of hand. I used to do it all myself, but since the strip club took off, I'm always behind," Blade said, watching me take in his words.

"But I already have a job. Two, to be exact. And one of those is at one of your businesses," I said, looking at Sebastian.

"We'd pay you enough that you can ditch your other two jobs. And you'll be added to our health care plan after four weeks of probation," Blade explained.

The mention of health care nearly made me want to hug him. But I wanted to make sure they were doing this for the right reason and wouldn't regret their decision. "Why me? I have no experience as an office manager."

Blade waved me off. "You have experience as a personal assistant and are incredibly well organized. We know everyone at Pepper's loves you, and you always show up for your shift, even if you're occasionally late."

That was a nice way of putting that I wasn't on time very often. "Is this because I'm going out with Sebastian?" I asked, questioning their motives. The job sounded like a dream come true. Regular hours. Health insurance.

Be still, my beating heart. We don't have the job quite yet.

Sebastian tugged on my hand, and I turned to him.

"I understand if you don't want to take the job because it's not the work you want to do. But don't refuse it because you think it's a pity offer. Blade doesn't employ people out of the goodness of his heart," he said. "And if you want to study while working, you can."

Well, he was right about Blade not giving handouts. It was the only reason why I didn't flat-out refuse to take the job. But I also didn't want to take advantage of my relationship with Sebastian. I never wanted him to think I was using him.

I turned my attention back to Blade. "So you're definitely not offering me the job because of Sebastian?"

"You're a smart girl. You already know the answer to that question. Ace heard I was looking for someone to help out and suggested you. Now stop letting your misguided pride lead you down the wrong path. I know you can do the job, and *you* know you can do the job. And you can take the kids to the office. Nobody will mind having them there," he said.

I knew he had a point, but I had to make sure this wouldn't change my relationship with Sebastian. Working for the club meant I would be around a lot.

I turned to him and asked, "Do you want me to take the job?"

"Whenever we stand outside Pepper's, the look on your face breaks my heart," he said, looking pained just thinking about it. "If I can stop you from doing something that sends you close to a nervous breakdown every time you have to do it, I will. So yes, I want you to take the job."

I bit my lip, thinking this was a fantastic offer. And this man just kept getting better and better.

"Okay, I'll take it," I said. The offer was good. Better than good, it was great and would mean my life changing for the better.

"Great. You start in two weeks," Blade said, handing me a stack of papers. "That's the contract. Read it, then sign it and get it back to me. We can negotiate the salary."

Wow, guess I'm really doing this.

"Okay, thanks, Blade," I said, clutching the papers against my chest.

"Now get out. I have work to do. If you have any questions, ask Sebastian."

We all filed out, and Grim patted my back. "Good to have you on board. You'll love it here. Blade's a great boss."

I found that hard to believe but didn't say anything. They all seemed to think highly of him and maybe with time I would come to like him too. *Maybe.*

We didn't stay; instead, Sebastian got us back on the road and pulled up in front of Pepper's a few minutes later.

I froze in front of the door. Despite feeling more settled than I had in a year, I still had to go inside, and

I still had to do my job. That hadn't changed. I had two more weeks left before I could get out of there for good.

Sebastian stepped in front of me and cupped my cheek, tilting my chin up. "Hey, I'm here with you. I'll be on the main floor the whole night. You're safe. I won't let anything happen to you."

I nodded and dropped my forehead onto his chest, breathing him in. "I know. I'm sorry for still freaking out. I've survived this long. Two more weeks shouldn't matter."

He kissed my hair and held me tight. "Don't ever apologize for the way you feel."

After I counted to a hundred and ten, I was ready to go inside. Sebastian took my hand again, something that had become a beautiful habit I loved.

He walked me straight to Smitty's office and knocked on the closed door, not waiting for an answer. Smitty's head shot up and his eyes went wide when he saw us standing in the door.

"Ace, what are you doing here?" Smitty asked, his voice high. And by the looks of the white powder on his desk, that wasn't the only thing that was high.

"Get out. You're fired," Sebastian said, his hands balled into fists.

"It's… it's not what it looks like," Smitty stuttered, wiping the powder off his desk.

Sebastian stepped closer. "You know the rules. We don't do warnings. Either you listen or you're out.

And you're a stupid fuck who didn't listen. Now you're out."

Smitty jumped up, his chair rolling backward. "That's fucking bullshit. This place is nothing without me."

"This place will be just fine without you. Now get your shit and go."

Smitty opened his mouth to say something else, but Sebastian cut him off. "You don't want to know what happens if you don't get your ass out of here in the next five minutes."

I stood by, watching the scene with wide eyes. I knew Sebastian could be scary, but I'd never seen him in action. And this was something else. His eyes were dark, his posture rigid, and his tone emotionless.

Smitty finally grew a brain and emptied his drawers. He stalked past us, sputtering curses, his face a red mask of fury. I really, really wanted to give him the finger on his way by.

Sebastian and I followed him out to the main floor and watched the girls stop what they were doing, staring at an enraged Smitty stomping past them.

"What are you looking at?" he yelled, spittle flying from his mouth.

When everyone realized what was happening, they started clapping, a few giving him the finger, others hollering. Guess he hadn't made many friends during his time at the club.

Sebastian watched him shove through the door,

then waved Kai over. "Make sure he leaves."

Kai nodded and followed Smitty outside.

"Well, you don't have to hand in your resignation anymore," Sebastian said, pulling me into his side. "I'll let the guys know."

"You're better off without him anyway," I said, my hands around Sebastian's waist. I couldn't seem to stop touching him. A very annoying little tic I'd developed.

"I'm starting to think that too. Pity we didn't notice sooner."

I shrugged. "I guess you don't talk to the girls much."

Sebastian looked down at me, raising a brow. "Not really. The only one in here I've ever talked to about anything besides work is you."

Now what did he go and do that for? We had five minutes before my shift started and his words only made me think of one thing I wanted to do right now. And it didn't include waiting tables.

"I'll walk you to the dressing room. Then I'll have to make a few calls to clean up this mess."

We stopped in front of the door and he kissed me, his lips lingering on mine in a gentle caress. "Find me if you need anything."

I walked through the door in a daze, almost forgetting where I was. Until an avalanche of half-dressed bodies hit me.

"Are you okay?"

"Why are you back already?"

"Did they kill him?"

"Here, sit down."

Elle untangled me from everyone else and pushed me down on a chair. "Give her some room, girls."

Tia pushed her way through. "Fucking Clive. He was always a creep. You okay, honey?"

I nodded, smiling a wobbly smile at everyone. "I'm fine, just glad it's finally over. Clive was denied bail, so he won't be able to come after me again."

"I hope he rots in hell," Star said, her hands braced on her hips, a scowl on her face.

Tia leaned down and hugged me, pressing my face into her teased-out hair that was doused in hairspray. I coughed as soon as my nose made contact. "At least now you're safe, honey."

I pulled back and looked at the girls, deciding this was the best time to tell them about changing jobs. "I need to tell you something."

"Oh. My. God. You're pregnant," Elle screeched, eyeing my belly.

"Are you getting married?" Tia asked at the same time, releasing me and jumping up and down, clapping her hands.

"Did you finally decide to change your conditioner?" Star asked, blinking at me.

"Hello, little darling," Elle said, kneeling in front of

me, talking to my stomach.

I put my hand up, and they fell silent. "I'm leaving Pepper's. Well, kind of. I'll still be working for the club, doing office work instead."

"That's fantastic. I'm so happy for you," Elle said, getting up but still eyeing my belly.

The other girls chimed in, everyone telling me they were glad I was getting out of there. I hoped they didn't think my dislike of the club had anything to do with them, because I would miss everyone. We'd become a little family, and I knew they always had my back and I had theirs.

"And guess what? Smitty just got fired," I said, grinning. It was always good to follow bad news with good news.

Their response was similar to the girls outside as everyone started hooting and hollering. They grew even louder when I told them how it all went down.

"Just when you think that man couldn't get any better, he goes and kicks out the weasel," Tia said, a dreamy look on her face.

"I know." I sighed, most likely sporting a similar expression.

The rest of the night was boring compared to how it started. I served a lot of rowdy eejits, and the girls killed it onstage. Sebastian was around as promised, and every time I looked up, he was watching me.

That might sound creepy, but to me it was everything. And it made me feel safe and cared for, two things I hadn't felt in a long time.

When the night was finally over, I couldn't run out of there fast enough. Sebastian helped me up onto his bike, and I got as close as I could, leaving no space between us. He put his hand on my leg before starting the bike, giving me a reassuring squeeze.

I held on tight and enjoyed the ride instead of doing what I really wanted, which was letting my hands wander. When we pulled up in front of my house, I was squirming on the seat, holding Sebastian in a tight grip.

He signaled for me to get off, his bemused expression floating over me once I was standing next to the bike. "Enjoy the ride?"

"As a matter of fact, I did. We should do it again soon."

"No doubt we will," he said and kicked the stand down. Once the bike was safely parked in my driveway, Sebastian caught my hand and walked us to the front door.

I'd barely closed the door behind us when he was on me, pressing my back against the closest wall. His eyes filled with love and desire, his hands roamed my body as if mapping every inch.

"I didn't think I could ever feel about another person the way I feel about you," Sebastian said against my cheek, his voice a husky whisper. "But you're a part of me now, one I couldn't survive without."

My legs went soft, my breathing stalled, and my

voice broke when I said, "Ditto."

"Ahem, did you forget about the other person in your house?" Stella interrupted us.

I squeaked and pushed at Sebastian to let me go. He chuckled but stepped back, releasing me.

"Sorry, Stella," I said, my face hot with embarrassment.

"Guess this is my cue to go home," she said, grinning at us.

After waving goodbye, she left, closing the door softly behind her. I went to the window to make sure she got inside her car safely. Once she was gone, I turned back to Sebastian.

His hair was disheveled, and he looked ready to charge me. Which he did, not breaking stride until he had me back against the wall. "Now where were we?"

Sebastian pulled my leg up to his hip and pressed himself against me. His head descended, and he took my mouth in a slow, drugging kiss, one I never wanted to end.

He lifted me up, and I wound my legs around him and held on tight, his lips never leaving mine. When we broke apart, we were holding on to each other like Luca did to the last jellybean in the jar.

"Let's take this somewhere else," Sebastian said, not wanting a repeat of the last time we couldn't wait to jump each other. We were in a similar position in front of the door when Luca stumbled out of his room.

He screamed when he saw us because he thought Sebastian was attacking me. Well, he kind of was, but it was the good kind of attack. And it took me over an hour to calm Luca down enough for him to fall asleep. He still eyed Sebastian suspiciously every time he touched me, three days later.

Sebastian walked us into my bedroom, closing the door and turning the lock. My kids knew how to open doors, so locking them was the only thing we could do.

"Never thought I'd have to sneak around again," he said, his voice a velvet murmur.

Joy bubbled in my laugh, and my heart was full to bursting. An invisible thread pulled me closer to him, connecting us heart and soul.

He was looking down at me with reverence, our lips almost touching. "And I don't even care. Because as long as I'm with you, nothing else matters."

"I love you," I said, my throat thick with emotion.

His arms tightened around me, and my lips instinctively found their way to his. We clawed at each other to get closer, our mouths clashing, our tongues dueling. My legs clamped around him, and I wished there were fewer clothes between us.

Forever reading me right, Sebastian eased me down onto the bed before stepping back. "I'll never get enough of looking at you." His eyes roamed my body.

Since I wanted nothing more than to please him, I wiggled out of my jeans, the horizontal position making it easier to pull them off. I sat up, taking off my shirt, a sense of urgency to my movements.

I should have been a lot better versed in taking my clothes off after working at a strip club for over a year, but my movements were jerky and unpracticed.

Sebastian watched me with hungry eyes, pulling his T-shirt over his head. I licked my lips, my eyes glued to his body. The hard ridges of his stomach looked more pronounced in the low light of my bedside lamp, and the sharp contours of his face gave his already masculine appearance an edge.

I hoped I would never lose the feeling of unwrapping a present every time he took his clothes off. My heart took a flying leap when he pushed his jeans off, leaving him in nothing but his boxers.

He kneeled on the bed, his big body coming down on top of mine, his hands braced next to my head. Our mouths met in a soul-bending kiss as his hands mapped my body.

He eased the cup of my bra aside, and his lips brushed my nipples. I wound my arms around him, holding him close, craving each touch of his hands and caress of his lips.

I was alight with the need to be close to him, his touch hypnotizing me, making every cell of my body tingle.

But the feeling was much more than desire; it was love and need.

His lips traced a path down my body, making me burn with passion. He devoured me, his kisses drugging, his hands searching. The telltale crinkle of foil nearly made me weep with relief, the need to be connected to him all-consuming.

And when I didn't think I could take anymore, he entered me with an aching slowness. There was a dreamy intimacy to our lovemaking that I'd never experienced before.

We groaned in unison, our mouths clashing, our bodies moving against each other in perfect harmony.

He took me to the height of passion, my body his completely. A deep feeling of peace surrounded me, and I came with quivering lips, my eyes locked on his. He soon followed me, his gaze never leaving mine.

And when we curled up in bed together— unfortunately in our pajamas, because kids—I knew I had everything I could ever need in my house at that moment.

My last waking thought before I drifted into sleep safely cocooned in his arms was that everything that happened to me in my life was worth it if this was where my path had taken me. And I'd go through it all again if it would lead me to him in the end.

Chapter Twenty

"Luca," I called through the huge office, sure the guys downstairs would be able to hear me.

"It wasn't me," my son yelled back.

I looked at the ceiling, hoping for divine intervention. Or a donut. I'd settle for the latter in a heartbeat.

The last few weeks had been like living a dream. Or someone else's life. I'd finished out my two weeks at Pepper's and started working in the office four days ago. Turned out the club owned a few buildings in town, one of them housing a tattoo shop downstairs and their offices upstairs.

I had my own space, right next to Sebastian's office. He was looking for someone to replace him as head of security at Pepper's so he could take over as the MC's security firm. He had more experience in that space than anyone else, and he could mostly keep normal working hours.

Talon had cleared out an office, and the guys had turned it into a playroom for the kids. It was opposite my room, and I had a clear path to look inside from behind my desk. Luca and Lena were currently playing with Talon, who was taking an extended lunch break that so far had lasted two hours.

I eyed the mess of sticky tape on my desk again and sighed. On the grand scale of things, sticky-taping my mouse, drawers, and keyboard wasn't the worst.

But since he had to understand that I was serious when I asked him to stay away from the contents of my desk drawers, I got up to talk to him.

"Hey." Sebastian came inside as I was rounding my desk.

My breath hitched and my heart broke out in an embarrassing dance routine. My feelings for him seemed to intensify the more we saw each other instead of tapering down to normal, sane levels.

"I thought you were out on a job," I said, making my way to him.

He pulled me close as soon as I was within reach and pressed a chaste kiss to my lips. "Everything was fine, and I missed you, so I came back."

I wound my arms around his neck and sank my hands into his hair, brushing through the silky strands.

"Missed you too," I whispered against his lips and kissed him.

"Stop with the kissing already," Talon complained from the playroom. "Did you forget this is an office?"

I leaned around Sebastian, watching Talon pretend to drink tea from a cup that was half the size of his hand. He was also wearing a gold tiara and pink bracelets.

"I didn't, but you seem to. Don't you have work to do?" I asked, struggling to hold back the laughter.

"Is that glitter on your face?" Sebastian asked, turning us so we were facing Lena and Talon. Luca was still in hiding.

"As a matter of fact, it is," Talon said, putting his middle finger on the side of his cup, discreetly flipping Sebastian off.

"Excellent. Since you're watching the kids, you won't mind if I take Nora out for a bit, right?" Sebastian asked.

"You got an hour. Then I have to meet with one of our suppliers over in Butler," Talon said, taking another pretend sip from his cup.

"Let me just have a chat with Luca first," I said and walked into the room.

Luca was hiding under the blanket on the couch, the big lump unmistakable.

I sat down next to him and tapped his legs. "Don't you have something to say to me?"

"Shmorry, Mommy," he mumbled from underneath the blanket.

"It's okay. But no more going through my desk drawers."

He pulled the blankets back and nodded. "Okay."

I leaned over and kissed his forehead. "I'm just going out with Sebastian. Talon is going to play with you."

"Where you going?" he asked.

I looked to Sebastian, who was sitting on the floor next to Talon, Lena standing in front of him, putting glitter in his hair. He'd be finding glitter for the next week if he didn't stop her soon.

"I'm not sure. But we won't be gone long, promise," I said, getting up.

Luca nodded, pulling a Superman comic out from underneath him. He was already lost in a world of superheroes by the time I stood up.

Lena was even less concerned about me leaving, fighting me off when I tried to kiss her goodbye.

"No kissing," she said, wagging her finger at me.

I grinned at her and blew a kiss instead. She grudgingly accepted it before getting back to her tea party.

Sebastian took my hand and walked me out to his bike, handing me my helmet. "So where are we going?" I asked when I sat behind him on the seat.

"It's a surprise," he said before putting his own helmet on.

We drove to the outskirts of Humptulips and turned onto a dirt road. All that was out here were fields and trees and a few farms. I recognized the area, since Stella and Mason lived out this way. I could never remember which dirt road to turn down to get to their place, but I'd been a few times. The kids loved going since Mason had a soft spot for animals and rescued them, meaning his farm was better than going to the zoo.

I watched with interest as we pulled up to an old farmhouse. There was a big shed off to the right, and the two-story house was nestled between huge trees on one side and empty fields on the other.

We parked in front of the porch steps leading up to the front door. I climbed off and removed my helmet, looking around. The ground was covered in long grass and weeds, but the buildings looked to be in good shape.

"Where are we?" I asked once Sebastian had taken off his helmet as well.

"Do you like it?" he asked, a tentative smile on his face.

Why is he shifting from foot to foot?

"It's beautiful. But what are we doing here?"

"I made an offer on it, and they accepted this morning," he said, watching me for a reaction.

My eyes went wide, and I stared at him. "You bought it?"

"I did, right after I sold my apartment in Chicago."

"When did you put it on the market?" I asked, astonished that he would be able to sell it so quickly and ecstatic that he did. It finally sank in that he was really staying.

"Seven weeks ago. The sale went through four days ago. I made the offer on this place right after."

"Seven weeks ago?" I asked, my voice a few octaves higher than usual.

"It's in a great location, and I've renovated it. Got a good price for it. And my money goes a lot further out here than it does in Chicago."

I swallowed, looking around again. "But it's a lot of land. That would have cost a lot, even in Humptulips."

"I've always worked, never really spent much. Never had anything I wanted to spend it on. Now I do, so I figured why wait?"

He took my hand, pulling it up and kissing my palm. "I know you're not there yet, but I want you to think about moving in when you're ready. There's five bedrooms, and the kids would love it out here."

They definitely would. It was perfect, and I could see how amazing it would look with a little TLC.

"This is amazing, Sebastian," I said, my voice wavering. "And it means the world to me that you included us when you made the decision to buy it."

"Of course I did. I love you, and I don't ever want to be without you. You're part of my life now. You and the kids."

I threw myself at him, Sebastian catching me and taking a step back to steady us. "Does that mean you like it?"

He sounded hesitant, and I looked up at him with wide eyes. "I love it."

"I know I should have talked to you first, but I saw it and thought it was perfect. I made the offer the day it came on the market."

"It's your money. You don't have to ask me before spending it," I said, placing a kiss on his chest.

"I want you to be comfortable here. If you don't like it, I'm sure we can sell it again. It's in a great location and comes with a lot of land."

I held him tighter. "Don't you dare sell my dream house."

He grinned, his body relaxing into me. "Just wait until you meet the neighbors."

"The neighbors? Why? Do I know them?"

He nodded over my shoulder, and I released him and turned around. Mason and Stella came walking across the field, followed by a rooster, a pig, and a dog.

Stella was the first to reach me and shrieked, pulling me into a hug. "We're going to be neighbors."

I chuckled, jumping up and down with her or risk getting my arms pulled out of their sockets. "I just found out."

Mason shook Sebastian's hand and greeted me with a kiss to my cheek. "Does this mean I have to find a new tenant?"

I flushed at everyone's attention. "Not yet. We'll give it a few months first."

"A few months?" Sebastian grumbled. "You mean a few weeks."

I raised my brows. "Didn't you just say you didn't want to rush me?"

"A few weeks is plenty of time to get used to the idea of living together," he said, looking serious.

If I didn't have two little humans to think about, I would jump at the chance to move in with him. But I had a responsibility to not rush this.

"Can we see the inside?" Stella asked, linking her arm with mine. "And I agree, a few weeks is plenty of time."

I elbowed her, but she dodged me by contorting her body. "You're supposed to be on my side."

"I am. That's why I'm telling you to give it a few weeks to think about it. You're basically living together already anyway."

We followed the guys inside and I stopped, thinking Sebastian couldn't have chosen a more perfect house. The bottom floor housed the kitchen, living room, laundry, and a bathroom, with a big wooden staircase to the right of the door.

The living room and kitchen were one big room, taking up almost the entire bottom floor. Big windows looked out over the mountains on one side and the trees on the other. The kitchen had seen better days, but it was huge and had a rustic charm with its wooden cabinets.

"I'll give you a hand to replace the kitchen if you want," Mason said.

"I hope he means he'll help once he's finished his own house," Stella whispered for only me to hear.

I chuckled, and we explored the rest of the house. The bedrooms were upstairs and all a decent size. The master bedroom had its own bathroom and a huge walk-in closet. The view was even more spectacular from up there.

"What do you think?" Sebastian asked, stopping next to me.

"I love it," I said, beaming at him.

"Good," he responded and walked to where Mason was inspecting the balcony railing, pointing at a few things.

"He didn't bring his tools, did he?" I asked Stella.

"I wouldn't let him. We'd never make it back home before it gets dark. And Porcahontas doesn't like the dark and freaks out."

"Who's Porcahontas?"

"The pig who's currently waiting in your yard for us to come back out. Or more specifically Mason, since he's like the animal whisperer. She belongs to Brielle, my friend Kinsley's sister, but she's getting too big for their yard, so we're looking after her."

"Okay, I'll take it. But what's with the rooster?"

Neither one of the animals had been there last time I visited. I wondered how many they were up to by now.

"That's Cluck Norris. We saved him three weeks ago, and he hasn't left our side since. Thinks he's a dog."

We stayed for another thirty minutes, the guys inspecting every inch of the house while Stella and I hung out with the animals. Porcahontas tried pushing me over whenever I stopped petting her, so I was stuck until the guys came back out. But she was a gorgeous—if huge—pig, so I didn't mind.

When we went back to the office, my heart was full and my head filled with decorating ideas. Maybe the kids could finally get a dog.

I had to thank Jim if I ever saw him again since his screwup led me to everything I now had.

Epilogue

"Pee, pee," Lena sang, dancing into the kitchen.

She was wearing a pink dress but seemed to have lost the tights she'd been wearing not ten minutes ago.

"Do you want to go to the potty?" I asked, eyeing her. She'd started showing interest in going to the potty, and I tried to encourage her.

"I did," she replied.

Oh no. Please don't let there be another mystery pee somewhere in the house. "Where did you go?" I asked and held out my hand for her to lead me to this supposed pee she'd done. "Show me, gorgeous."

We made our way past the moving boxes that were piled up everywhere and to the kids' bedroom. Lena pointed at a suitcase I'd packed that morning.

I walked around the room, looking inside the suitcase, then studying the floor and sniffing the air. No wet spots and no smell was a good sign. But it also meant I had to search the house for a potential accident.

"Come on, let's go on an expedition," I said and led the way out of the room.

I was on my knees, looking under the coffee table, when Sebastian and Luca walked in. They'd been at the farmhouse, dropping off a load of boxes. Luca had become Sebastian's shadow over the last three months, accepting him like he'd always been there.

And yes, that's how long it took for me to agree to move in with him. I figured since we hadn't been apart for even one night in all that time, we basically lived together already. The kids loved the farmhouse and Sebastian, so we might as well make it official.

"Well, now that's a view I don't mind coming back to," Sebastian growled, and I shot up, hitting my head.

"Ouch," I cried and backed out from under the table.

"Are you okay, baby?" Sebastian asked, helping me up. He studied my head and felt for a lump. When he was satisfied I would live, he whispered a kiss over my lips and released me.

"I'm fine," I said and then looked at my son. "Did you like the color for your bedroom?"

We'd been painting the rooms and letting the kids pick out their colors. Luca had been unsure of what color he wanted, but in the end he settled on blue.

He nodded, his eyes shining. "It's blue, like water. Seb said we can put sharks on the wall too."

Something else he'd discovered over the last few months were sharks. He devoured every morsel of information he could find on them.

"Great choice," I said, smiling at him.

Sebastian put his arms around me and pulled me into his side. "What were you doing under the coffee table?"

I sighed. "I'm 89.65 percent certain Lena peed somewhere in the house. But I haven't been able to find it yet."

He chuckled. "Want me to help you look?"

I put a hand to my chest and looked up at him. "My hero."

The kids were running around the living room, Luca chasing Lena, pretending to be the Grinch.

We left them to it and continued the search for the mystery pee. Maybe she didn't do one after all. The house wasn't big; it shouldn't be this hard to find it. I inspected the kitchen floor again, but besides dust mites and food scraps, there wasn't much to see.

A loud crash and then a groan came from the back door, making me pause in my search. I turned on my heels and speed-walked down the hallway, the kids right behind me.

Sebastian was lying on the ground, moaning. "I found it."

I suppressed the giggle wanting to escape. After all, he hurt himself slipping on my daughter's pee.

"I'm sorry," I said, my voice laced with amusement.

He got up, turning from side to side to assess the damage. "You may laugh now, but you'll be the one waiting on me when I can't get up off the couch because I hurt myself."

He had a point. "And I'll be happy to fulfill your every wish," I said.

"Maybe we should put that to the test tonight," he said, his eyes blazing with heat.

My whole body flushed, and I chastised myself for my inappropriate reaction. After all, there were kids present.

"Happy to," I said, my voice breathy.

He strolled past me, not looking like he'd hurt himself at all.

Sebastian took a shower while I cleaned the floor. My phone binged a few times, but I was on a mission and mopped the whole house while I had the water out.

I made the kids a snack and pulled myself up onto the counter, checking my messages. I had four unread texts and two missed calls.

I took a sip of water that I nearly spat out again when an image popped up on my screen.

It was Malena, doing a perfectly executed upside-down split on the pole. No idea what the move was called, but it was hot. She was hot. And barely wearing any clothes.

Elle had sent the image first and then a text message.

Elle: Your girl is killing it. Shame we can't talk her into working for us a few nights a week.

The other two messages were from Malena.

Malena: We missed you at pole dance last night.

Malena: Delete the photo Elle sent you or I'll get out the one of you on the mechanical bull.

I chuckled and replied to her, thinking me not going to a few of the lessons was better for everyone's health. Elle had started teaching pole dancing at the club during the day when it was closed to customers. It was a popular class, and she even had a waiting list.

Me: I feel no shame over that night. Do your worst.

Sebastian came back in, his hair wet, his white T-shirt clinging to his body. I licked my lips at the sight like Pavlov's dog when he heard a bell and thought he was getting food. Or in my case, a hot biker.

"Talon just messaged. They'll be here soon," he said, fitting himself between my legs.

We'd both taken the week off for the move, and the guys were coming over to help with the heavy stuff. We'd rented a truck and were just waiting for them to arrive.

"Perfect. You think you'll get it all in one load?"

Sebastian trailed his hands up my leg, resting them on my hips. "Not sure if we can fit all your nail polish in. I don't think I've ever seen so many shades of the same colors."

I slapped his chest playfully and grinned. "I like nail polish."

"I noticed," he said and kissed my cheek.

The front door smashed open and heavy footsteps pounded on the floor. "We're here," Talon bellowed. "Where's my princess?"

The pitter-patter of small feet rang through the house, and then a loud shriek sounded. Lena loved Sebastian, but Talon held a special place in her heart, and nobody existed but him whenever he was around.

"There she is," Talon called out and came into the kitchen a few seconds later, holding Lena.

Grim, Gears, and Blaze followed, crowding the small space.

"Hey, honey," Grim greeted me. "Where do you want us?"

Gears and Blaze called out greetings as well, and Sebastian showed them where everything was. Stella and Mason would meet us at the house to help unload.

They were planning on being here this morning to take the kids, but the three baby goats they'd taken in a few days ago escaped.

Stella had only just called me before the pee incident to let me know they'd found them. I didn't want to add to her already stressful day and talked her into just meeting us at the farmhouse. Willa and Jameson would be there as well to give us a hand.

For the next few hours, the guys emptied out the house. It was a bittersweet moment since I had a lot of great memories there, but the thought of officially moving in with Sebastian made me ecstatic.

When the last box had left the house, I stood in my empty bedroom, looking around what used to be my home.

Sebastian joined me, pulling my back to his front. "You ready?"

I turned in his embrace and beamed at him. "Let's do it."

I walked out holding Sebastian's hand, a huge smile on my face.

THE END

This series continues with Malena's story, coming out in November 2021. Don't miss the release and sign up for my newsletter http://bit.ly/SarahPeisNewsletter to find out when it will be available.

About the Author

I love the written word in all forms and shapes and if I'm not glued to a book, I'm attempting to write one. I'm a frequent blonde moment sufferer and still haven't figured out how to adult. Lucky google always has an answer, so I don't have to.

I live in Melbourne, Victoria, with my two kids, the holder of my heart and two fur babies. If you want to accompany me on my path to enlightenment, check out my publications or get in touch, I would love to hear from you!

Where you can find me

Join my Blonde Moment Support Group (all hair colours welcome!) on Facebook to talk about books, books and books! @blondemomentsupportgroup

Facebook @sarahpeisbooks

Instagram @sarahpeis

Pinterest @sarahpeisbooks

Website www.sarahpeis.com

Booklist

Sweet Dreams Series

Some Call It Love (#1)

Some Call It Temptation (#2)

Some Call It Fate (#3)

Some Call It Devotion (#4)

Worship (A Sweet Dreams novella)

Kismet (A Sweet Dreams novella, exclusive to newsletter subscribers. Sign up now https://mailchi.mp/11937aa98a67/newsletter-sign-up)

Standalone

Happily Never Forever

Adult Supervision Required

Thank you

Thank you for taking a chance on this book and making it all the way to this part. I hope you enjoyed this story as much as I loved writing it. <- still true

These are just a few of the people who have helped me along the way and I'm forever grateful for everything they've done (don't hate me if I forgot anyone, kids have turned my brain into a lost & found box where nothing ever gets found).

Natasha: you rock my socks off. Thank you for believing in me and my books. They wouldn't be the same without you. <- yes, times a thousand. <- You're all that and a bag of chips.

Robyn: #LYLT <- always.

Ben: your designs are one-of-a-kind and I'm in awe of your mad skills. You're also a pretty great human, so there's that.

Kristin: sorry for all the comma splices. I'd like to say it will never happen again buuuuuut….. (seriously, thanks for all your work polishing my manuscript). <- and guess what, there were just as many comma splices in this manuscript than in the last. This time it was the repetition…I've moved on to screwing up the simplest of words. Like The End.

The lovely humans at Hot Tree Editing: You guys are the best. Thanks for being so awesome. <- honestly, these guys are game changes!

Sim: love of my life, kettle to my pot, holder of my heart. Couldn't do this without you. <- don't ever change!

Sandy: kickass MIL. Thanks for still supporting me, even after reading my shitty first draft of my (even) shittier first book (shudder). <- and she's still reading my books people!! <- yup, still reading them!

CPSIA information can be obtained
at www.ICGtesting.com
Printed in the USA
BVHW082217140521
607267BV00003B/285

9 780648 975762